STORM'S CHILD

JOHN ORTEGA

SMASH BEAR
-PUBLISHING-

SmashBear Publishing

Office 48276

PO Box 6945

London

W1A 6US

www.smashbearpublishing.com

Or email:

info@smashbearpublishing.com

PROLOGUE

TEN YEARS AGO

The forest gave off an oppressive aura, a chill breeze swept between the branches sending shivers down my spine. I ducked beneath the branches of a large pine before moving between a cluster of trees as we slowly made our way through the thicket. The musky scent of the woods permeated the air the deeper we went and, mixed with the copper scent of blood, stung the back of my throat.

We stopped next to a large tree to gather our bearings. Why would she come here? I turned towards the knight beside me. Like many of the Fae he was tall but managed to walk through the forest with graceful elegance, his ash-colored hair tied in a ponytail revealed his slightly pointed ears. His intricate silver armor shone like a beacon in the dark forest, unlike mine which, whilst simple and less ornate, let me blend in with the darkness around us. Two swords were sheathed across his back and a small dagger tied to his waist.

It had been years since I saw Galesh have so much as a paper cut, yet now the fae had blood dripping from his face and neck, marring his otherwise perfect complexion. But if there was one knight I would have guarding my back in this godforsaken forest, it would be him.

"Galesh, where did you last leave her?" I palmed the hilt of my sword, ready to draw it at the sign of any movement, eying the forest for any movement. "What the hell were you guys doing here?"

"We were following orders, Nathan," He answered softly, his gaze darting around. "She wanted to hunt a boar to clear her mind before the festival preparations started, and she knew you were called away by the Queen, so she brought a squad of knights." We stepped over a fallen log, careful not to make too much noise before he continued. "We came upon the tracks of a drake and the Princess thought it would prove more of a challenge. During the middle of the hunt, about four miles from the base of the mountain, we were besieged by a squad from Summer and chased like dogs to this shit hole."

"Of course she did, only she would do something as stupid as switch hunts from a boar to a drake." I frowned, something about the story not making sense: drakes were massive lizards, about twelve feet tall at the shoulder and covered in thick scales with huge spiked tails covered in poison. Though they lacked the ability to fly like their wyvern cousins and thank the gods they couldn't breathe fire or ice like a dragon, they were a savage breed requiring a full squad of knights to hunt it.

Drakes were foul tempered beasts and resistant to magic, not that it stopped moronic nobles from trying to tame them in the hopes of turning them into a cavalry force. I frowned as we moved again, recalling drakes made their dens in caves and mountains. The peaks outside Fuar Dorcha, the capital of Winter, were perfect for them. The Queen had to keep sending out squads of knights to deal with them.

How did Summer's knights cross the border without raising any alarms? I turned to Galesh, looked him straight in the eyes and asked, "But why would you abandon her?"

"I did not abandon her!" He glared at me. "Those bastards ran us down, Mihael and Blyte were the first to fall, shot down by arrows just as we made it to the entrance of the forest." His shoulders shook as he looked down. "We were being cut down one after the other and our only choice was to go deeper, she ordered me to get help and now here we are."

A cohort of Winter's best would be here at any moment. Today I had been preparing for the Bicentennial Kinship Ball, where the monarchs and nobles of all four courts gathered to mingle and tried not to kill each other: key word being *tried*. It was Queen Mab's time to host, so preparations were already underway even if the ball wasn't for another decade or so.

Since the point of the ball was to promote friendship between beings that hated each other's guts, violence was forbidden. Not that it stopped any of the Fae from trying to pull one over on the hosting monarch. As a precaution, the host began preparing things a decade or two in advance.

Earlier today the Queen summoned all her retainers to discuss the upcoming ball. She went into excruciating detail that if anything went wrong during the ball, heads would roll. At the end of the meeting, she handed a scroll to each captain with their individual assignments. As I was walking to the stables, with my scroll in hand, I ran into a wounded Galesh: the fae was bleeding from half a dozen cuts and had branches in his hair.

"Crooked Man's Forest" and "Princess in danger," was all he needed to say before I pulled the nearest knight and ordered a cohort to mount up before riding ahead with Galesh.

The deeper we went, the harder it was to see where we were going, even with my enhanced vision I could only see five feet in front of me.

Eventually, we left the horses tied to a nearby tree as they wouldn't be able to carry us any deeper, the foliage was just too thick. Lighting a torch wasn't an option, we were no longer in Winter's lands and the Crooked Man didn't take kindly to fire in his forest.

"How much farther Galesh?" I turned just in time to see a flash of steel as I felt a sharp piercing pain in my side. A pained gasp escaped me as I looked to see my armor pierced by Galesh's dagger. The knight had a smirk on his face as he pulled the dagger out and stabbed me again.

The weapon went through my armor like it wasn't even there - this wasn't supposed to happen, my armor was bespelled to stop knives. As the dagger plunged deeper into me, I tried to steady myself against a tree, coughing up mouthfuls of blood. I tried to speak, to call my magic to me, but through the blood loss and pain it was no use. The pain was too much, the magic slipped through my fingers like dry sand.

Galesh twisted the dagger before he leaned forward and whispered in my ear,

"The Princess sends her love."

1

PRESENT DAY

I looked out of the window, noticing how the grey clouds formed a dim atmosphere on the grounds. The satyr father and son duo ran through the rain, rejoicing in the cleansing the fresh water brought. The large windows of the Inn gave the guests a great view whilst enjoying the comfort of chilling by the roaring fire, but it also meant I could see the mud that would be dragged in and require cleaning. Looking at my floors, I regretted not putting the 'wipe your feet if you have them' mat out.

It was a slow morning. The family of centaurs took to the woods at sunrise and wouldn't be back until lunch, which left me with plenty of time to catch up on work. I put one of my favourite records on and the soft tunes of Beirut played in the background as I turned to my current project: reorganizing the living room. I tapped my foot to the beat of the song as I tilted my head, thinking of the best way to improve my guest's comfort. The fireplace sat in a cozy corner with two leather chairs and a small tea table, while on the other side of the room a black leather couch lay behind an oak wood piano. A fine layer of dust covered the couch and with winter around the corner, my guests would probably appreciate an extra seat next to the fireplace.

"That's it, I quit." said a frustrated voice behind me, followed by the absence of music.

I sighed and turned to the bane of my existence. Standing at five-foot-something, Lucas wasn't the first person you imagined as a mage in training; his shabby, short blonde hair and gray overalls made him an unexpected candidate. I sighed again, softly - he wouldn't let me walk by until I heard whatever teenage ailment bothered him now. I could already feel the need for a soothing cup of hot tea.

I ignored him and looked about the living room again; the boy threatened to quit about three times a day since he'd started working at the Inn back in August. He lasted a month, which is more than could be said for the several others that came before him.

Maybe if I didn't say anything, he would go away? Then I could finish with the living room and move onto the next chore on the list. I walked to the couch, considering if I moved it a little more to the right the guests could have a nice view of the woods without getting baked in the afternoon sun...

"I mean it Nathan, that beast almost killed me."

I rolled my eyes, got to give the kid points for drama at the very least. Still undecided as to how I wanted the room to look, I grabbed the back of the couch and frowned, now wondering if I moved it to the left, the guests would get nice and cozy by the fireplace at night when it gets cold. Decisions, decisions. Woods or Fireplace?

Lucas parked himself in front of me just as I was about to move the couch to the left. "Nathan, are you even listening?" He had a deter-mined look on his face that told me, this time, he was trying to be serious. "That thing tried to kill me."

I looked dubiously towards said thing napping by the fireplace without a care in the world. "What did you do to her?"

Lucas threw his hands in the air with all the angst a teenage mage in training could muster, "You *always* take her side over mine."

I let go of the couch, accepting he wouldn't let me move it until I heard his side of the story. The sooner this was over, the sooner I could make some tea.

"Okay, you have my undivided attention. What happened?"

He took a deep and calming breath before looking at me. "I just got in from the college and was about to make myself something to eat before getting started on the lunch rush, and she just bolted at me and nearly took my whole damn leg off!" He glared at the aforementioned beast who was busy kicking her paws at the air while making soft growly noises. "I told you that if I kept working here you'd need to keep that demon chained. I'm a mage for Merlin's sake!"

It was only then I noticed he was missing the bottom half of his pants, hanging in tatters, like a grass skirt around his calf. Today was Friday so Lucas had probably come straight from his class at the college which meant he stank of magic and other interesting things which usually set Sabine off.

I raised a finger at him. "You're not a mage...yet." I raised another finger, "Second, did you shower before coming to work?" I cut him off before he could answer. "Let me answer that for you, that would be a no, because if you showered like you were supposed to, this wouldn't have happened." I pointed towards the fireplace. "You know Sabine is sensitive to magic and she's not a demon, a thing or a beast. She's a beagle."

A look of resentment washed over his face, "So, it's my fault then?"

I sighed and pinched the bridge of my nose, thinking about every regretful decision leading me to this very moment, all for paying back a favour to Lucas's father, Cassius. He helped me out some time ago and now here was my comeuppance. His little bundle of joy got into trouble at school for unauthorized use of magic in the girls' locker room and he'd rung me asking if I had any jobs lying around to keep the kid busy.

It just so happened my last kitchen boy quit after a near-death experience with my cook for screwing up a guest's order - who knew minotaurs were allergic to peanuts? Lucas was a hard worker no doubt, but his constant insistence on quitting was draining.

"Lucas how about you take the rest of the day off and come back tomorrow?"

Lucas crossed his arms over his chest and lifted his chin defiantly.

"I don't need to be in a place where a dog is more appreciated than me." He spun on his heel and slammed the door on the way out.

Sabine looked up from her spot and wagged her tail at me.

I sighed, "You see what you did? Now what am I going to tell Julia?"

"Tell Julia what?"

I cringed before turning around to look at the suspicious dryad. "Er, hey Julia, did you do something new with your hair? I have to say it looks great."

She stood in the middle of the room and arched an eyebrow at me. "Don't bullshit me Nathan, what did you do?"

Of average height and slim build, Julia looked more like a college student than a dryad, she still managed to scare the bejeezus out of me though. Not that I would ever tell her that. Today she wore her hair in a tight ponytail which highlighted her sharp eyes and made her look quite severe.

I took a deep breath and tried to think quickly the best way to explain what just happened. "Sabine fired Lucas. I tried to stop her but she wouldn't listen to reason."

Sabine whined behind me.

Julia's eyes swirled and shifted, glowing like liquid steel. She walked towards me poking my chest with her finger. "What do you mean Sabine fired him? Wait, don't answer that." She pinched her nose in frustration and growled. "What the hell am I going to do now? Lunch is in two hours!"

I gave her my best smile. "I'm sure you'll figure it out, you always do."

She rolled her eyes at me in exasperation. "How in Pan's ass do you stay in business?"

I smiled at her and nodded towards the outside. "Where else in the world could you see something like that?" The satyr family were playing a mud version of a snowball fight, laughing like idiots. One of the mud balls missed the kid and splattered onto one of the windows. I frowned, that would need a good scrubbing. "Tír na nÓg is the only inn for supernatural folks where people feel safe enough to-"

"Be their true selves." She rolled her eyes and I could practically see her counting to ten. "I didn't ask for the sales pitch. Get your ass in the kitchen."

I took a couple of steps back from her. "Wait, what?"

She crossed her arms over her chest and gave me the stink eye. "You didn't stop Lucas from quitting so until you can replace him, guess what?" She reached over and poked me on the shoulder, "Tag, you're it."

By the time I finished, it was almost midnight. Julia couldn't stand my incompetence for more than a couple of minutes before grumpily kicking me out of the kitchen, muttering she was faster by herself. Unfortunately, my day didn't stop there: one of the joys of running an inn for things that go bump in the night was that there was always something to do. Most of my afternoon was spent replacing the attic window which managed to stay relatively intact despite boasting three arrows, courtesy of the centaurs and their 'target practice'. Xaris, the dragon who permanently rented the attic, was not amused. I had to spend the rest of the afternoon convincing him centaurs leave a bad taste in your mouth.

After that, I'd made my way back towards the living room where the couch still sat at an awkward angle next to the piano. The fireplace crackled with faint, dying flames still warming the room. I stood by the entrance and gave the living room a cursory glance, the record player stood to my left on top of an eighteenth century oak table Xaris gifted the inn to commemorate his fifth year staying here.

I smiled remembering the dragon making a whole show of it and how it was our honor to receive a part of his hoard. To my right stood a worn bookshelf. I bagged it for an absolute steal after a local bookstore closed and sold their furniture. A wine colored rug covered the wooden floors, it was one of Sabine's favorite spots as she loved to roll around in it. Across from me were a pair of wooden double doors with circular windows in the middle, it had taken a bit of elbow grease but the mud had finally come off of it.

The windows gave a clear view of the woods and it was never difficult to see what inspired Shakespeare's 'A Midsummer Night's Dream' on nights like this. I could imagine the Fair Folk dancing between the silver light and the shadows cast by the moonlight shining through the trees.

I started moving the couch towards the doors when the front desk bell rang, announcing the arrival of a new guest. I sighed, letting go of the couch before making my way to the reception hall.

The hall was at the heart of the inn, an open space that connected the downstairs to the upper parts through a wooden staircase. Snuggled between the entrance to the living and dining rooms was my little piece of the kingdom. A dark cherry wooden desk sat perfectly in the corner, it took me more than two weeks to find it. Funds were tight at the beginning but it was worth it. The large table and chairs were collecting a fine layer of dust needing to be cleaned tomorrow. It was rarely used unless we had a big party or a formal gathering, most guests like to take their meals in their rooms or the upstairs balcony. There was no better spot for going through paperwork and enjoying a cup of peppermint tea.

Sabine was lying down on her bed next to the stairs. The word 'manager' was embroidered on the side of the bed: the guests thought it was cute.

A young man was standing at the desk, in his mid-twenties with light brown hair, his skin had a ruddy tone from spending too much time in the sun. Wearing a tattered jacket with a black shirt and blue jeans that had seen better days, he looked rather worse for wear. Even his shoes looked like they were about to fall apart.

I mentally checked the protective wards, the familiar tingle at the back of my neck gave me a brief pause of relief.

"Welcome to Tir na nÓg, I'm Nathan. How can I help you?" I smiled, extending my hand.

He hesitated, before slowly shaking it. "I heard this is a safe place, is that true?"

I gave him a reassuring smile. "As long as guests abide by the inn's laws, it's the safest place in Portland. They have our full protection."

He shifted his weight from one foot to the other as he let go of my hand. "What laws?"

I pointed to a small plaque on the wall next to the stairs where a cartoon version of Sabine was reading the text:

"Come in peace. Do not harm the other guests. Don't run out on your bill. Be courteous to the staff."

Normally guests came to the inn for one of three reasons. Some wanted to escape the mortals oblivious to the darker side of the world and let their supernatural side shine. Some needed a quiet place to rest. Others were running from something big and bad.

The kid wet his chapped lips before nodding to himself as if he was coming to a decision. "How much for a room?"

I took another look at the prospective guest standing in front of me; he didn't have any luggage to speak of except for a small black leather hip pouch that was in pristine condition, unlike the rest of him. The only jewelry he had on was a small silver ring with a dark blue gem with a faint glow of magic, now that was odd. Jewelry was usually the first thing to be sold or pawned when someone's this down on their luck. There was a slight tangy, sweet smell wafting from him, reminiscent of when Sabine thought it was a good idea to go dumpster diving. Even if he didn't have the money for a room, I'd at least offer him a shower. Then again, with supernatural folk, appearances are most definitely deceiving. He could be a one thousand-year-old prince with more money than I make in a year just sitting in his pocket.

"It's five gold pieces a night, you can pay up front if you know how long your stay is going to be. If not, then we collect weekly payments on Sundays." I stood behind the front desk. "Do you know how long you'll be staying with us?"

Gold was the universal currency of the supernatural world - empires rose and fell every other century, but gold would never devalue. Each piece was the size of a Girl Scout cookie and would go for about $100 dollars each. I didn't think the kid had that much money. Which surprised me when he pulled out thirty-five gold pieces from his hip pouch and laid them down on the counter.

I nodded and pulled out the registration form. "Please sign your name on the bottom." He gave me that same deer in headlights look from before. "Don't worry, it's not a magical contract. Just your consent of the inn's laws."

He signed his name, I smiled and took the form back before grabbing one of the keys from inside the desk. "Okay Mr..." I looked at the flowing cursive writing. "Roel. Please follow me."

Sabine stood up from her bed and shook herself off before bolting for the stairs. Welcoming a new guest was one of her favorite things to do.

As we walked to his room on the second floor, I tried to get a feel for the kid. He didn't have any of the usual smells of a shifter (although it would be difficult to tell considering the only thing I could smell at the moment was garbage), or the unnatural stillness of the undead, and he sure as hell wasn't any type of Fae, which my wards would have warned me against.

He did have magic though. I could sense that much, just not what flavor. The only vibe I got off this kid was that he needed somewhere safe to crash.

I let my magic gather around my thumb and traced a small symbol, two white parallel lines inside a circle, at the base of the key. All the keys had different runes needing to be drawn by me to allow the doors to open, an extra safety measure the guests appreciated, no one but myself and the guest could use the key to access the room. We arrived at his room, where Sabine as expected was already waiting impatiently outside the reddish brown door.

The door opened to reveal a large sandalwood bed in the center of the room, dark blue linens adorning it, with a small nightstand on each side, both with brass candle holders. At the foot of the bed stood a soft blue lounging chair positioned on woolen grey carpet. Opposite the bed, two large doors lead to a marble-tiled bathroom and walk-in closet. Two arched windows gave a perfect view of the woods outside while a wooden door led to the second floor balcony.

I turned towards the kid and the look of relief in his eyes as I handed him the key made me happy, at least here he could sleep knowing he would be safe. "Here you go, Mr. Roel. Breakfast is at seven, lunch at noon and dinner just after sunset. You need anything, call me. The number is next to the phone, have a good night."

He stood by the door for a good twenty seconds before Sabine let out a small bark of annoyance and sat in the middle of the room, giving the new guest a look. Roel looked at me.

I shrugged. "She won't feel her job is done until you step inside."

He chuckled a little then caught himself and stopped. He walked inside, passing by Sabine and sat on the bed. My little manager gave him a nod before she sneezed in his general direction and walked out of the room.

I waved at the kid and smiled. "You have a good night." I closed the door and turned to Sabine, who was giving me the stink eye.

"What?" She looked at the door, sneezed again then looked back to me.

I looked at her, annoyed, as we walked downstairs. "Don't be a busybody, his business is none of our business."

She whined before lying down on her bed.

I ran my hand through my hair, a dark strand falling next to her paws. I still wasn't used to how short it was now. "No, I'm not making things hard on you. If he feels up to it, he will let us know. If not then we'll deal with whatever it is when it comes knocking."

She gave me a small growl of acceptance before laying on her back. I laughed and knelt to give her a belly rub. "Now you're just being a spoiled brat."

After Sabine got her fill, she dashed towards the kitchen, probably to beg for some treats off Julia. I walked back towards the couch. "Okay, time to get you out of the way."

I bent over to grab the couch, about to move it, when a knock on the door stopped me. I laid my head on the armrest and rolled my eyes. "You gotta be kidding me." I gave the couch a glare, mumbling, "this isn't over," and made my way towards the door.

I looked through the peephole of the large oak door to see a tall woman standing on my porch. She was probably in her mid-thirties with piercing dark brown eyes with bags beneath them, and dark curly hair that fell just below her neck. She was wearing a dark blue pant suit. The glint of a gun could be seen beneath her jacket.

I opened the door and put on my most charming voice. She was either a cop, or someone ready to make trouble. Or even worse, a door to door salesman, although I dismissed that idea given the hour and the gun. "Good evening Miss, how can I help you?"

"Nathaniel Mercer?" She asked in a stern tone.

From the way she carried herself and spoke, she was definitely a cop. I extended my senses around her and found she was vanilla human... Lucky me. "Nathan please, Nathaniel makes me sound like a grumpy old man."

The joke bounced off her like dry peas on a wall. She pulled up her credentials confirming my cop suspicion. "I'm Detective Garcia, Portland PD. Can we speak for a moment?"

A shiver ran down my spine. I ran a mental note of my guests; none of them were of the violent variety... well, except for the dragon in the attic and maybe Roel, but the kid was too new for me to get a read on. I was apprehensive, concerned that I was in for a world of trouble. What could my guests have done?

I stepped outside, closing the door behind me and motioned to a couple of chairs on the porch. "Sure Detective, I hope it's okay that we talk outside. As you can see, I run an inn and don't want my guests feeling uncomfortable. I hope you understand."

The inn sat in the middle of a five hundred acre property west of the Willamette River. It gave enough privacy to my less-than-human guests to shed their disguises while being relatively close to civilization for a nice cup of coffee.

The cool night breeze swept through the front porch, carrying the musky scent of the woods with the undertones of the sweet citrusy Red Verbena and St. John's Wort circling the whole property. Several chairs sat around an ash wooden table: it was a particular favourite spot of the guests, who liked to sit around amongst nature and drink a glass of iced tea. A halfway filled ashtray told me Xaris had been sitting here recently. That dragon enjoyed his cigars a little too much for my liking, not that he'd be too put out if he burned the place down, being fireproof had its perks. A blue sedan parked next to my truck caught the corner of my eye, must be the detective's.

She gave me a stiff nod before following to the table as I pulled out a chair for her, but she shook her head. "No thank you, how long have you known Lucas Gray?"

I frowned at her, a bad feeling slowly creeping up my spine. "His dad and I have been friends for years. I have known Lucas since he was in grade school. Why? Has he done something?"

She took out a little notepad and began writing on it. "Was he having trouble at school? History of bullying? Anyone that might want to hurt him?"

What the hell? Did something happen to the kid? Shit, Cassius is going to kill me.

"No, not at all. He started going to college this year and his dad asked me to look out for him. So, I gave him a job in the kitchen, helping with the meals. He's new to town so he mostly spends his time here or at school. Detective, what is this about? Is Lucas okay?"

She took a few notes before putting the notebook away. "Mr. Mercer, I'm sorry to say this but we found Lucas floating beneath the Hawthorne Bridge. Paramedics at the scene tried everything they could. I'm sorry."

2

_____

My mind blanked, failing to process what she was saying. *Lucas, dead? How? Why?*

The detective kept talking but I didn't hear her. The kid didn't have any enemies, aside from annoying anyone who he spent more than five minutes with, but that wasn't a reason to kill him.

"Mr. Mercer... Nathaniel... Are you okay?" The detective waved her hand in front of my face.

I shook my head and sat down. "Sorry Detective, but are you sure it was Lucas? We just spoke this morning and he was fine."

The tight corners of her mouth softened a little before she nodded. "We haven't been able to officially identify the body yet but he had his wallet on him which is also how we found you, he had a list of emergency contacts. We tried reaching his parents but had no luck. The NYPD made a drive by their residence but no one was home."

"Did he jump?" I stood and started pacing the length of the porch, sitting wasn't going to cut it right now. "Was he pushed? Can you tell me what happened?"

Lucas was many things but suicidal wasn't one of them, at least to my knowledge. Extremely annoying? Yes, but that was every teenager ever. If the police tried to contact Cassius and he didn't answer, something must've happened. I raked my hand through my hair. How do you tell someone their child is dead?

"We still don't know the cause of death; the medical examiner is doing the autopsy as we speak." She sat down and pulled out her notebook again. "We're still in the preliminary stages of the investigation so we don't know much right now. Which is why any information you know can help us figure out what happened. Was he having trouble adjusting to Portland?"

I shook my head and leaned against the wooden railing. "He is…" I caught myself, "…was a good kid, a little bit aggravating but what teenager isn't, right?" I took a deep breath, trying to remember if there was anything odd about him in the last couple of days… well, odder than usual. "He'd never said anything about running into any trouble, and as far as I know he had no history with drugs or alcohol, his parents would kill him." I looked at her with a forced smile, "Figuratively speaking, of course."

Magic and drugs were a lethal combination, there was no way in hell a mage would go within a mile of the stuff. The Sahara was a prime example of why it was a bad idea.

The detective took out a card with her contact information and handed it to me. I frowned at the crisp off-white paper, making the dark block letters stand out: 'Detective Penelope Garcia, Homicide Division'.

I looked at the stern officer. "Detective Garcia, why is homicide on a suicide case? Is there something you're not telling me?"

Detective Garcia shook her head as she stood up. "I was the detective on call when it came in. I've told you everything we can at this point." I leaned away from the railing, a couple of owls hooting in the distance. The detective paid them no mind as she walked towards the end of the porch. "As soon as the ME is done with the autopsy, we'll give you a call. I'll keep trying to reach his family, but if they get in touch with you please let them know we want to talk to them."

I nodded and escorted her to the car. Once she was gone, I made my way inside to find Julia staring at me with a serious face. Sabine was sitting next to her. "Is it true?" Being a dryad came with several quirks, such as incredible hearing. She'd probably heard the entire conversation.

I shook my head frowning, "It doesn't make any sense. The kid wasn't suicidal, at least he never mentioned anything like that to me, and unless he was having more trouble than he let on, there's something more going on."

I discarded the local supernatural community in an instant; it would be stupid for any of them to hurt my staff, as they would no longer be able to stay at the inn and enjoy its protection. Tir na nÓg was the only neutral ground in the city, getting barred from it meant you had nowhere to hide and were free game. More importantly, I would hunt whoever it was and make an example out of them - it wouldn't be the first time I'd had to bloody my hands.

Julia bent down to pick up Sabine, scratching her between the ears. "Are you going to call Cassius?"

I shook my head. "Not yet, the police tried and he didn't pick up or answer his door, which probably means he's secluded in chambers with the rest of the Assembly or might not even be on this plane." I let out a slow breath. "I heard it's pretty tense over there."

"What about the mirror? Can't you use it?" She started walking over to the sofa and sat down with Sabine on her lap.

I went to the front desk, pulled out a bottle of bourbon and poured two glasses before joining her. "What am I going to tell him? 'Hey Cassius, your kid may or may not have been killed while he was under my watch, sorry can you come over?' Besides you know I hate using the mirror."

I shook my head and took a sip, after the last hour it was necessary. Anyone with a drop of magic could use mirrors to communicate, it was the simplest use for them. But there was the risk that the mirror would absorb too much magic and become sentient. Look how well that turned out for Snow White's stepmother. Lately mine had been showing signs of sentience, nothing that I could prove but every now and then out of the corner of my eye I could feel it looking at me.

Julia took the other glass and scratched Sabine's ear with her free hand. "That's not a conversation you can put off indefinitely," she took a sip of her glass, "The longer you wait the worse it's going to be." She frowned as if she tasted something bitter. "There's nothing more dangerous than being on the receiving end of a father's ire."

She sounded as if she spoke from experience, but I didn't pry into what she meant. Everyone was entitled to their secrets.

"Well, the police are waiting on the medical examiner, but luckily for us I have a friend there."

I pulled out my phone and started dialing.

"You don't sound confident, what does this friend do? And since when do you have friends? Most of the time you're cooped up in here."

As the phone started ringing, I turned to glare at her. "I have plenty of friends and I went out just the other day."

She snorted taking another sip of her drink. "Going out for errands doesn't count. Seriously, who is this guy?"

I was about to respond when the call connected on the other end. Music could be heard in the background, jazz maybe? The music was lowered to reasonable standards before Devon's cheerful voice answered. The man was never down; he would smile at midnight while performing an autopsy, or at seven in the morning while dropping his daughter off at school.

"Nathan, glad you called. Margie's birthday party is coming up soon and I need a venue, think you can hook a brother up?"

"Devon, I run an inn, not a community center. My guests need to feel relaxed and at home, and that's kind of hard to do with a horde of zombies making balloon animals and serving cotton candy."

Not only was he an excellent medical examiner with PhDs in biology and chemistry, but Devon was also the most powerful necromancer this side of the Atlantic. I once asked why a necromancer would take such a cliché job as a medical examiner. He said he liked helping people get closure.

"There were only three zombies, and the kids loved it." The sounds of bones breaking could be heard over the music. "Come on Nathan, she's turning ten. Tenth birthdays are very important, she's going into double digits."

I sighed in defeat - using a nine-year-old girl's happiness as leverage should be a crime. "Fine, but no zombies, I mean it Devon. In fact, leave the staffing to me. "

"Sure, sure, no zombies making balloon animals or cotton candy, you made yourself very clear. Now what did you want to talk about that was so important that you rang me up so late?"

My mouth was moving but no words were coming out. It hadn't dawned on me until then that Lucas might actually be dead. I struggled for a moment before pushing the thought away. As ridiculous as it sounded, I was still hanging onto the hope that the cops made a mistake and it wasn't him.

"Listen, a body might've come through tonight, a drowning victim pulled from beneath Hawthorne Bridge. It's one of us, Devon... it's Lucas."

Silence fell on the other side of the line. Devon liked Lucas, the kid had babysat Margie a couple of times and they had hit it off right away.

"I'm sorry Nathan, he was a good kid. Damn shame. The cops know what happened?"

I took another sip before filling him in on what I knew, "Not yet, they're waiting for the autopsy report, think you can see what's going on?"

"Hold on let me check, I've not been notified of a body coming in."

"Is that strange?"

I could hear a door being closed in the back as well as hurried pacing. "A little, since I'm the attending ME tonight. If a body came in, I should've been notified. I'm in the office now, let me check the system."

"Has that happened before? Not being notified a body came in?"

"Not really, especially if the cops are involved, they become prickly when an autopsy is not done on their time. I mean, do you know how long it takes to perform an autopsy? A couple of hours if you're lucky." I rolled my eyes at him and took another sip of my drink. "Now give me a moment, keep drinking your bourbon and let me do me."

I pulled the phone away from my ear and gave it a glare hoping it would burn the man on the other side. "How the hell did you know I was drinking bourbon?"

"Educated guess, you wouldn't be telling me any of this without some liquid pick-me-up." More typing could be heard in the background, "Not that I would know what a drink tastes like, my jailer has me on this new diet and it's killing me." He stopped for a moment as if realizing what he said, before shooting, "You tell Alice any of this and I will deny it."

I rolled my eyes. Devon adored his wife and would do anything for her. "Like she'd believe you."

He gave me a small chuckle before turning serious. "Now here's something you might like to know. A body did come in, a John Doe, blonde, late teens... Sounds like our boy. It was sent directly to Jason, the autopsy is scheduled for tomorrow morning."

"Is that weird?" Jason was Devon's boss and Head ME for the city.

"Extremely. An official identification is required by a next of kin but from what you told me the cops already identified the body using his ID that was found on the scene, so why is it registered here as a John Doe?" Devon sounded confused.

'Makes two of us,' I thought to myself.

"Jason is currently on vacation and won't be back for another two weeks," He continued as the sound of a door opening rang in the background, "I'll tell you something, the man's taste in music sucks. I mean who performs an autopsy to O Sole Mio?"

"Is it possible that he cut his vacation short?" I asked, ignoring the jab at his boss.

Devon snorted, "Not likely, the man is an egomaniac with a god complex. He wouldn't cut his precious fishing trip for anything short of a celebrity or politician."

Julia stood up and poured herself another glass. Given her incredible hearing, I had no doubts she could hear both sides of the conversation from the front desk. Guess you need good hearing when you're running from lovesick gods.

"Is Jason one of us, or at least in the know?" If he was that would make things simpler.

Another chuckled answered. "He's as mortal as they come, hell he doesn't even watch horror movies because it gives him the willies or something of that sort." Devon sighed, I could practically hear him shaking his head. "I mean who doesn't like a good horror movie?"

"Given the type of guests I have every other day, horror doesn't make it to my top three favorite genres."

"That's because you're a wuss." He snorted, as I heard another door close. "Anyways, how long will it take you to come here?" Jazz music rang in the background again. "I'll leave word with the front desk to let you in while I work on our boy."

I frowned and was about to ask if that will get him into trouble, but knowing Devon he wouldn't care. "Give me half an hour and I'll be there."

"Sure, just tell Janine to buzz you in. I'll be neck-deep in guts by then," Devon inhaled sharply. "Sorry, gallows humour. You know I didn't mean it like that."

I scratched Sabine's ears as she laid down next to me and shook my head. "I know. See you soon." I hung up the phone and took a deep breath, a heavy feeling settling on my shoulders.

"You should've said it was Devon instead of being all mysterious" Julia sat back down with her drink.

I gave her a small smile. "Sorry my mind is all over the place. Think you can hold the fort while I'm gone?"

She rolled her eyes and gave me a mock salute with her glass while rubbing Sabine's ears with her other hand. "Aye aye, Sarge. Sabine and I have got it covered," Julia's eyes flashed a deep emerald for a moment. "Be careful out there Nathaniel, something doesn't feel right about this."

"It's not me who has to be careful." I scratched Sabine beneath the chin. "Keep an eye on our new guest, okay girl?"

Julia frowned. "We have a new guest?" She stood up and followed me. "Why does he need to be watched?"

I made my way towards the front desk where I kept two silver bracelets: one had a morningstar, a spiked mace, while the other had a

22

shield. I put the mace one my left wrist while the shield went on my right. "I don't know yet, he seems like a good kid. Just keep an eye ok?"

"Sure thing, my lord." She gave me another salute with her glass before downing it.

Sabine sneezed before making her way up the stairs. I watched her go before grabbing my keys. "Guess I don't have anything to worry about."

I grabbed my jacket off the coat hanger by the door, and made sure to shut it quietly behind me as I escaped into the crisp night, my dark mood matching my surroundings as I walked to the car. Hopefully, Devon would at least be able to shed some light on the situation.

3

Devon worked out of the Multnomah County Medical Examiner's office, which was only a couple of minutes away from Hawthorne Bridge where Lucas's body had been discovered. If you were a part of the supernatural community, and died within the city's limits, your body was sent to Multnomah. It was standard procedure ever since Devon started working there.

I parked my truck across the street at the Pearl of Wisdom Bookstore, run by a merfolk couple who couldn't resist a pun. Selenic and his wife kept a good selection of rare and old books in stock, which came in helpful for me when the rare sea creature that no one had seen for centuries decided to holiday at the inn and I needed to know what the heck to feed it.

They wouldn't mind me leaving my truck parked in their driveway, although I hoped to be out before that became an issue.

The two-story dark brick building sat in between a couple of trees, the orange and yellow leaves yet another reminder that fall was here. I made my way up the stairs and knocked on the white double doors.

My favourite nurse appeared behind the door. Five foot three, slightly on the plumper side and an infectious smile made Janine the kryptonite for any hardcore detective or anyone with a pulse in fact, male or female. Much to my amusement she was wearing her 'The Nightmare Before Christmas' scrubs that had Oogie Boogie dancing all over them. Her chestnut hair was tucked beneath her cap but a few strands had started to escape.

We'd dated for a while when she'd first started working at the morgue after Devon had insisted on setting us up, but I broke it off when things started to get serious. It wasn't fair to her that I couldn't let go of my past and commit to any kind of future besides running my inn. She'd understood and we'd still managed to maintain a good friendship.

She opened the door and smiled. "Hey Nathan, Devon said you'd be dropping by."

I gave her a quick kiss on the cheek and stepped inside. "You look lovelier every time I see you, it's been too long."

"I've missed your accent." She pretended to swoon, holding her hand to her forehead. "I could listen to you speak all night long, but boy do you need a shower and a shave."

I screwed my face up at her, but she had a point. I'd caught my reflection in a window on my way in and almost did a double take. My dark hair, normally neatly styled with the longer top gelled to the side, was now skewed and spiked from where I'd constantly been running my hands through it. A hint of stubble could be seen along my jaw and fatigued grey eyes stared back at me, heavy bags weighing them down. I wanted a shower and sleep, but I had a feeling I wouldn't be getting either for a while. Although it was reassuring that she still liked my accent. Working at the inn, I met all kinds of creatures with international accents so I often forgot that my Irish accent was not native to Portland.

It was then that I noticed a familiar purple napkin in her hand.

"Russell's? Isn't it a little late for BBQ?"

She rolled her eyes at me. "Don't start, I have finals coming up soon and they are riding me into the ground - and not in a good way." I followed her inside to the reception desk where she had a plate of half-eaten ribs with fries. "So, a little comfort food while studying is absolutely required."

Janine had been working on her master's degree for a while. She'd had to quit for a couple of years to take care of her sick mother who sadly passed away last year, but after a small period of mourning, Janine went back to work and her studies.

"I know how smart you are, this test is nothing but a formality to you." I reached down and stole a fry. "Once you ace it, we'll celebrate with an all-you-can-eat BBQ. My treat."

She slapped me on the arm before going back to her meal, where next to the food was an opened biology book stained with sauce. "I'll take that as a promise," a familiar smile played across her mouth. "Anyways what brings you here so late? Devon didn't say anything other than to buzz you in."

I forced a grimace and said the first thing that I could think of: "Devon has been nagging me all day about Margie's birthday. So, to get a good night's sleep, I'll have to spend most of the night awake going over themes with him," I shrugged, "You know how he gets."

She rolled her eyes and bit into another fry. "He's been looking at birthday themes all day and asking anyone that comes near which one is best. Zombie superheroes or zombie princesses."

I laughed, "I'll try to talk the zombie out of him. See you later, Janine."

Sometimes that man took his job way too seriously. She waved at me before going back to her book while holding a rib in the other hand. I made my way down the dimly lit hall, past several small offices and through the large metal door which led to the stairs that took me where the underground examination rooms were located.

Due to the otherworldly nature of his patients, Devon worked out of the underground examination rooms instead of the ones on the second floor. If his patient suddenly felt the need to go for a snack, it would be harder to escape from an underground room with no windows. Movies get a lot about zombies wrong, according to Devon, but the one thing they get right is the corpse's hunger for flesh. A zombie that breaks away from his necromancer will consume anything in its path.

Zombies will always target those with a strong magical essence, but normal humans will do to keep the decomposition away. According to Devon, if a zombie ate enough flesh it would evolve into a ghoul, and no one wanted that.

I shook my head and continued down the stairs; this day had been strange enough without adding zombies into the mix.

The door to exam room 4 was ajar when I arrived, so I took the invitation and stepped in. Inside were two metal tables, a body lay on one, covered with a white sheet. On the far wall, from floor to ceiling, were what looked like metal cabinets, presumably there for body storage. A large fluorescent light, that reminded me of the ones they had at the dentist's office, hovered above the tables.

I walked through the door, past the sinks and slowly made my way to the occupied table. "Gods, please let it be someone else," I said through gritted teeth, and pulled the sheet from the body's face.

I hadn't realized until that moment that a small part of me was still hoping against all odds that the body on the table wasn't Lucas, and that the cops had it all wrong. But the gods were never on my side, the capricious bastards.

The body on the table had short blonde hair, and while the skin around the face was paler than usual, there was no doubt in my mind. I had seen his face just a few short hours ago as we argued about pants. His chest was smooth and pale, without any cuts: Devon hadn't begun the autopsy yet.

Rage bubbled inside me; my hands simmered with magic. The more I looked at Lucas' still form, the angrier I became. "Damn it kid, what the hell happened?"

A hand grabbed me by the shoulder and before my mind could process who it was, I grabbed it by the wrist, twisting as I turned around, and my magic arced towards the spiked mace charm dangling from my left hand.

"Ag Fás!" The words thundered through the room and the almost indecipherable rune, an ellipse overlapping a circle, glowed white on the surface of the charm before it grew into a familiar four feet long silver and iron morningstar.

The man who was now on the floor was in his late thirties with short sandy blonde hair, and a pair of pale blue eyes looked up at me in surprise from behind a pair of glasses. Peeking from the top of his purple shirt the hint of a scar could be seen. I knew it went from his clavicle all the way to his ribs, where an animated suit of armor almost killed him.

"Friend! I'm a friend, remember?" Devon panted from the floor. "Best friend I should add! Now would you mind not bashing my brains in before my daughter turns twenty-one?" His blue eyes looked at me with worry, "I still have boyfriends to scare, and a pregnant and upset wife to pamper."

That last bit shook me out of my rage more than the best friend part, and my magic receded. "Alice is pregnant?"

Devon rolled his eyes at me. "That's what made you stop? Not the whole best friend thing?" He clutched his chest with his free hand, "I'm hurt Nathan, really hurt." He wiped away a nonexistent tear.

I let go of his wrist and helped him up with my free hand while keeping my mace away. "I barely lived through her last pregnancy," I shrugged, "but I could always get another best friend."

"Ha-ha-ha. You're hilarious, ever thought of taking your show on the road?" He gave me a wide happy smile, "I'm going to be a dad again." The realisation seemed to dawn on him as Devon's smile melted into a frown. "Shit, I'm going to be a dad again, feels so real when you tell someone else."

I couldn't help it and started laughing. "Congratulations man." I gave him a hug. "When did you find out?"

He hugged me back tightly, his body shaking from excitement before pulling a metal stool to sit on. "About ten minutes ago, she'd been feeling sick for a while now and called me as soon as the test came back positive." He shook his head. "I didn't even know that she'd bought a test." He looked at the spiked mace in my hand. "Are you going to put that away?"

I gave the morningstar a mock swing at his head. "I don't know, some idiot might try to jump me again." Devon rolled his eyes and slapped the weapon away.

"Fine, just keep it away from me." He sighed and then turned to Lucas with a complicated look on his face before turning back to me.

"I was going to ask if you wanted the good or bad news first but the first one is out of the bag. So that leaves us with the bad one, are you ready for this?"

"What do you mean?"

He gave me another of those looks that cut straight through the bullshit. "How long have we known each other? Since before my daughter was born, right?" He crossed his arms and stared me down with those piercing blue eyes. "You could've waited for the cops to call you with the results, but you didn't. So, I'll ask again. Are you ready for this?"

I glared at him wanting to deny it, but he was right. "I need to know what happened; he wasn't suicidal. Someone pushed him and I need to know who."

Devon's eyes softened before nodding. He pulled a knife from a sheath beneath his lab coat, as large as his forearm, so it worked more as a short sword than as a knife. The blade was black and shaped like a kukri with a large belly towards the edge.

As soon as the blade was out the lights in the room dimmed and the temperature dropped. A shiver ran down my spine just looking at it. I've seen what that blade can do, how every time it came out blood had to be spilled. If not someone else's, then Devon's.

I didn't know where he got it from and he never spoke about it. All he would say was that it was a family heirloom.

Devon carefully leaned over Lucas's upper body and made a small X-shaped cut over his heart. He slowly pulled his own right sleeve up revealing a mass of scars, some old while others were still scabbing. I turned to look at Devon's eyes, which had turned a sickly green color, before he chose a fresh spot on his arm and made a cut. From the cut, a small drop of black blood fell onto the X on Lucas's body before being sucked inside.

The air was charged with power as a slow, sickening feeling crept over my spine as the ritual started: there was no chanting or candles involved in raising the dead, or at least I'd never seen Devon use them.

Two cuts, a drop of blood, creepy knife and spooky atmosphere was all he needed to bake you a zombie.

"Now leave it in the oven at 450 degrees for two hours and boom," I muttered under my breath.

"You know I can hear you right?" His voice vibrated with power as he channeled it into Lucas.

"You know I find this creepy," I shot back. Devon's magic always felt like staring into a dark abyss and having it stare right back, something primal and cold that raked its claws along my skin.

He was about to answer back when the almost-tangible tension in the air snapped. Devon's eyes faded from their glowing green back to their usual blue, his face a shade paler than it was a moment ago. The knife dropped as he slumped against the table, needing both hands to support himself.

"Son of a bitch!" He breathed through his teeth as he tried to steady himself.

I put my arm around him and helped him to the stool. "Are you ok? What happened?"

Sweat matted his brow as he struggled to keep himself upright. "Please hand me my knife... Ugh, that hurts."

The knife was lying underneath the empty table. I scooped it up, trying as hard as I could to ignore the burning cold feeling it was giving me. Devon took the knife, carefully placing it back inside his coat. I rubbed my hands together to try and get rid of the feeling as the lights suddenly glowed back to their usual brilliance.

"Why didn't you tell me the kid wasn't human?" He pressed the palm of his hand to his eye. "I'm going to be feeling that for a while."

I looked at him confused. "What do you mean? The kid's a mage but that's it," I pointed towards Lucas's body, "Your magic should've worked without a hitch."

Devon pointed to his covered eye with his free hand. "Well it didn't, the kid isn't completely mortal and he must've never told you." He closed his eyes and started rubbing his temples. "Gods above and below, I haven't felt pain like this since we tried to raise that Naga that was killed at the inn."

During my first year in business, one of my guests had been murdered. I'd needed answers, and Devon was the person to go to. We'd had a couple of near-death experiences, although the worst was with an animated suit of armor. It's amazing how fast you become friends with someone after you have to put their insides back... well, inside.

"I remember you saying something about your magic working best on humans, and how half humans like satyrs wouldn't work," I crossed my arms frowning, "But Lucas is mortal, he's not adopted. Cassius has shown me pictures of Ava pregnant."

"Satyrs are just spirits of nature," He waved his hand in the air before groaning in pain at the motion, "They die and reincarnate as a tree, bush or some flower, so reanimation doesn't exactly work. Merfolk, maybe?" He shrugged. "I don't know, never tried, but they are so intricately tied to the ocean that it might not work."

I look back to the body. "So anyway, this isn't Lucas?"

Devon opened his eyes and met my gaze. "If the kid was just a plain old strawberry mage like you've said, then no. Whatever *that* is, it's just wearing his face - it isn't *him*. It can't be. Which begs the question, if this isn't Lucas..."

I murmured, "Then who the hell is it and where *is* the kid?"

"You got me there brother, as you saw there's not much else I can do. Some spells allow you to disguise yourself as someone else," He waved his hand over his face as if putting a mask on, "But that magic is temporary, and it wouldn't explain why I couldn't raise him." He shook his fingers off and tapped his chin in thought. "Some of the old school shifters could take on the appearance of others but they would revert back to their natural forms when they died." He pointed towards the fresh cut he'd made on the body. "He could be a golem made to look like Lucas, but once I made the cut he would've bled whatever material he was made off, which didn't happen."

The more Devon talked, the more I could see the pieces of the puzzle slowly coming together in my head.

"There's another possibility. I'm running on fumes so after I do this be ready to catch me." Before he could answer, I moved towards the body, magic bubbling at my fingertips, fed by my fear, anxiety and slow-burning anger. The tip of my finger glowed with a bright white light as I slowly traced a half open eye on the forehead of the body.

"Nochtadh."

The word rang through the room and magic flowed through me. It was in these moments that I felt most myself. My magic knew me as no one else could and accepted me for it. There was no pretense, no deceptions: just me and the magic.

"Unveil yourself. Show me who you really are."

The magic crashed into the body but was met by a wall of resistance. I pushed my powers forward, but the wall held.

I gathered the force of my magic, shaping it into a spear, and rammed it against the resistance. The wall shook trying to repel but I kept hammering the spear into it, and eventually the wall started to crack under the assault.

A little more, just a little more...

BOOM! BOOM! BOOM!

I gathered the last traces of my magic, throwing it against the wall. With one resounding crack that reverberated through my brain, the wall of magic surrounding the body crumbled. The sudden release was more powerful than I expected. The residual magic pushed me off my feet - one moment I was standing next to the body, and the next I found myself lying beneath one of the exam tables.

"Jesus, Nathan, are you ok?"

Devon rushed over to me and helped me up. I grabbed his hand to pull myself up. The spell had drained me completely. Right now, even a falling leaf would be enough to knock me on my ass.

I centered myself with Devon's help and nodded towards the body. "Enough about me. Let's see who this guy really is."

"Not sure it is a guy. Here, I'll help you."

With the help of Devon, I made it to the body and my stomach cramped into a knot. "Damn it."

The illusion had been shattered and now something that was definitely not Lucas lay on the table. The skin a light shade of gray with darker patches along its body. Its head was smooth without a hint of hair, and it had no ears, just small holes on either side of its head. Beneath the eyelids, two black and soulless beads replaced its eyes. Its mouth was its most distinctive feature, short and wide like the snout of a seal.

"Well, the cause of death is pretty clear." Devon pointed towards the fist-sized hole in the creature's stomach. The edges of the hole were scorched, and black veins spread throughout the chest. Looking at the wound, I found myself smiling.

"Good one, kid."

Devon turned to me with a confused look on his face. "I take it you know what caused this? And, more importantly, what the hell this thing on my table is?"

I looked at the body again. "That, my friend, is one of the fae - a selkie, to be exact. Pretty low level in terms of power and influence as far as the fae go. They can do basic glamour and in their human shape are slightly stronger than the average human." I shrugged. "They're born as seals and once they reach maturity they shed their skins for this humanoid appearance," I pointed towards the body, "They keep the skin which allows them to shapeshift into their seal forms, and they're stronger and faster than regular seals but that's about it. Unless you're in the water with them, they aren't a threat. The nobles use them as hired muscle."

Devon looked at the body. "If being in the water makes them stronger, and this body was found floating beneath a bridge, then what happened?"

I shrugged, and gestured at the body. "I'm guessing they were waiting for the kid, and jumped him when he appeared. He must've gotten enough time to fire off a spell that hit this guy here," I reached down to trace the charred hole with my finger, where the skin felt rough and dry, "Which would explain how he came to be *here*, but not why they would pull something like this." I frowned and wiped my hands together. "Selkie are followers, not leaders, haven't been for centuries since their kingdom was destroyed." I looked at Devon, trying to keep myself steady where the spell had drained me. "Someone with a lot of magic and influence is behind this. An illusion like that is not something to scoff at, and it tells me they knew who Lucas was and targeted him specifically."

Devon gave me a look of concern. "How come you know so much about the fae?"

Memories of violence and blood flashed through my mind. A dark ominous forest surrounded by monstrosities, my sword plunging into the neck of one of them as the others converged on me, and the feeling of betrayal that had led me there.

I sighed and pushed the memories back. "Because once upon a time, I used to live among them."

4

After my little reveal there wasn't much to discuss. Devon could tell I wasn't in the mood to talk about my past, and luckily he didn't press the issue, although he did forbid me from driving home in my state. He settled me down on the couch in his office and while I tried to protest, he wasn't having any of it, and he was quickly proved right because I was out like a light before he had even turned around.

The thing about overexerting one's magic is that it leaves your mind defenseless. Things that you normally kept at bay pounce into your consciousness at the slightest hint of weakness.

I found myself at the edge of a snow-covered cliff overlooking the dark ocean. The skies were dark with storm clouds; lightning flashed in the distance followed by the clap of thunder. The waves roared in defiance at the sky as they rose and crashed against the cliff.

Water battered my face as the sea grew more restless. I took a step back, the snow crunching beneath my boots. I looked down at myself, dressed in my old black-plated armor, a sword with a white hilt at my hip and a shield decorated with a howling timber wolf tied to my wrist.

"The sea grows ever restless; soon it will come for us. We must make our

stand here." An alluring feminine voice whispered behind me. It sounded vaguely familiar and a tight sensation gripped my chest as I tried to remember.

I turned around to see a woman standing a few feet away, her long auburn hair obscuring her features as it danced with the wind. An intimate scent made its way towards me over the sea salt; winterberries and primrose. She looked delicate yet unbreakable, her gown a deep indigo, a splash of color in the gray landscape. In her hand, a double-edged leaf-bladed longsword glowed light blue, encrusted with snowflakes and sharp ice. The hilt was wrapped in white leather, ending in a dark blue gemstone carved into a four-pointed star.

"Who are you? What's going on?" I could barely even hear myself over the howling wind.

"It's time for you to show your fangs once more and face what's coming." She pointed to my sword. "Find the storm's child before the sea pulls him into her embrace, otherwise all will be lost."

I could barely make out what she was saying. "What are you talking about? Whose child? Who wants to pull him where?"

The woman raised her blade at something behind me and whispered. "It's coming."

I turned around. The sea was churning violently, the waves crashing with more fervor against the cliff, as though the land would give out at any moment. From the center of the dark ocean a massive whirlpool roared to life, and where the currents spun in a mad dash a thresh of tentacles broke the surface, rose up and swiped at the cliff, taking huge chunks from it. I turned to make sure the woman was okay but she was gone. It was just me and whatever was in the sea. An earth-shaking roar cut through the sound of the storm, like a primal titan come to life.

As if alerted to my presence, a pale green tentacle covered with gray slime, larger than the others, rose and swung down violently towards me, too big and too fast to stop. I tried to scramble away, to escape but my legs couldn't hold my weight. I stumbled onto the ground, chips of stone digging into my face. I turned on my back and saw the massive tentacle looming over me, but all I could do was raise my hands and close my eyes against the inevitable.

I was startled awake by Devon shaking me, and I stared up at him. "Are you ok? You've been shivering for a while now."

The room looked normal: no cliff, no ocean and certainly no giant tentacles. I shook my head and sat up, "Just weird dreams, I guess."

He passed me a mug of coffee. "That bad, huh?"

"Thank you," I took a sip, hot and with a hint of hazelnut... perfect. "Let's say I won't be eating sushi in the near future."

Devon raised an eyebrow. "Ooo-kay. Anyway, while you were counting wasabis I spent the night trying to get some answers," He grimaced and sat next to me, "I tried to get in contact with my boss, but it went straight to voicemail with some annoying message that said unless it was life or death, he would be fishing and unreachable for the next couple of weeks. So, there's no way to know why this selkie was sent directly to him."

"Well isn't that convenient." I looked at the clock above the wall which read ten-past-nine. "Look, why don't you go home and get some rest, and I'll start to ask around, see if there's been any weird fae movement in the city."

He gave me a dubious look. "Are you sure? I could go with you, knock a couple of heads, shake some trees, that kind of thing."

I shook my head and finished my coffee. "No, when it concerns the Fae. You've got your family to worry about, not to mention a new baby. The less attention you attract the better, but I promise to keep you in the loop."

He smacked me on the back of my head. "Moron, you are family. I worry about you too, and you know Alice will kill me if I let anything happen to you."

"Not this time my friend," I stood up and stretched before turning to him. "You have zero experience with the Fae, and they have ways of turning your life into a living hell with just a sweet smile. I'll call you if things get hairy, promise."

He sighed before going to unhook his jacket from the back of the door. "Fine, but if I don't hear from you for more than a day, I'm coming after you." He slung his jacket over his shoulder, and pointed to my spiked mace sitting at his coffee table. "Can you put that away please, it's going to look weird when we get out of here."

I looked at the mace; Devon must have brought it in from where I left it in the exam room sometime during the night. I grabbed the familiar leather handle and let my magic surge towards the second rune on the mace, a circle with two smaller ones inside it.

"Laghdaigh".

The rune flared with white light before the mace shrunk back into its charm form. I gave Devon a smile. "Like it wasn't even there."

He rolled his eyes at me. "Your magic is the weirdest I've ever seen, and this is coming from a guy who raises corpses. Come on, I'll escort you outside."

I laughed but didn't comment: the nature of my magic was a sensitive subject. I followed him out of the office, noting how the building was filled with people as they went about their business. It made me miss the quietness of last night. Most people gave Devon a salute or nod, but plainly ignored me. Just the way I liked it.

We made it outside, and Devon turned to grab me by the shoulder. "Hey, I meant it before. You are family, always have been and always will be," He wiggled his finger at me, "You can get into trouble following the rabbit down the hole, so just call me before you drink any weird potions or go through snoring doors."

"You went there? Really?" I sighed, crossed my heart and held up my hand. "Fine *mom*, I promise not to have tea with people in weird hats or farm animals, and if someone comes for my head, you'll be my first call."

He smacked me in the shoulder and shook his head, "Smartass."

I smiled at him. "Say hi to the girls for me and congratulations again on the baby."

He gave me a toothy grin before walking to his car. My car was still parked in front of the bookstore, and I walked over, expecting it to be open. When I got there, however, it was strangely closed.

That's odd... Selenic usually has the store opened at the crack of dawn. The merman was borderline insane about punctuality, although I'd never understood why.

I walked up the steps of the store to check if everything was okay. Taped to the front door, hastily scribbled on a scrap of paper in permanent marker, was a note.

'Gone for the holidays. Back in two weeks.'

That was strange. As far as I knew there were no holidays this month, magical or otherwise. September had rolled in with more rains than usual and some people took the month off to go on road-trips but Selenic was practically allergic to taking time off. Between his work as a mage and the store, the man never took a day's holiday. I examined the note closely, noting that the writing was lopsided with sharp lines instead of the meticulous cursive that Selenic usually used. What could've made him close his store and leave in what appeared to be such a hurry?

The image from last night's dream of the tentacle about to turn me into a pancake came to mind. *There's no such thing as coincidence.*

Given Portland's proximity to the ocean, the city had a wider variety of sea denizens than other parts of the country. Merfolk, Naids, Nereids and sea-based shifters, among other creatures, made their home here. Hell, we even had a hydra.

Nothing short of an emergency would drive Selenic to pack his things and skip town, I was sure. After looking back at the store and not finding anything outwardly or obviously abnormal with it, I got in my truck and drove away. Was it the fae? Selkies didn't have the magical 'oomph' to drive Selenic away, although honestly I couldn't think of any fae that did either. Were Selenic's abrupt 'vacation' and what happened to Lucas somehow connected?

There were too many questions with no answers dropping from the sky.

I needed to focus on Lucas, Selenic could look after himself.

MY HISTORY WITH THE FAE WAS TOO LONG, TOO COMPLICATED, AND ended with them thinking I was dead. If it were anybody else, I would've looked the other way rather than risk the fae knowing that I was in fact alive, but this was Lucas; if the fae had anything to do with his disappearance I'd bathe myself in their blood to get him back.

If I wanted information on the fae, there was only one other man in town who had as much history with 'the Good Neighbors', as the fae are sometimes called. In the past, he had been a captive of the Summer Court, forced to fight in their coliseum for amusement. When he was not fighting for his life, he was being experimented on by a sadistic lord who wanted to improve his abilities. During one of the experiments, the spell they had on him loosened enough and he slaughtered the entire castle before escaping into the mortal world.

I had found Travis collapsed in front of the inn, bleeding from a dozen different wounds. It was only when I helped him that I recognized the feel of Summer's magic on him. At the time I had just escaped from the fae and was barely keeping it together, and although his presence at the inn threatened the life that I had built, I couldn't bring myself to kill him. I offered him food and shelter for as long as he needed until one day he just left. During his stay, we bonded over our shared pasts with the Good Neighbors and struck an unusual friendship; we had kept an eye out for each other during the years. He had settled himself into his new life, and opened a garage.

I'd give it to him: for someone who lived most of his life with the iron-phobic fae, he was a damn fine mechanic.

I pulled over to the black and red building after stopping for some more coffee and bacon bribes. Travis had turned an abandoned firehouse into a fully functioning garage; the bottom part of the building served as the workspace while he lived up in the top. There were several cars in different states of repair in the workspace when I arrived. A bus had its whole motor dug out, a Buick had three wheels off, and from underneath a Beetle I could see a pair of huge legs which seemed to be emitting a large amount of loud cursing.

I took another sip of my coffee and grabbed the bag of bacon burgers from the passenger's side of my car before making my way over.

"Son of a whore! I hope your sister gives you parvo." Another round of cussing came from beneath the hideous multicolor beetle.

"Isn't parvo a dog thing?" I asked before downing my coffee and throwing the cup into the wastebasket.

"Don't you start with me, Mercer," A loud bang came from beneath the beetle, "Whoever it was that fixed this transmission must be roasted in the Pyres of Hal'Greydian."

Given that Hal'Greydian was Queen Titania's special room, used to torture traitors and winter spies, I pitied the poor fool who managed to get himself sent there.

"Yeah well I doubt the Bright One will care about someone messing with a transmission," I remarked at him, "Doubt she even knows what a car is."

As smart as Titania was, from what I heard she had trouble keeping up with the times, unlike her counterpart Mab, Queen of Air and Darkness and ruler of the Winter Court. Mab made sure she was on top of everything that could give her an edge against her enemies and was scarily efficient.

A snort came from beneath the beetle before Travis pushed himself out from underneath it, standing up and stretching. I looked up at his tall frame. Don't get me wrong, at six feet tall I'm not short but Travis was a good six inches taller than me, with broad shoulders and enough muscle to break you over his knee. He was undoubtedly an intimidating man, and that was without considering the scars he had from the neck down.

But it was his pale lavender eyes that told his story; those tormented eyes had seen more blood and carnage than any war veteran, and behind them a slow amber shadow lurked. It let me know that Travis's other self was watching me.

Travis looked at the bag and snorted. "Don't let the stories fool you, the Bright One only lets her enemies think she is stuck in the olden days," He gave me a knowing look, "Remember out of the other three courts, she's the one with the power to rival Winter."

And that was as scary a thought as anything else, since Mab was the original bad guy. Vlad the Impaler, Genghis Khan, Ivan the Terrible, Hitler, Stalin... all those guys were just playground bullies compared to her.

I held up the bag. "I brought a bribe."

"I could smell it all the way from your car, which needs an oil change by the way. Bring it over next week and I'll take care of it." He nodded, took the bag, and headed up the stairs to his loft.

For all the tools and cars lying around, the garage was neat and organized. I knew the reason for it: Travis had made this garage into an iron fortress, quite literally. It served as a great deterrent to any fae, as none of them would ever dare to come into a place with so much cold iron.

I followed Travis upstairs to the small kitchen on the balcony which overlooked the workspace and sat down as he served me a new cup of coffee with a hint of hazelnut. I breathed in the aromas with happiness, "Ah, bless you man."

"Still don't understand why you like that garbage so much," He gave the coffee a disgusted look, "I only keep it for the occasions when you drop by."

"You try running an inn for the supernatural where everyone has different hours that need accommodating," I took a sip of coffee, "Satyrs waking up at the crack of dawn for a little nookie, vampires that are still stuck in the past playing The Beegees at all hours of the night, or a dragon with a cold." I shuddered remembering that particular summer. "I didn't even know they could get sick. The only way you survive all that is with buttloads of coffee."

He cracked a grinned before taking a bite of his burger. "Is a buttload a real measurement?" He asked between bites.

I took another sip. "Yeah, it's slightly more than a fuckton but less than a shitload."

Travis growled at me before taking another bite of his burger. "You're not as funny as you think."

I aimed my mug at him. "I object to that, your honor. I'm extremely hilarious, Sabine said so."

"Probably because you were holding her food hostage." He'd finished his third burger and was starting on the fourth.

"Hey, no need to get into the details. She said it and that's that." I chuckled and continued drinking my coffee.

Once Travis finished eating, he lay back in his chair, wiping his mouth with a napkin. "Are you ready to tell me what's going on? Not that I don't enjoy the meal, but something's obviously up."

"What makes you say that?" I gave him a weak smile. "Can't I come and say hi to a friend?"

His eyes glowed with faint amber light, and his voice took on a rough timbre. "You know bullshitting won't work on me, Wolf. Now what is it that brought you over to my domain?"

There it was, Travis's other self. I had thought, even hoped, that the meal would've lulled the beast to sleep, but no dice. "You know I'm no longer the Wolf. I need to speak to Travis."

An amused growl came from my friend, alien and predatory. "But you are. You may have put down your fangs, but the song of the hunt still vibrates within you," Travis purred. "You didn't come here to speak with Travis," Amber eyes regarded me with predatory glee, "You came to see if I knew anything of our new visitors."

I could see Travis's nails slowly elongating into claws as he scratched the table. His purr morphed into a snarl. "You think that you can come into my domain, stinking of the fae, and I wouldn't notice?" He slapped the empty bag of food away. "That the promise of meat will save you from my wrath?!"

Faster than I could see, he launched at me from the other side of the table, claws reaching for my throat. Years of battling for my life were the only thing that saved me as I jumped back at the last second. The claws missed my throat by a hair's breadth.

Or so I thought. I touched my fingers to my throat, and pulled them away to see them stained with blood. The *thing* inside my friend licked the drops of blood off his claws, and gave me a predatory smile. "You're getting slow, Wolf. Years of looking after sheep have rusted your skills."

Anger bubbled inside me and my hands tingled as I reached for my magic. "Damn it, Travis, get your other self under control. I really don't want to draw steel on a friend but if you force me, I will."

"Travis is not here right now. You have led them straight to us, didn't you Wolf?" The beast roared. "The exile was too much that you ran back to your mistress." He pounced at me without second thought.

I let my magic run through me and reached for my shield. "Ag Fás!"

The rune on the charm flared white as a small buckler shield appeared in my hand, black and eighteen inches in diameter with a stylized hammer in the middle. I parried Travis's claws, using his momentum to send him to the side. "What are you talking about? I haven't had contact with the fae in decades." I turned to him, the shield extended in front of me.

Travis whipped around, his eyes now glowed like molten amber. "Lies, why else would the fae suddenly start swarming the city like locusts?"

The muscles beneath his face started to bulge and shift, and I knew that if I didn't stop this soon, he would change all the way and there would be no reasoning with him. I had to keep him talking. "I have no idea what you're talking about. I haven't sensed any fae in the city. Hell, I didn't know they were in town until this morning when I discovered a dead selkie."

Travis pounced at me again, claws outstretched in front of his body ready to render me limb from limb. I dodged the incoming strike, lowering myself to the ground before coming up and punching him in the face with the shield. A crunching sound rang through the room, probably a broken nose. The blow evidently caught him by surprise as his own momentum shot him back against the balcony railing.

The reason why I prefer bucklers to other shields, besides the fact that they're small and great for parrying, was that they also do a great job at punching enraged shifters back to their senses. Blood slowly trickled down from his crooked nose. Travis slowly reached up to touch it before growling at me in rage.

Shit, I'd drawn blood. Now it was personal. "I swear to you by the

Evernight that I have not contacted the fae, and if I'm lying let it swallow me whole."

"If you didn't call the fae then why the hell is that damnable Hobgoblin in town" Long canines extended from his upper jaw. "He is of Winter and I don't know of anyone else with ties to them than you!" He roared at me.

A shiver ran down my spine. "Wait, what? He's in Portland?"

He roared in response, rage completely overtaking his reasoning. Magic saturated the air as the smell of hawthorn and alder spread through the garage, his broken and crooked nose straightening as rust-colored fur grew to cover his body, his bones snapping with a loud bang as the full transformation began.

Damn it, I really needed him to calm down enough to tell me where he saw him. If he finished transforming, there was no way he could tell me in the imminent future. "Damn it Travis, you forced me to do this."

I let my magic surge reach for my morningstar. "Ag Fás!"

The mace grew in my hand, the familiar weight comforting and solid. I rushed towards Travis, his transformation already halfway done: a nightmare of both human and beast. Elongated arms that ended in five-inch claws, teeth sharpened into fangs inside a human mouth, amber eyes filled with wrath. The only parts that were remotely human were his legs, but even that wouldn't be for long.

Before he could finish transforming, I rushed in and swung my mace down on his kneecap, wincing at the sound of bones crunching underneath my weapon. Travis howled in pain and tried to swipe at me, but the pain from the blow made him miss me by a mile. I swung twice more, once to the other kneecap and the other to an elbow, snapping it out of place. Pain flared in the nightmare creature that was my friend.

His body was now bulging uncontrollably, torn between finishing the transformation or healing the inflicted damage. Human and beast fought for dominance in one body; one wanted to render me limb from limb, the other just wanted a nap, possibly some more burgers. In the end, the need to heal the damage won the body over and he started to slowly revert back to human form. I breathed a sigh of relief and exhaustion, and turned my back on my friend to look for some spare clothes. Travis would need some time to put himself back together, physically and mentally, and I needed a few minutes to gather myself.

5

By the time I'd returned with a spare coverall, Travis was sitting on a chair, his brow matted with sweat and trying to get his breath back. The remnants of his shirt hung on his chest like dirty rags. Beneath the tatters, a multitude of scars told his story of captivity with the fae and the cruelty they inflicted upon him. Shifters almost never scar, but when they did it was because the damage was so intense, more than they could heal completely.

He saw me walking towards him, and his eyes flashed amber for a second before they returned to their usual lavender color. "Since when did you start using a morningstar? Last I recalled you were a swordsman."

I handed him the clothes and shrugged. "Necessity. When you run an inn where most of the guests have stupid levels of healing, I needed something else to motivate them to behave." I nodded towards his elbow, "Healing broken bones takes time and energy, as we just found out, and swords never felt right after..." A bitter taste rose in my mouth, the memory of a dark forest tried to rear its head before I pushed it back down. "Well, you know."

He snorted, stripping off the remnants of his shredded coveralls. "Yeah, I already know I will be in bed for the rest of the day. The elbow should be fine in a couple of hours but the knees..." He grunted in pain as he put his legs into the clean garment. "Was it necessary to crush both my knees?" He zipped up the coveralls, shaking out the sleeves, and glared at my bracelets. "And what the hell is that thing made of anyways? It burns like a motherfucker and it's making my healing more prickly than it normally is."

I went to the kitchen, poured him a glass of milk and grabbed a calcium vitamin from the cupboards. "Mithril and silver, works great against shifters, the undead and fae, just in case they come knocking on my door." I walked back and gave them to him. "One of my regulars, a dwarf who comes to holiday at the inn every Yule, made it for me. Since silver is such a soft material to work with it needed to be mixed with something else, and the dwarves are the only ones that can make it besides the Fae."

He grimaced at the milk and vitamin but downed them in one go, knowing the extra bit of calcium would help with the healing. "Now," I raised my eyebrow at Travis, "Want to tell me what the hell that was all about?"

He sighed and motioned for me to sit. "Three days ago, I was making a house call to Goose Hollow. This old lady had a problem with her minivan and wanted to get it looked at but couldn't make it to the shop," He moved his arm grunting in pain and glared at me. "Anyways, I saw the Hobgoblin walking to the athletic club next door. Safe to say, I didn't make it to the old lady's house, I came straight back home to prepare. And then along you come, out of nowhere, stinking of dead fae." He gestured to his head. "It made my brother... upset."

"Upset is an understatement," I snorted and sat down to think.

Goose Hollow is north of Downtown Portland, one of the nicer parts of the city, with some nice restaurants but mostly just apartment complexes. From what I know, it didn't have any solid or prominent supernatural group. However, rather worryingly, the athletic complex was just a hop away from the bridge where the selkie's body had been found.

"What's Goodfellow doing here?" I muttered out loud. "He wouldn't move unless ordered by the Queen."

Robin Goodfellow, also known as Puck or the Hobgoblin, was a lord of the fae. When people heard his name, they imagined a mischievous, bubbling little fae of Shakespeare's *A Midsummer's Night's Dream*. The bard had *some* of the facts about what happened that night right, but he had mostly been used by King Oberon to spread his version of events.

The real Goodfellow was not a sweet impish trickster, but a powerful fae. Devious and cunning, he had previously been the King's right-hand man. The English play script made him look like a fool at Oberon's behest, in order to hide the fact that Goodfellow's schemes had almost lost Oberon his crown.

Seeing his plan to get rid of Oberon and cause civil war among Summer, the Fae was ultimately foiled at the last minute. He sought refuge with Queen Mab and the Winter court, and has been one of her most loyal subjects ever since.

"I've had some dealing with Goodfellow in the past, and that's stretching it. He mostly stays by the Queen's side as one of her advisers," I tapped my fingers on the table.

"I know." He said flatly.

"What the fuck is he doing in Portland?" I swore, this was not good; I had spent years without coming anywhere near any of the fae, and in the span of twenty-four hours I was somehow up to my elbows with them.

"You already asked that, and I'll repeat that I have no idea," He shrugged his wide shoulders and gave me a questioning look, "Which reminds me, why do you smell of dead fae?"

I explained everything to him, from Detective Garcia's visit to finding out that the body of Lucas was actually a dead selkie, and my thoughts on his disappearance.

A sheen of amber flickered within his eyes. "That sounds disturbing. Either they didn't know who he was, which means that they are indiscriminately taking anyone they can, or they knew who his father was and specifically targeted him. Either way, this doesn't sound good Wolf."

I scoffed at him. "Tell me something I don't know."

He gave me a serious look. "You know that if you get involved in whatever this is, there's a chance that the fae might never leave you alone, especially given what happened last time."

He left the thought hanging, and after a sigh I nodded gravely. "Yeah I know, but Lucas is a friend, and if they think they can come into my town and start shit up then they have another thing coming."

Travis crossed his arms over his chest and raised an eyebrow. "What are you going to do? Take on the whole of the fae by yourself? You tried that before, and look where it got you."

"I'm not the same as before, and maybe it's time they were reminded of why they call me Winter's Wolf."

I talked with Travis for another ten minutes, discussing the situation in hand. He firmly told me that he wouldn't go out of his way to help me as it might draw Summer's attention, but that if I was ever in a pinch, he would do what he could to help.

It was a quarter after noon by the time I got out of his garage, my whole body sore and still coming down from the adrenaline and physical shock of the fight. God, it had been so long since I'd been in a proper fight. Sure, a guest might get rowdy every now and again, or the dragon might get pissed about something, but it never got to the point of life or death.

Fighting Travis brought back all sorts of memories, both pleasant and unpleasant. If Goodfellow was in town then something big must have happened at court.

"Well, no time like the present to say hi to some old friends." Having pulled out of Travis' garage, I turned the car around the corner and made my way towards the athletic club.

The Multnomah Athletic Complex, commonly known as The MAC, sat between a clothing store and a church off by Salmon Street. As I parked on the side of the street, I looked up to the red brick building and felt a rush of anxiety surge through me. I was not ready to fight someone as powerful as Goodfellow.

My magic didn't have a fancy name like evocation or abjuration. In all my years, I haven't seen anyone perform the kind of magic I could; not even the fae, who were literal beings of magic. I was a rune caster, who drew magical runes either on an object or in the air to serve a specific purpose. The mass and material properties limited how many runes I could draw on an object; my morningstar could hold two runes while my shield could hold three. I could also write a rune in the air and cast my magic that way, but it took more power than just activating a pre-existing one.

I looked down at my bracelets where my charms hang. Normally, they were all the firepower I needed, but today wasn't a normal day. I looked around in my car to see if there was anything useful. Couple of pens, a pair of sunglasses, a receipt for gas and a deck of playing cards. Figuring it will have to do, I grabbed two cards from it and let my magic surge from within me, carving two runes on the cards just to be on the safe side. I could feel the drain on my reserves but it was a manageable one, easily replenished. I put the rune cards in my back pocket and threw the sunglasses on before stepping out of my car.

Much to my chagrin I'd parked at the back of the MAC and had to walk around the corner to get to the entrance. The double glass doors opened into a large reception hall, where soft music gave the room a relaxed ambiance. The walls were lined with sports photos and trophies, from cross country to fencing and everything in between.

Members were running to and from places, wearing all sorts of sports uniforms and equipment. If I wanted to blend in it would be difficult given my flannel shirt, jeans and boots ensemble.

I was only at the door and was already in way over my head. Back when I was living among the fae the ability to see beyond their glamour was paramount for surviving and the only way I could defend myself was with my runes. So one day, I carved a pair of illusion-piercing runes on my eyes, which when activated would let me pierce through their illusions. It hurt like hell and turned my eyes from blue to gray, but it worked.

Better safe than sorry. I sighed and let my magic seep behind my eyes. "Féach"

The veil of magic that clouded the supernatural world from the mortal one parted before me revealing the true nature of the building. Surprisingly it looked just about the same, no couches turning into man-eating monsters, or carpets with eyes ready to smother anyone stupid enough to walk on them.

The members on the other hand were a different story; goblins, bugbears, trolls and all sorts of fae were wandering around. Some were carrying bowling balls and tennis rackets, others were walking around with spears and swords. A bugbear passed by wearing only swim trunks - something *that* hairy needed to be covered up and thrown in a closet.

I had truly fooled myself into thinking that Portland didn't have a large fae community. Yet, here I was, looking at a whole club whose membership was made up of Winter Fae.

"Oh, frack me." I swore beneath my breath.

I must have been standing at the front like an idiot for a while, because I snapped out of my stupor to see one of the employees making a beeline for me. She was short, about five feet tall, with dark bobbed hair. Her eyes were polished obsidian and her skin black, like wet earth after a thunderstorm.

"A bwca, just my luck", I muttered grimly. Pronounced 'bucca', they are the Welsh cousins of the friendly brownies. While brownies were predominantly found among the Summer and Spring courts, bwca preferred to make their home amongst the denizens of Winter. Unlike the brownies, bwcas have nastier tempers and don't take well to criticism: they've been known to cut off someone's head at the slightest hint of it.

"Good day sir, this is a member's only club so I'm going to have to ask you to leave." She said with a thousand-watt smile. I looked at her name tag that spelled *Darling*. Sure she was.

"How do you know I'm not a member?" Seeing a bwca smile was more jarring than I thought, as normally they just snarled.

Her smile alarmingly got even brighter, if that was possible. "I've been working here a long time and pride myself on knowing every member, and you're not one of them," Her tone took a hard edge, "So, I'm going to ask you to leave or I'll call security."

Security seemed to be a couple of twelve-foot-tall trolls, armed with large spiked clubs, who were making their way towards us. Well, that officially made bluffing my way inside impossible. "What you mean is that I'm not fae, and thus not a member."

A slight tension of the shoulders was the only reaction I got. Her smile never faltered. "I don't know what you mean, sir."

I gave her my own smile, letting my magic surge forward as I moved my hand to my pocket where the cards lay, just in case. "Sure you do honey, now be a good dear and tell Puck that Nathaniel Mercer is here to see him." I nodded towards the incoming trolls that had picked up their pace, adding, "I would hate to decorate this lovely carpet with troll brains, so keep your goons away."

The smile dropped from the bwca as her eyes glowed scarlet and hair whirled in the air. "A hairless ape like you has no right to give me orders, or call our lord by name."

My grin widened as I shifted my weight to the balls of my feet in case this got out of hand. "The last time a fairy called me an ape, I spilled his guts all over the banquet hall then made him clean the mess before going back to my pie." I took off my sunglasses and levelled my glare at her. "Call me an ape one more time, please," I grinned at her, "It's been so long since I've spilled fae blood."

The rage in the bwca's eyes grew for a moment before her face suddenly paled as she looked at me. "You're Winter's Wolf." She shook her head in denial, taking a step back and muttering, "That's impossible. You're supposed to be dead."

I let my magic swirl around us then leaned slowly towards her. "Want to test me, little maid?"

Her eyes darted around, panicking, brown tears streaming down her face. "Master, please save me!" She screamed, taking another step back, drawing a ragged breath but stopped short by the force of my magic sealing us in.

Any other time I would've felt bad for her, but if I showed her any weakness she would've taken my throat out in an instant, and my whole show and tell would've been for nothing. The trolls had finally reached us, but they were staying outside of the range of my magic. They didn't know what I could do, but they were of Winter, and recognized a predator when they saw one.

"How low our Princess's captain of the guards has fallen to. Making little ones cry, shame on you Nathaniel." A lazy voice with a hint of mirth came from somewhere to my right.

I turned to look at the fae who had spoken. He was about my height, with hair falling to his shoulders in waves the color of dried wheat. Wearing a white business suit with a light blue tie, he regarded me with bright ruby eyes that shone with intelligence. His soft features would never make you think of him as handsome, but instead... beautiful. I felt my expression harden.

"I would say that since she's standing here, alive and not a stain on the floor, that shows remarkable self restraint on my behalf." My voice hardened as my magic pulsed outward in a gale of red and silver, swirling faster around the bwca and myself. "If it were any other time, her intestines would already be splattered over the walls." I turned towards the bwca with a grim smile. "Wouldn't you say so, *Darling?*"

She fell to her knees, her mascara mixing with her tears as she continued to cry and splutter, "Master please, save me, I've always been faithful to you."

Goodfellow raised his hand and she stopped. "Don't worry my dear, he won't kill you, our former captain just wanted to get my attention." He then turned to me. "You got what you wanted, so could you please let this little one go?"

I gave the bwca another smirk, before pulling my magic back. The red and silver winds vanished as if they were never there, and she slowly got to her feet with the help of one of the trolls before making her escape down the hallway. I turned to look at Goodfellow. "That was awfully altruistic of you."

His ruby eyes narrowed before motioning me to follow him; I trailed behind as he led me through a series of corridors to the heart of the complex. The deeper we went, the colder the air felt. The walls were painted a soft white and blue, and paintings depicting different regions of Winter decorated the walls. Fae of all shapes and sizes were minding their own business, either participating in sport or practicing combat maneuvers. A goblin was berating a group of pixies, the neon pink and blue globules of light flying around the goblin's head revealed his anger. I had not been around so many fae since I left the court, and it was disconcerting to say the least. Everyone that passed us stopped to give Goodfellow a bow before continuing with what they were doing.

What was this place? On the surface it looked like a private sports complex that helped the young athletes of the city, but beneath the complex was teeming with fae running drills on how to storm a castle. I looked around and... was that *lava* coming from the top of that wall? I suppose for some of the fae, wielding a sword and learning how to best chop someone's head off could be considered a sport. What was the play here?

"Is it really so strange?" Goodfellow asked as he led me further into the building.

The question caught me off guard, breaking my train of thought. "I don't follow."

"Do you truly find it strange that I would care for the wellbeing of those under me?" He explained.

I snorted and gave him an incredulous look as we walked. "Are you seriously asking me that question? Since when has the nobility cared about anything other than their own self-interest?"

He opened a pair of white, wooden double doors that led into a small but beautifully decorated studio, with wooden bookshelves of ash lining the walls from floor to ceiling. A dark brick fireplace crackled with faint golden flames to our right, and a white leather couch and chairs sat in front of it with a small tea table in between them.

Above the fireplace was a gorgeous painting of a sun kissed forest, the trees vibrant with life, the sunlight hitting the leaves in such a way that gave the illusion that they were made of gold. It was The Golden Woods, one of the most dangerous and beautiful forests of the Summer Court.

"While you're not wrong about the selfishness of the nobility, we do take care of our underlings," Goodfellow said as he strode towards the huge mahogany desk that sat to the left of the studio and poured two glasses of some orange-colored drink. "They provide us with their loyalty and service, and in return we protect them from anything that might cause harm to them."

He offered me one of the glasses. I looked at it, was he testing me? You never take food or drink from the fae; it's a quick way to get yourself dutifully bound to them. He noticed my look and rolled his eyes. "I offer this drink in my role as host to a guest, neither I nor one of mine will do you harm for the remainder of your stay."

He was invoking guesting laws. That caught my attention. If I were to accept the drink, then he would have to do everything in his power to keep me safe while I was under his roof, and the same would apply to me. I would have to be courteous and do no harm to my host.

Breaking guesting laws was a taboo for anyone in the magical community, but even more so for the fae. Due to their nature, if they broke the laws, untold calamities would fall upon them. Not to say that you were a hundred percent safe - there's no such thing when dealing with the fae, but it would give me an extra layer of protection.

"I appreciate your generous gift of hospitality." I took the drink from him, taking a sip. The alcohol went down smoothly, leaving an aftertaste of berries on my tongue.

Goodfellow took his own drink and sat on the couch by the fireplace. "Sunshine's Laughter, an exquisite concoction straight from Summer," He took a sip and revelled in the taste, "Quite hard to find in the lands of Winter, but not impossible in the mortal world. You just have to know the right pixie."

I took one of the chairs and sat down, and looking at my host pointed towards the painting and then the drink in his hand. "Missing your old haunts, Puck?"

If the nickname bothered him, he didn't show it. "Sometimes. When the waves of nostalgia grip my heart, I gaze into the horizon wishing to stride once more through the woods, letting the sun kiss my skin." He waved his hand in the air, dismissing the imagined image. "Then I remember that I value my life more than any nostalgia and it passes."

He gave me a smile behind the rim of his glass as he took another sip. "How long has it been? Ten years? I remember the commotion your death caused at court. Can you imagine?" He motioned towards me. "Winter's Wolf, our lovely Princess's mighty human captain, killed in battle," He snorted before taking another sip of his drink. "Blue-beard was especially thrilled; he threw a three-day banquet where he met his newest bride." Goodfellow gave me an inquisitive look. "What none of us could figure out was what you were doing in the Crooked Man's forest to start with."

6

The name triggered a slew of memories that had been haunting me for years; half-formed monstrosities howling for blood, the smell of rotting bodies that permeated the air that was so thick it made you gag, the cries of children scared out of their minds which fell on deaf ears. But worst of all was the cackling laughter that rose above the madness as he feasted on his latest victim.

I took another sip of my drink to wash away the memories, ignoring his probe for information. "Last night the body of a young man was found floating beneath Hawthorne Bridge. During the autopsy the glamour on the body vanished, revealing the corpse of a selkie."

His expression turned solemn and he regarded me with a stoic demeanor. "And your interest in this is? As I recall, you never cared for the death of a selkie, or any fae for that matter. Well, except perhaps one."

I put the glass down, the time for niceties long past. "The boy is one of mine, Goodfellow, and he was obviously taken by the fae who left a double presumably to not arouse suspicions. Where is he?"

A smirk formed in the corner of his lips as he stood up to refill his drink. "One of yours? Now that's amusing. The boy must be really important for you to make your presence known to us after so long." He leaned against the desk and regarded me with a curious look. "Is he your lover? No, that's not right, your taste never ran in that direction. Pity." He seemed laughably forlorn at the notion as he tapped the glass to his lips in thought. "You wouldn't reveal yourself for simple friendship or duty. Is he perhaps your child, Nathaniel?" He looked at me with his ruby eyes as he smiled.

I ignored the question and continued, "The body presented clear signs of a struggle. Someone went to great lengths to capture the boy and make sure no one went looking for him." I glared at Goodfellow trying to keep myself under control. "If they hadn't made a mistake with the glamour they might have gotten away without me noticing it. Now they have my undivided attention." I repeated, "Where is the boy?"

He looked at the ceiling in thought as he drank. "Well, that was foolish of them. Straight kidnapping is much easier than falsifying someone's death. So many variables are needed to be taken into account. First you need a double for the body, and then you have to make the death seem ordinary. Make it so ordinary that it could happen to anyone." He lifted the glass to his eyes and gave it a cursory look. "Drowning beneath a bridge is moronic unless the person is depressed and suicidal. Much easier making people think he was run over by a car or attacked in some dark alley."

"Well thank you for your insights on kidnapping, that wasn't creepy at all," I stood up, muscles tense in case things get dicey. "Selkie are muscle, just one step above vermin in the eyes of the fae. They don't have the smarts or the balls to kidnap someone off the street, and in such a messy matter." I crossed my arms over my chest. "And they certainly don't have the juice to glamour a body. Where is the boy? Thrice asked."

There's a lot of conflicting information about the fae, most of it construed at their behest to appear mysterious. The main myth that mortals get right about them is that the fae can't lie. They can twist the truth into a pretzel, but they cannot outright lie, due to an ancient curse placed on their kind centuries ago. The curse strikes when they're asked a question three times, compelling them to answer to the best of their abilities. No lies, no deceptions, just the truth. Every fae in existence was a control freak and they hated to be forced into something against their own will, so you were unlikely to make it to asking them something three times. It struck me as strange that Goodfellow let me ask the question three times: most fae would've attacked by the time the second question was asked.

He took a sip of his drink before answering, "I don't know where the boy is. As a matter of fact, I had no idea any of this took place before you walked through my door and told me about it."

I frowned, confused. Goodfellow was a meticulous old bastard, he didn't make a move on someone if he didn't have every bit of information about his target, from their favorite tie to how much a cup of coffee cost at their local diner.

"Why so forthcoming with information, Goodfellow? This is unlike you." He could've simply answered with 'I don't know' and that would've fulfilled the requirements of the question. So why was he being so helpful? What was his angle?

He waved his hand dismissively. "My reasons are my own, call it a greeting gift after not seeing each other for so long, a boon after that marvelous display of ruthlessness at the entrance." He closed his eyes, biting his lip for a moment before looking at me, his face stoic. "Or simply me wanting you out of my premises as fast as possible. I do have orders and obligations to fulfill and you're in the way of them."

I rolled my eyes at him. "We were never on any terms that would require a meeting gift,and as for the boon, you can shove it." I pushed my luck, "Do you know anybody that keeps close ties to the selkie community? Someone as knowledgeable as you would know a name or two?"

He took another sip of his drink before shaking a finger at me. "I have answered your questions to the best of my abilities, and while it's been a pleasure seeing you again Nathaniel, I do have other appointments so if you'll please."

The door to the studio suddenly opened revealing a couple of security trolls ready to throw my butt to the curb. I turned to Goodfellow, there was more he wasn't telling me. But he had fulfilled his obligations as host, asked me to leave, and under the guesting laws I had no way to force the information out of him.

He had basically given me nothing, and I had the feeling that he got more information out of our little meeting than I did. I gave him my best innkeeper smile, forcing, "Thank you for your time, Lord Puck, I'm sure we'll be seeing each other soon."

The lord of the fae returned my smile and said nothing. I walked towards the trolls, exiting the room as Goodfellow called behind me, "Be advised Captain, selkies swim in murky waters, the murkier the better. They hide themselves before snatching their prey and have no love for the frozen waters of Winter."

And with that cryptic message, the doors closed behind me. I sighed. "Freaking faeries always resorting to riddles."

A growl next to me caught my attention. I looked up to see one of the trolls snarling at me and raised my hands. "Slip of the tongue, gentleman, my mistake. Shall we continue?"

After my little faux pas they escorted me out of the building. I got into my car, luckily without incident; I had feared perhaps assassins ready to take off my head. I sat back and considered the meeting. Honestly, it had been one of the nicest interactions I've had with one of the Fae, the whole bwca incident included.

The athletic complex gave me an uneasy feeling, perhaps because that many fae put together were basically a garrison. If this was a recent move, then they were surely planning something that needed large numbers. Given the size of the building, it could host and train a couple thousand fae.

Something big must've happened at court for them to mobilize such a large force to the mortal world. Did it have something to do with the selkies that took Lucas? I frowned - what had Goodfellow meant by 'they have no love for Winter's waters'? I scratched my head furiously. Damn faeries and their love of riddles. Even though I had cut all ties with them, they still found ways to screw with me.

Although, Goodfellow *had* sounded surprised when he saw I was alive, and acted like he hadn't known I'd survived... although with the

Fae you could never trust anything that came out of their mouths. Just because they couldn't lie, didn't mean they couldn't twist the truth. I shook my head and decided to put those thoughts behind me. My priority was finding Lucas, even though I had no leads except for that cryptic message.

I pulled out my phone and scrolled through my contacts until Cassius's number came up. I had put this off for far too long. He deserved to know that his child was alive and that I was doing everything in my power to get him back. I looked back at the building before taking a deep breath and made the call.

The phone rang and rang. I eyed the street to see if any unfriendlies were coming but it was empty. I looked back at my phone and frowned. What was taking him so long? I cranked the A/C to max, letting the cool air hit my face while my stomach did the rumba.

"Hello, this Cassius. I can't come over the phone but if you leave a short message I'll get back to you at my earliest convenience."

I took a deep breath while the voicemail beeped and let it out. "Hey man, I need to talk to you about Lucas. He's okay so don't worry but things are complicated here and... just call me okay..." I struggled to find the words and ended the call, throwing my phone on the passenger seat in defeat.

With no other choice, I started the car and made my way back to the inn. Maybe something will hit me on the head on the way, or a clue might fall into my lap.

IT WAS ALMOST SUNSET WHEN I MADE IT BACK TO THE INN WITH TWO boxes of pepperoni alfredo pizza. After the whole Goodfellow fiasco, a little comfort food seemed like a good idea. I looked at the inn, still in one piece, and breathed a sigh of relief; every time I left, there was a nagging feeling in the pit of my stomach that the inn wouldn't be there by the time I came back.

I let my magic flow through me and into the land, checking that all my wards were up and in good condition. I paid special attention to the circle of red verbena and St. John's Wort circling the inn, keeping it hidden from fae eyes; they would have to be strengthened at some point now that the fae knew my current living status.

That could wait until after dinner, I thought as my stomach noticeably growled. I picked up my pizza and made my way towards the door, suddenly noticing a silver Audi pulling up and parking on my driveway.

A new guest perhaps, or someone with more sinister intentions?

"One afternoon with the Fae and I'm already seeing threats jumping from every shadow," I mocked myself before stepping through the door.

The foyer and front desk were empty, which was odd considering normally when I come back Sabine would be at the desk waiting for me. I looked towards the living room and saw that none of the guests were there either. It wasn't *that* strange considering that the inn currently only had two guests: Xaris the dragon, who'd been a permanent lodger for years, and Roel the magical human. The centaur herd that was staying should've left this morning along with the satyr father and son. I guess pissing off a cranky dragon put a damper on any family reunion.

I put the pizzas on the front desk and was about to call for Sabine when my wards started to scream at me, just as the front door opened. I turned around and saw a middle-aged woman enter the foyer with magic swirling around her like a cloak. She was wearing a tight dark green and black gown, platinum curls falling below her waist in soft waves, with sharp brown eyes taking in every detail as she slowly walked forward. Behind her stood a young woman, probably in her mid-twenties, with short dark hair and light brown eyes, wearing a similar outfit in a paler shade of green.

Witches. Great, just my luck!

I gave them my warmest smile. "Good evening ladies, welcome to Tir na nÓg. How can I help you tonight?"

"You're the owner?" Asked the younger of the two in a haughty tone.

The older woman's magic coiled around her like an ancient

serpent, and cold spikes pricked my skin as she filled the foyer with her magic; it crested attempting to move past the foyer and up the stairs. I smiled and let her. The wards I carved on the wooden floors activated, grounding the magic before it could reach the first step. The woman frowned for a moment and I could feel her gathering another pass when the floorboards shook, sending a warning spike back to her.

She raised her brows in surprise and tried to shield herself from the spike, but it was useless as the floorboards redirected the witch's magic against her, and she stumbled backwards. Her brow was matted with sweat and the first hint of caution shone in her eyes. She started gathering large quantities of magic, the air around her thickening with the smell of iron and sea water.

Okay, enough is enough... I glared at them. "I recommend you stop, any further probing will be considered a hostile action and I will respond in kind."

I didn't reach for my magic, it wasn't necessary, as I knew the wards around the inn would turn the witches' insides into a bubbling puddle of grease at the moment they turned hostile.

The younger witch looked at the sweating older woman before glaring at me. "Is that how you treat your guests? What a sorry excuse for a host are you?"

"That is where you're wrong, miss." I smiled at her, leaning against the front desk. "You're not currently guests of Tir na nÓg, and given your actions you can be considered a threat to my *actual* guests. As the host, it is my duty to protect the safety of my lodgers with utmost zeal," I pointed towards the plaque with the inn rules, "I'll give you your first and final warning, behave within the walls of Tir na nÓg, or die."

The young witch was about to retort when the matronly woman touched her shoulder and glared at me. "Do you think you can threaten me, little man?" She raised her chin and I fought hard not to roll my eyes at her as she continued. "Do you know who I am? What I can do to you with just a flick of my wrist?"

Fiery anger sizzled my insides. All my life I had been looked down upon by the fae and there was no way I was going to let some pointy-hatted, wart-nosed cackling witch speak to me like that in my own inn. "I don't give a damn about who you are or what you can do," I said, crossing my arms and glared at her. "If you don't start talking like a civilized person instead of a shrieking hag, I'll wipe my floors with you and use your body as compost for my trees."

The woman's face turned purple with anger and she opened her mouth to speak, but I had enough of her and was getting seriously annoyed. I called to the inn, feeding my magic to the runes I had previously prepared for such occasions. "Tost!"

The broken wing shaped rune above the door flared white sending a pulse of magic through the inn. The woman tried to cast a spell, but no words came out of her mouth. Shock and fear clouded her face as she tried several more times but still no sound came. The younger woman tried to mutter to her, but similarly her mouth moved and no sound came.

"Kind of hard to cast spells without a voice, don't you think?" I said with a saccharine smile.

The woman's eyes flared with rage and she aimed a finger at me in some vague attempt to either cuss at me or put a spell; either was impossible to do without a voice. I opened one of the pizza boxes, grabbed a slice and bit into it while they continued their futile attempts to kill me.

"Mmm delicious, Marny just makes the best pizza." I gushed, ignoring them standing there in outrage. If they were going to insult and belittle me then I had no reason to be polite to them - besides, my pizza was getting cold.

"Mmm, so good." I moaned while taking another bite.

The two witches began gathering large amounts of magic, but without a way to release it they were pretty harmless. Casting a spell at its most basic was a two step process, you gathered the magic and then released it. The easiest way was to call out your intent out loud, with only really old and powerful magic users being able to do it without speaking.

I finished my slice and made a show of licking my fingers loudly before turning my attention to them, but by this point they had given up their attempts to cast magic and were glaring daggers at me. "Done already?" I looked at the box mournfully. "Shame, I wanted another slice."

If looks could kill, I would've been a stain on the floor, or a toad. You could never know with witches.

Time to get serious. I turned towards the elder of the two. "I'm sure Matilda warned you to be on your best behavior before coming to meet me. You probably thought she was just being courteous and didn't pay her any mind," I wagged my finger at her and clicked my tongue, "You should've listened to her, this is my domain and the safety of those inside are my priority. I'm going to release the spell, try anything like that again or say anything bothersome and you'll find out what the inside of a toad feels like. Are we clear?"

The younger woman was shaking with rage and flipped me the bird. The matronly woman grabbed her by the shoulder, lowering her arm with a shake of her head before turning towards me and giving me a stiff nod.

"Saor." I called out and felt another drain on my reserves, but that was okay: I had pizza to spare.

Another rune in the shape of a cloud glowed with power above the door, pulling the magic back into itself along with a little bit from both women to recharge. "Now, who are you and why have you come to disturb the peace of my guests?"

The women glared at me. "I'm Valentina Hall, Voice of the Waves and Blade of the Goddess. My companion is Teresa Wright, Child of the Breeze." She announced grandly.

I fought hard not to roll my eyes at them again - all witches had a flare for the dramatic. They were the child of this, the pulse of that, heart of the other. They took titles based on their own magical affinity, although only the leader of the coven could take a second title related to the goddess of magic, Hecate.

Matilda, the leader of the local coven that also provided the cleaning service for the inn, was pretty much the same. Her full title was Tempest's Dancer and Torchbearer of the Goddess. She was a pragmatic woman and didn't like to cause any waves, however she ran her coven with an iron fist and didn't tolerate any funny business from the witch community.

If a witch as powerful as Valentina was in my inn, then she would've first gone to Matilda as a courtesy call to get the layout of the city, and a warning not to make trouble.

So, whatever made Valentina come here was witch-related.

"And you're here because?" Seeing as they didn't answer immediately, I pointed towards the pizza boxes. "Come on, woman, out with it, can't you see that my pizza is getting cold?"

I normally try to be as polite as possible, but the day had been shitty and she was making it even shittier. I just wanted them out of my inn.

Her eyes flared with rage, but she swallowed it as her accent got even thicker. "Is this how you normally treat your guests? Matilda assured us that you were an understanding and helpful man, not some uncultured monkey without the slightest sense of decorum."

What was it about today that everyone started calling me a monkey? I arched an eyebrow at her; she had blown past the last shred of my patience.

"We've already covered that you're not guests in my inn. If you have trouble remembering that, I would suggest seeing a doctor - they do say the memory is the first thing to go as we age. Now, I'll ask one last time. What do you want, Puddle Screech, or whatever your name is?"

The younger woman, Teresa, roared at me. "You insignificant cur, how dare you be so disrespectful to the Chosen of the Goddess! You should be groveling and begging for her forgiveness. It's your honor that she decided to grace your shack with her pre...aaghhhh!!!" She screamed as thick vines rose from the floorboards and wrapped themselves around her. She tried to fight them off, but they were too strong as they coiled around her, encasing the young witch in a green cocoon.

I turned to the stairs where Julia was coming down, wearing a light blue shirt with a dancing bear on it, a pair of cut off shorts and some sandals. Sabine was trailing behind her with a doggie grin on her face. "I see you didn't learn your lesson this morning," She scoffed at the witch before inspecting her nails, as if wrapping people in cocoons was an everyday thing. She sighed dramatically, "You humans are all the same; you get a little power and suddenly think you're above the rest."

Valentina's face was burning, and if you squinted at her in just the right way you could see steam coming out of her ears. She was about to speak when Julia looked up and cut her off. "Choose your next words carefully or you will share her fate."

The witch swallowed her anger and righted herself, sneering at both of us, "I've never been more insulted in my whole life. Just you wait, the Goddess will avenge my slight today."

"As if," Julia laughed, looking at the witch with disdain and mockery. "It's amazing how you humans think the gods care about you just because you light a few scented candles and say a prayer or two. If you ever actually *see* Hecate, tell her she still owes me a hundred bucks."

"Insolent mongrel, I will pour maggots down your throat and sew your mouth shut for such insolence!" Valentina screamed, her eyes shining with rage.

"Okay, enough is enough," I had to cut this off or we'd be here the whole night, "You have violated the rules of the inn and it's only out of consideration for Matilda that you're not a puddle of boiling piss on the floor, so state your business and leave. Any more delays and your companion will suffocate."

Valentina glared at Julia who only winked in response, and Sabine barked at her for good measure. Maybe it was the audacity of a twenty-pound beagle barking at her, or that her companion might run out of air at any moment, but she finally realized how screwed she was.

"One of the members of my coven was set to stand trial for his crimes but escaped custody last month. During his escape he injured three members, two of them will never be the same again after what he did." Her mouth thinned into a hard line as she looked around the inn. "We've been tracking him using divination spells and know he made it to Portland but after that our vision has been clouded. We contacted the local coven and found out about this… *place*."

She put so much disgust into that last word I felt the need to clobber her with a mop. Who did she think she was?

I thought about our newest guest, and suddenly a lot of things made sense. I was hardly surprised that they lost track of him, the inn was protected against divination magic. "What crimes did this person commit to be hunted down by the coven's Head Priestess personally?"

She sneered and pointed a finger at me. "That's none of your business. If you're harboring Roel Theron then you must hand him over at once." She crossed her arms and smiled smugly. "After he stands trial before the coven, he will be punished and we can all get on with our lives."

"Seems to me that his sentence has already been decided. Not that I care, but I'm afraid you've had a wasted trip." I chuckled and crossed my arms over my chest. "The safety and identity of our guests is our top priority. If such a person is or becomes a guest of the inn, then there's no way in hell we would hand him over."

Shock colored Valentina's face. Did she really think that after what just happened I would happily hand over a guest willy nilly? Even if she had comported herself with utmost grace and amiability, there was no way I would hand any guest over.

"You're going to stand against us?" She threatened in a low and dangerous tone.

I didn't say anything and just looked at the green cocoon next to her. Julia had made her way downstairs and stood next to me, Sabine right on her heels.

The witch raised her head high. "If that is your wish then so be it, we will take our leave now."

I gave her my best checkout smile and pointed at the door. "Thank you for visiting Tir na nÓg, we hope you had a pleasant experience and *don't* come again."

Julia snorted and waved her hand, and the cocoon started compressing before the vines opened up, spitting a disheveled Teresa on the floor. She looked nothing like the arrogant young lady from a few minutes ago; her skin was swollen red and blistered, spewing green pus from her face onto her throat and hands.

Valentina gasped in shock and knelt by Teresa, as the younger witch madly scratched her face and neck. Teresa saw her and recoiled in fear, "No, don't touch me!"

Valentina turned to Julia, fear and anger shining in her eyes. "What did you do to her?"

"I wrapped her in a vine cocoon to teach her a lesson about manners." Julia looked confused, tapping her finger to her lower lip. "Didn't you see it?"

I fought hard not to laugh, Valentina looked like she might spit fire at any moment. Teresa was scratching herself like a madman, her nails drawing blood with every scratch.

"Vines wouldn't have done this." Valentina argued as she watched Teresa moaning in pain and continuing to scratch herself.

"They would if they were made from poison ivy." Julia clicked her tongue and seemed to think about it for a second before she corrected herself. "Well actually that's not true, my vines are a hybrid breed of sumac, oak and ivy making their toxins double in their efficacy. The person feels like a thousand needles are poking them, the skin becomes hypersensitive and the mind gets clouded by the desire to get relief."

Teresa glared at Julia and was about to say something when her skin started to turn blue, she clutched at her throat making a waving motion. Julia looked at it and shook her head. "She's starting to suffocate, it would be best if you take her to a hospital as soon as possible."

Valentina swerved towards Julia, her eyes alight with magic. "Give me the antidote now!"

"There isn't one," Julia gave her another confused look, "Why would I make an antidote to something that's clearly meant for an enemy?"

Valentina growled at us; it was an impressive growl, kind of like a pissed off raccoon. She turned towards Teresa and muttered a few words as the young witch's eyes closed before she fell to her side. The older witch then picked her up fireman-style and walked towards the door. Before she left, she turned back towards us, rage and humiliation coming off in waves.

"I won't forget this. We won't forget this. You will suffer the wrath of the Goddess so swears her Blade!" And with that declaration she walked out of the inn slamming the door behind her.

I turned to Julia and clapped my hands together. "Well that was ominous. Pizza?"

7

W e made our way to the dinner table with the boxes of pizza and a bottle of wine. I put a plate down with three slices for Sabine, who dove into them with gusto while Julia served the wine.

"I'm guessing the younger one came in during the day and was rude?" I asked while setting the plates for ourselves.

She nodded as she handed me a glass of wine. "Around noon, Sabine came to get me in the kitchen because someone was at the door. She basically said the same things, 'in the name of the goddess, hand over the criminal, harbor him and we will suffer the consequences, blah blah', then she tried to muscle her way upstairs." She poured herself a glass and took a seat next to me. "In the end I slapped some manners back into her, some teeth fell out and she tried to cast a spell but got another slap for her troubles. We went back and forth for a good minute until she'd lost most of her teeth," She took a sip of her wine, "I'm surprised she grew them back so fast."

I took a bite of pizza and moaned in pleasure. Marny's made the best pizza in the world: thin crispy crust with garlic spread around it, with lots of cheese and homemade sauce. Julia was having her own heavenly experience and for a few minutes we enjoyed the marvels of

Italian cuisine in silence. I came back up for air after scarfing my fifth slice and second glass of wine.

"Now, that hit the spot. She probably had Valentina magic them back. Should be a simple spell for a witch of her caliber, did the kid come out of the room while she was here?"

Julia wiped her mouth with a napkin before taking another sip of wine. "He came down for meals after Teresa left. I asked him if he was alright and he just nodded before going back to his room." She leaned back in her chair, her eyes fixed on the spiral chandelier above. "I was going to talk to you about it when you got back but those wenches beat me to the punch."

I looked in the direction of the stairs. "Yeah, I'll talk to him. From the sounds of it, those two aren't going to give up so easily."

Julia shrugged. "Let them come again, if they think we're afraid of them they got another thing coming." She put her glass on the table and pinned me with a hard stare. "Anyways, what happened last night? I thought you were going to make a quick stop, not stay away for the whole night."

I sighed and downed my glass in one gulp before bringing her up to speed on everything that happened; from discovering that the body in the morgue was fake to my visit with Goodfellow and everything in between. It was about an hour before I got the whole story out, though in fairness it had been quite a day. The only thing I didn't tell her was about the dream in Devon's office - it was too random to make anything out of it.

She leaned back in her chair and whistled. "Wow. So, we've got a dead fae, missing mage, run away mermen, a fugitive witch being hunted by his coven and you were a fae lackey." She looked towards the ceiling. "Is it a full moon or something?"

I glowered at her. "You know it's not a full moon, we'd be neck deep in shifters."

The inn sat on five hundred acres of woods and so every full moon the out of town shifters came here to shed their humanity in order to roar, howl and shriek at the moon. Since they couldn't join the local pack, as shifters were ornery about hanging only with their own flavor of animal, they came here and spent quite a bit of money.

"But you're not denying being a fae lackey?" She picked up her glass and I refilled it. "Interesting, how long were you with them?"

I shrugged and filled my own glass. "It's the truth, so why would I deny it?" I rubbed my head, trying to keep the memories away. "I was with them for too long."

She leaned forward with a concerned look on her face. "How long is too long? I've never heard you mention them once in the eight years I've been here."

I sighed and shook my head before taking a sip of wine. "I don't know, could've been years or centuries. You've probably heard rumours that time in Faerie works differently than in the real world."

She put her arms on the table and nodded. "Everyone has."

"Well it's mostly true; time is finicky in the lands of the fae." I grimaced, thinking back on my time at court. "In some places time moves so slowly that you could spend a decade inside while on the outside only a minute has passed, and in others time moves so fast a baby will turn into an old man by sunset." I took a deep breath and let it out slowly; this was harder than I thought. "The only places that are remotely close to normal are the courts themselves, as they are so closely tied to the seasons that time passes there at a more normal rate. Most fae don't mind since they are so long-lived, but it's a different story if you're human," I winced thinking back, "Far more cruel."

Julia frowned, going to take a sip from her glass but noticing it was empty. She reached across and poured herself another glass. "What do you mean?"

I finished my glass and put it on the table. "Faerie treats humans as something special, maybe because we're so weak compared to the rest of her denizens. While we're in Faerie we do grow and mature but at a certain point we just stop aging. But the minute we step outside of Faerie, time catches up to us." I clasped my hands together to keep them from shaking, the memories threatened to overwhelm me. "I once saw someone that looked about ten years old turn into a skeleton the second she walked out of that bastard's sphere of influence." I looked at her and gave her a half smile. "It's why you hear so many stories of the fae stealing children. Free labor. If we leave, we die. Staying meant we got to live but under the control of the Fae."

Julia put her hand above mine and squeezed it tight. "You were one of those kidnapped children, weren't you?"

I nodded, squeezing her back. "I don't remember anything before my time with the fae. Not my parents, place of birth, hell - I don't even know if Nathaniel is my real name." I sighed, trying to keep my voice under control. "As a child I worked in the kitchens where they would use us to taste some of the dishes the cooks made, and if we survived we had to help prepare them or risk punishment. Then puberty hit me and my magic manifested."

I let go of her hand and filled my glass with the last drop of wine in the bottle. "One of the nobles found out, and thought it would be amusing to show a monkey how to wield a sword," I drank the glass in one gulp but the alcohol did nothing to chase away the memories. "Biggest mistake of his life. I took to the sword like a fish to water. They used to make me fight for their amusement until one day the Princess saw me fight and requested for me to join her personal retinue. Some time later I rose to the rank of captain of the guard. I made a lot of enemies but I didn't care, for the first time in my life I was... not happy, but content at least."

"Then what happened? How did you end up here?" She picked up Sabine from the floor and petted her behind her ears. "From what you're telling me, you spent quite a number of years at court, yet you look no older than thirty, how is that possible?"

I was going to refill my glass again, but the bottle was empty. "Dumb luck." Just thinking about it sent shivers down my spine.

"You must've been very lucky, given you're here and all?" She stood up and brought back a bottle of tequila before serving a couple of shots. Sabine jumped to the chair next to it and began to scratch herself behind the ears.

"Sometimes I wonder about that, but for some reason I didn't die."
I downed a shot, hoping the alcohol would burn the memories away.
"After coming through, I was bleeding from a dozen different wounds
and passed out only to later wake up in Cassius' house."

Julia took another shot and served me a double. "So that's how you
two met."

I nodded chuckling. "Apparently, I came out of some tree in
Central Park screaming in Gaelic, at a time when he was teaching
Lucas a new spell. Scared the crap out of them, I can imagine how it
would look to see an armored man appearing out of nowhere covered
in guts and blood." I drank my shot and smiled at the memory. "Cassius is a good man, strict with his kid, but good. He nursed me back to
health, taught me how to live a life in the mortal world, basically gave
me a second chance. Which is why I can't tell him about Lucas until I
have him safe and sound."

"Nathan I'm sorry about what the fae did to you, I truly am." There
was a complicated look in Julia's eyes, and she started to speak several
times but in the end shook her head and gave me a small smile. "I
know you feel indebted to Cassius for being there for you in your
darkest moments but you have to call him - he deserves to know
what's going on with his son."

"I already did and he didn't pick up. I'll try again tomorrow." I said
before going for another drink as she let out an exasperated breath
and stopped me, moving the bottle. "Fine, we'll do it your way, but
first you need to talk with our new guest about his deal with the
witches and then get some rest." She shooed me from the table. "Go,
I'll clean this up."

"Thanks Julia, for everything." She might be dictator in the kitchen,
but she was a good friend.

She rolled her eyes at me and picked up the glasses as Sabine
jumped to the floor. "Don't get all mushy on me. Now get the hell out
of here."

I smiled and gave her a mock salute. "Aye aye, Captain."

"That's General to you, butter fingers." She said with a smile as she
left to go wash the dishes.

I turned to Sabine who was wagging her tail at me. "Ready to have a talk with our witchy friend?"

She sneezed at me.

"Yes, you were right, he was in trouble. Satisfied?"

She flopped on her back and showed me her belly.

I gave her my death stare. "Now you're just being a brat."

She gave me a doggy grin and wagged her tail once. I caved in and rubbed her belly. "A spoiled brat."

She growled at me and I rubbed her with more gusto. Satisfied with the belly rubs, she darted up the stairs. "Somedays I wonder who's the owner between the two of us," I mused out loud before following her.

I walked up to Roel's room and found the door open, where he was sitting on the bed facing the window with a lost look on his face. He looked cleaner, though he was still wearing the same clothes as when he arrived - we'd have to fix that as soon as possible. Sabine was already inside and lying down on the floor by the bed. I knocked on the door a few times before he noticed me. "Can I come in?"

He turned to look at me, his eyes weary and filled with regret. After a few seconds he nodded his head. I walked in slowly and motioned towards the bed. "Would it be okay if I sit down?"

"You're here to ask me to leave, aren't you?" His body was so tense that I was afraid he'd snap at any moment.

I hated this. My guests didn't need to be afraid here, the inn was supposed to be a place where people could escape their daily troubles and relax.

"Why would I ask you to leave?"

The tension visibly left his body as he took a deep breath and let out slowly. He still looked weary but at least he appeared calmer. "I heard Valentina and Teresa threaten you. I don't want to cause you any trouble."

"They're not the first, and nor will they be the last." I waved his concerns away and smiled at him. "I've dealt with scarier and more powerful beings than some has-been witch on a power trip. Hell, I deal with two every day, have you seen my chef? Now *she's* scary."

He chuckled for a moment and I could see a hint of the young man he was supposed to be, not the haunted soul that first walked in yesterday; it wasn't much but at least it was a start. "Who's the second one?"

I turned my head to look at Sabine who was trying to eat her paw in a *highly* dignified manner. Roel followed my gaze and laughed. I took that as a good sign and sat down on the edge of the bed. "You laugh because you think she's all cute and fluffy, but don't get her riled up or you'll be sorry."

He gave me a skeptical look before his face turned stoic again.

"The secret to enjoying life is knowing how much trouble you're willing to invite into your home," I raised my palms mimicking a balance scale, "Not enough and you've lived a meaningless life, too much and you might not survive it. If they want to come and stir the pot, let them, we'll see who gets burned."

He thought about it for a moment before nodding his head. "Thank you, and I'm sorry for all this. I knew she was hunting me and that I shouldn't stop but I've been running for so long," He let out a tired breath, "I needed a place to rest."

I patted him on the shoulder. "It's okay, even if we have the most powerful magic in the world at the end of the day, we're only human," A soft gowl interrupted me, "And dog. Now, enough of this sorry business, it's my policy not to intrude in my guests' private affairs but I do have to know. How much of what Valentina said is true?"

"Everything." Roel held my gaze before looking down and smiling weakly at my little manager as she ran in circles trying to catch her tail. He took a deep breath before standing up and pacing the room. "I'm part of the Night Wanderers Coven, we're based in Odessa, Texas. My mother was the head priestess, but she passed away when I was six, along with my dad." He stopped in front of the window, his gaze sad and lost. "They were picking up my birthday cake when a drunk driver crashed into them. Valentina is my paternal aunt, but she and my father didn't have a good relationship and once my parents were gone she took over the coven."

"That's an interesting name for a coven," I crossed my arms over my chest, "How powerful are they compared to the other covens in Texas?"

Witches were a territorial bunch that did not always play nice with each other. Five years ago Portland had two covens, but then Matilda moved into town... Two months later, the covens were gone and the survivors formed into one.

Roel turned back and smiled. "Most covens are made up of witches who didn't know who or what they were before they joined, but our members come from generations of witches who can trace their lineage back to the Old World," He shrugged half heartedly, "While we're the only coven in the state, each of the families help by protecting a main city."

I could handle a couple of witches, especially if they were stupid enough to attack at the inn, but several families... I shook my head, that was more than I could handle. "Fuck."

Roel stopped pacing and gave me a confident smile. "I told you. At least she won't call upon the families to capture me."

"Why is that? She would be stupid not to use them to nuke the hell out of us, especially after the humble pie we shoved down her gullet."

"Because the Therons - that's my mother's family - wouldn't stand for it. Neither would my dad's." He started playing with the ring on his finger, though I don't think he noticed he was doing it. "She's had me locked up for the past two years because she's afraid of what I know. If the families knew what she did, they would rally the other families to remove her from power."

"They would?" I asked dubiously.

He nodded. "The coven exists to protect the families, attacking one of our own without cause is forbidden." His gaze turned hard and he stopped playing with his ring. "Valentina knows this and it's why she has worked hard to admit members that are only loyal to her. Right now, only half the coven is in her pocket and I took out three of them already. Besides her and Teresa, that only leaves two other witches that she can call for help."

"Why is she so obsessed with you?" I stood up and looked at him in the eye. "Why imprison her own nephew?"

Rage filled his eyes, and I could see a well of deep hatred and power swirling in those hazel eyes as tears started flowing from them. "Because my parents weren't killed by a drunk driver. She killed them, and once I'm back to full strength, I will rip out her still-beating heart and shove it down her throat."

8

I chatted for a couple more minutes with Roel, but it was obvious that he wasn't in the mood to continue talking. I requested his measurements to buy new clothes, and ordered him to stay inside the inn.

Looking back to Roel's door as I walked away, I felt sorry for the kid. Family should make you feel safe no matter what, yet his own aunt had killed his parents and locked him away for two years. I wondered for the millionth time what having a family would feel like; the soft kiss of a mother, the firm embrace of a father. Did I have siblings.? I shook my head. There was no time to waste on pointless thoughts as I made a mental note to talk to Matilda about Roel and see how she could help.

Today had been one hell of a day, not just physically but emotionally. Meeting the fae again after so many years had been exhausting; since opening the inn I had been living my days in peace, but I knew now that was over. Goodfellow hadn't known anything about Lucas, and divination magic was not within my repertoire, so that was out. I could make a tracking rune, but that wouldn't be of any help now since I really needed to have put one on him before he went missing.

I walked towards the end of the hall where it split into two stairways: a spiral one to the left that led to the attic where Xaris made his home and a second plain staircase that led to the third floor where mine and Julia's rooms were. The tension escaped me as I stepped through the dark wooden door to my room whilst letting out a tired breath. I took off my shirt, threw it into the clothes basket in the corner and sat on the bed.

What a day! I was glad to be back in my room after everything that had happened. The room wasn't much, just a bookcase with my favorite paperbacks, an old wooden closet with a few changes of clothes and a door that led to the bathroom. Yet it was my space, and I treasured it. I grabbed one of my fluffy pillows and lay back, looking out the window to try to clear my thoughts before sleep finally took over.

I WOKE UP WITH A START, SWEAT DRIPPING DOWN MY BROW. I RUBBED MY forehead with a shaky hand, trying to get my heartbeat under control as the dream faded from my consciousness, although the scent of copper and pine still seemed to burn my throat with each breath. The rush of running through the woods had felt so *real*. I slowly traced the scars along my side and gritted my teeth at the fading pain.

I wiped my damp forehead one last time and gave the room a cursory glance; once again, nothing seemed out of the ordinary. The morning sun was slowly peeking its way through the heavy drapes and Sabine, who had been sleeping at my feet, was giving me a dirty look while she yawned.

"Sorry girl, bad dreams." I leaned forward and rubbed her soft tummy.

She yawned again before thumping her tail against the bedding and I smiled, reassuring her that everything was okay. Not that it was going to fool her; sometimes I think that dog is smarter than me.

After a good ten minutes, Sabine wiggled her way out from underneath my hand, stretched herself and bolted out the doggie door I installed for her. I got up and once again found myself subconsciously tracing my fingers across the scars on my side.

"How long has it been since you hounded my dreams, Galesh?" I had been dreaming too much lately and I still didn't know what to make of that first dream, with the woman and tentacles. I sighed and made my way over to the closet, letting my magic flow from the tip of my finger to the small rune in the shape of a keyhole. "Oscaíl."

The rune began to glow with white light and a small compartment popped open from the side of the closet. Inside was a dagger: its blade fifteen inches of magically enchanted silver, able to pierce through most enchantments and armor. The hilt and pommel were made of a single piece of deep green malachite, the blade still covered in dark stains of my own dried blood.

Even now, looking at the dagger made my insides ache. "One day, Galesh."

Magic gathered around the tip of my finger, and I traced my usual runes for 'grow' and 'shrink' around the hilt of the dagger. Unlike when I enchanted my morningstar, which took almost no effort, this time it felt like writing on a cotton ball, largely due to the dagger's own magical enchantment. I frowned and fed more magic into the runes, pushing past the resistance, finally managing to put my own runes into the weapon.

Once the runes were carved, I shrunk the dagger down to a charm and linked it onto my bracelet next to my morningstar - I had a feeling that it might come in handy given the way things were shaping up recently. I picked up some clean clothes and went to take a shower. The cold water felt heavenly as it touched my skin, letting me clear my thoughts and push the nightmare back to the darkest corners of my mind where it belonged.

The first order of business would be to find out where the selkie crossed over. There were only two ways for someone to travel between Faerie and the mortal realm. The first was to locate a rift between the planes, somewhere where the veil that separates the human and fae world was thinnest. Typically those places had a strong magical concentration, or appear at certain dates. The problem with that, however, was that even if I found such a place there would be no guarantee that it was the same one that the selkie used. Also, there was no telling who or what was waiting for me on the other side.

The second way to cross was for a powerful fae to rip open a portal between the realms and bring a person or fae through, which seemed most likely as selkies are magical morons and need the extra help.

In theory, a mage could also open a portal. I'd have to look into Lucas's relationships at school, but I couldn't remember him saying he was having problems with anyone, other than Sabine. Cassius was a powerful member of the New York Assembly and had made plenty of enemies in his crusade for mages and shifters to coexist peacefully in the Big Apple, and it was for that very reason he sent Lucas to study here: he didn't want his son caught up in politics.

So yes, a mage could've taken the boy to get back at Cassius, but if they wanted something from his father why pass Lucas off as dead? You couldn't ask for a ransom if the person was dead. I discarded Winter out of the equation after my talk with Goodfellow yesterday as it was clear he didn't have anything to do with it. Was I wrong, and it actually had nothing to do with the fae?

I rubbed the back of my head frustrated. I needed more information, as what I had wasn't nearly enough.

Every cop show tells you that the first forty-eight hours are crucial in a missing persons case, and that after that time the odds of survival drop drastically. The problem was that no one was looking for Lucas except for me, as they all (understandably) thought he was dead. Whoever did this was smart and planned ahead; there's no way this was put together on the fly.

I finished getting dressed and walked downstairs to find Julia on her way to the kitchen, Sabine right at her heels.

"I'm going to put the 'No Vacancy' sign up until this whole Lucas thing is settled and we have the witches out of our hair."

She stopped at the bottom of the stairs and threw a cursory look at the second floor. "Did he tell you anything?"

"Yeah, basically we're in a witchy version of the Lion King. Only instead of his uncle killing his dad, it was his aunt that killed both his parents."

Julia rolled her eyes at me. "You're not funny, you know that right?"

Why does everyone keep saying that? "I'm hilarious, tell her Sabine."

My little manager looked at me, giving me a big doggie yawn and shaking her head.

Julia stepped onto the landing and poked me in the arm. "If I see a wild boar and meerkat near my kitchen, I'll chop them into stew." She paused for a moment and tapped her chin with her finger. "Stew, huh? Guess that's what we're having for lunch."

I was about to comment when there was a knock on the door.

I looked at Julia confused, but she turned, shrugging her shoulders. "I'm going to start working on lunch."

As she walked through the reception hall and into the kitchen, I looked at Sabine. "I am funny."

Sabine sneezed and went after Julia. "Ungrateful dog." I murmured under my breath and went to open the door.

On the other side of the door stood Detective Penelope Garcia. Her dark hair was pulled into a tight ponytail, her otherwise crisp grey suit marred by the odd wrinkle and the glint of her gun beneath her jacket, and I could see new bags under her eyes. Next to her stood a middle aged man, dark skinned, six feet tall, with dark blue eyes and short graying hair. He was wearing a dark blue suit and holding a yellow manila folder.

The cops? Again? Gods, what's happened now?

I gave them my warmest smile. "Detective Garcia, I wasn't expecting you, is this about Lucas?"

Detective Garcia shook her head. "We're still conducting our investigation but as soon as we know something, we'll let you know." She motioned stiffly to her partner. "Mr. Mercer, this is my partner Detective Kane, would it be okay if we come in and ask a couple of questions?"

I shook my head. "I was just heading out, can this wait?" I couldn't waste time entertaining a couple of normies when Lucas was out there, needing my help.

"We'll be brief." Detective Kane said in a rich baritone voice which left absolutely no room for argument.

I looked at them and sighed, opening the door wide enough for them to enter. Thank the gods the only current guests were relatively human, with the obvious exception of the dragon. "Please, come in."

We walked through the reception hall with the sounds of pots banging echoed from the kitchen into the living room. I eyed the two leather chairs by the fireplace. Not enough room for all of us to sit, which left the couch, although with everything going on it still sat at a frustratingly awkward angle behind the piano. "Please have a seat."

Neither one of them took a seat. I crossed my arms and turned to them. "How can I be of service?"

Detective Garcia looked around the living room. "This is a nice place Mr. Mercer, not a lot of guests though?"

Where was she going with this? I shrugged halfheartedly, "A big group checked out yesterday morning so it's fairly empty at the moment." I looked at her curiously. "Are any of my guests in trouble?"

The detective shook her head and continued to survey the living room while her partner stood next to her like a statue watching my every move. "Nothing of the sort. How many people are under your employment, Mr. Mercer?"

I frowned at her and put my hands in my pockets. "At the moment it's just me and my cook. Obviously we had a third employee, but... well, you know what happened to him." If they would stop wasting my time, I could be out there looking for him.

Detective Kane's stern face cracked a little and he nodded. "We're sorry for your loss, Mr. Mercer. Was your cook on the premises around eight last night?"

What was he talking about? "Yes. Detectives, forgive me for being blunt but what the hell is going on?"

"Early this morning we received a complaint from one Valentina Hall stating that you assaulted her and her companion, Ms. Teresa Wright, whilst they were seeking lodging at your inn." Detective

Kane opened the folder and handed me a couple of pictures while Detective Garcia went to the wooden doors and looked out towards the woods through the glass planes. "Ms. Hall states that you maliciously threw her companion into a shrub of poison ivy which caused a severe allergic reaction that sent Ms. Wright to the hospital."

I looked at the pictures and vowed to myself never to piss off Julia. The rash had turned a nasty shade of red, covering the witch's body and interrupted only by deep bloody scratch marks where she had almost dug out pieces of her own flesh in her scratching. "While I feel sorry for Ms. Wright, do you have any evidence that it was me?"

Detective Kane shook his head, "So far it is her word against yours, which is why we're here to get your version of events."

Those two-faced, wart-hugging, cauldron-humping no good wenches! How dare they call the cops, are they insane? It was in everyone's best interests to keep both worlds separate; mortals couldn't handle the supernatural. "They did come in last night but given our staff shortage I told them that we had no vacancy," I handed the pictures back to him, "They wouldn't take no for an answer and started making a scene and for fear of disrupting my other guests, I asked them to leave."

"And then what happened?" Asked Detective Garcia from the door.

My cook wrapped her like a tamale, but you don't need to know that, I thought to myself. "They left on their own two feet and in perfect health," I raised my hand like I was in court, "At no point, from the moment they entered to the moment they left, did I touch a hair on either of them."

Detective Kane took the pictures and put them back in the folder. "Any idea why they would accuse you of harming them?"

I shook my head. "Insurance scam maybe? Looking for a quick buck." I pointed to the glass door where Detective Garcia was standing. "You're welcome to walk the grounds; you won't actually find any poison ivy."

I led the detectives outside through the glass doors and took in a deep breath, the musky scents of the Western Hemlock trees mixed with the sweet citrusy scent of the red and yellow flowers around us always put me in a good mood.

Detective Garcia stood next me and noticed the flowers. "I saw those flowers when we pulled up in the driveway, what are they? Can't say I've ever seen them before."

I smiled at her as I walked towards one of the flower beds next to the door and caressed the red flowers. "These are Red Verbena," I pointed to yellow ones next to the reds, "And those are St. John's wort, that's the sweet citrusy aroma you can smell around the inn."

They not only look pretty, but they keep the inn hidden from the Fae.

"As you can see these are the only plants around the inn," I stood up and spread my arms, "But feel free to look around the grounds, I have nothing to hide."

"You have horses here?" I looked at Detective Kane who had walked towards the back of the inn and caught sight of the stables at the back of the inn.

I groaned internally. *Are you kidding me? I need to go!*

I smiled at him and nodded, "That's right, some of the guests love taking a ride in the woods."

There was a glint in his blue eyes that made him look several years younger than he appeared as he looked from the stables back to me. "Would it be okay if I take a look?"

I nodded, the faster they were out of here the better. Detective Garcia shook her head and turned to me. "I'm sorry about this, my partner fancies himself a cowboy."

"No worries, I know the type," I said and followed after Detective Kane. The stables were a large wooden building for my quadruped guests who couldn't fit in the main building. We kept a couple of horses on the rare occasion that a mortal came in and wondered why we had stables with no horses. It could fit up to twenty horses with each box stall being six feet wide and ten feet long.

I opened the doors and let the detectives in, the smell of hay and manure wafting from the inside, and the stern expression on Detective Kane's face melted into a boyish grin. He stopped by the first stall that housed a stocky chestnut mare, about fourteen hands in height with a flowing dark mane pulled to one side and a few strands of hay tangled in her mane. "She's beautiful, what breed is she?"

I looked at the mare as she made her way to the bars of the stall and snorted at me. "This is Millie, she's the baby of the family," I put my hand through bars and rubbed her forehead softly while picking the hay out of her mane, "Aren't you my dear?" Millie neighed softly, and I looked at Detective Kane. "She's a Morgan, perfect for riding along wooden trails like the ones we have out back, her Sire and Dam are next door."

Detective Kane slowly walked over to the stall next door where a taller version of Millie was drinking water. Unlike Millie, who got her black mane from her Sire, her mother's mane was a light blonde color. "That's Epona, you won't find a gentler horse in the world." I let go of Millie, who snorted before going to eat at the end of her stall.

Detective Kane was about to say something when he turned to the last stall and paused. I knew the feeling; Hades was a magnificent specimen. At eighteen hands in height he was taller than the average Morgan, with strong muscled legs and short back he was the epitome of the species, but what drew people's attention was his glossy black coat.

"That's Hades, he's what you called a Lippitt. He's got a bit of a temper but loyal as they come." I turned to the horse who looked at me with piercing dark eyes and I found myself smiling. "Fine, but only one."

I made my way towards a small fridge at the end of the hall and picked up a pomegranate from it before taking it back to Hades. "Here you go, boy." I handed him the fruit through the bars and rubbed his forehead while he ate.

Detective Garcia came to stand next to her partner with an amused smile on her face, and I realised it was the first real smile I've seen from her. It made her look softer. "Hades eating a pomegranate?"

I snorted and continued to rub his forehead as his lips tickled my palm. "Trust me, the irony isn't lost on me."

Detective Kane moved forward slowly and looked at me. "Can I?"

I looked at Hades who was engrossed in his treat and nodded. The detective reached forward and rubbed Hades's neck slowly with a small smile. "My family used to breed horses for a living back in South Carolina, Freisians."

I whistled softly. "Big horses, hard work but worth it."

Detective Kane nodded. "Those were the days."

I let Hades finish his fruit and gave him one last caress before turning to the detectives. "As you can see detectives, other than woods, flowers and horses there's nothing else in my inn."

The detectives shared a look, apparently coming to some unspoken agreement, and they turned to me. "We didn't find any evidence of poison ivy, sorry for having wasted your time, Mr. Mercer. We'll be on our way." Detective Kane said as he put his hands on his pocket.

I escorted the detectives back to their car, the same one from the other night, and turned to Detective Garcia as they climbed in. "Have you been able to locate Lucas' parents?"

The detective's smile fell back into that stoic cop face and shook her head. "We've reached out to our contacts in the NYPD but they haven't been able to contact them."

I frowned, it had been two days since 'Lucas's' body had been found and neither Cassius nor Ava were anywhere to be found. Detective Garcia turned to me, "Like I mentioned before, Mr. Mercer, as soon as we know anything, we'll contact you. Sorry to have wasted your time."

I smiled at them and waved. "Not at all, come back any time."

"I might take you up on that." Detective Kane looked at the stables and nodded before driving away.

As soon as they were gone I dropped my hand and frowned. "What a waste of time."

I walked back towards the inn and was about to call Julia when my cell phone started ringing. I didn't recognize the number but that was normal, it was probably a potential guest calling to make reservations. I accepted the call and pressed the phone to my ear. "Good afternoon, thank you for calling Tir na nÓg, how can I help you today?"

A soft and smooth voice replied, "If you want to know where Lucas Gray is, come to the road outside your inn now." The voice hung up.

I looked at my phone and frowned. I tried to call back but the line was busy. I put my phone in my pocket and weighed my options. I was faced with two choices: on the one hand, a suspicious phone call from a mystery person usually led to a kidnapping, or even torture. But on the other hand, a phone call from a mystery person could be a break-through lead to Lucas. I thought about it for a nano second, turned on my heel and sprinted towards the main road.

9

O kay, *mysterious voice, where the hell are you?*
A few cars had driven past without incident. I looked at my watch. It had been fifteen minutes since the phone call. I was about to head back when a dark blue SUV with tinted windows pulled up in front of me. The passenger door opened. I hesitated a moment before climbing in.

Seated across from me was a young woman in her early twenties, her dark hair glossy and wavey where it fell down her back, her eyes glowing blue with an unnatural brightness, the smell of wet earth and fish wafting through the car. A Naiad, a river spirit.

"Those witches were really petty to bring mortal authorities into this," She said as she pulled out her phone and started texting, "You must have pissed them off really bad for them to do that. I'm Irini, that's Hughey." She nodded towards the driver, a man so large he barely fit in the seat. The steering wheel looked like a kids toy, and the way he held it suggested he was having to be very conscious about not simply crushing it.

I looked around the car and noticed the doors weren't locked. It occured to me that I'd rather jump than give this Hughey a chance at me.

"I've always wanted to see what happens to a human who jumps out of a car going sixty miles per hour, but please, don't let me stop you. What do you think, Hughey? Splat or skid?" Hughey replied only with a twinge of his cheek that *might* have been a smile. Irini put her phone down, pulled out a manilla folder from an expensive looking bag at her feet and began reading, a small frown pulling on her features as she concentrated.

"Are you going to let me know where we're going?" My voice was the only noise in the car besides the surprisingly quiet engine.

"All I've been told is to pick you up and bring you to the boss and answer no questions. Now, I have court in the morning and quite an intricate case so I'd appreciate silence." Once again, she didn't even look up from her task whilst talking to me.

Naiads, being water spirits, didn't stray too far from the water, although that was hardly a problem in Portland. But a lawyer naiad was a first for me; normally that was a job common amongst vampires.

The car drove into the Pearl District, where the bars and restaurants were buzzing with activity as the different patrons came and went. The district had its own unique charm, with galleries and clubs that appealed to a variety of cultural and social tastes. As the city passed us by, it gave me time to think about my latest predicament.

Ever since I opened the inn, it was a policy of mine to not get involved with the local power structure of the city and to remain as neutral as possible. Whoever sent Irini had some serious clout and wasn't afraid to use it, especially if they were able to find out about the witches sending the cops just seconds after they left.

We stopped in front of a three-story red brick building; large arched windows gave the place a rustic feel, and below many people could be seen entering through the wide metal doors next to a sign that read 'Sea Cradle' in beautiful cursive script.

Irini exited the car and made a motion for me to follow her. I looked at the building again and sighed before following, glancing back to see Hughey and the car driving off into the Portland traffic.

The double doors opened straight onto the gallery floor where people were milling around, quietly murmuring about the various artworks. A giant crystal chandelier, probably the size of a small car, hung from the high ceiling, brightly illuminating the vivid paintings whilst also making its own art in the form of fractured rainbows cast by the individual crystals onto the walls. I almost felt bad walking on the oak floor in my work boots, but then remembered I hadn't wanted to be here in the first place.

The paintings were beautiful: a girl running across the water of a sun-lit lake, mermaids dancing beneath the waves with glowing jelly-fish of every color, a hippocampus - half-horse half-fish - jumping over the crest of a wave. On and on, every painting was more striking than the next yet they all shared the water as a common theme.

I looked around confused. Seriously, where were we? An art gallery? I looked towards the lawyer, who had taken a drink from one of the serving girls who were wearing pale blue and green uniforms with stylised wave details, and was now moving at a brisk pace towards an oak staircase while I had been gawking at the paintings. I rushed towards her.

As I was passing the painting with the girl running across the lake, something about it drew my attention. I couldn't see her face as she was running away from the perspective of the viewer, but her long auburn curls and pale skin reminded me of the figure from my dream. But it couldn't be her: the girl in the painting wore a green sundress and there was an aura of innocence to her, while the knight from my dreams epitomized power and sophistication.

I shook my head, throwing those thoughts to the back of my mind. The stairs radiated a soft hum of magic as I approached them; it was the first indication that we were not in an ordinary art gallery, as I was beginning to suspect.

I followed her up the stairs, where we found ourselves in a wide open space filled with dozens of tables where people were conversing and eating in a loud cacophony of voices, the smell of spices and cooked food permeating the air. I held onto the railing of the stairs for a moment, taking in the sudden change. *What the hell? What was a restaurant doing here? Why didn't I notice the smell and all this noise from downstairs?*

"Weird," I murmured, looking at the stairs which continued to vibrate with a soft hum and extending my magical senses towards it. They were brimming with magic. Was that how they made sure the noise of this hidden area didn't disturb the gallery below? I shook my head and let go of the stairs to catch up with my wrangler.

Like the gallery below, the restaurant walls were decorated with more art pieces, the most eye-catching being a huge canvas on the back wall. It depicted a gruesome battle between a wounded youth who looked no older than sixteen wearing a lion's pelt around his head; he held a broken sword in one hand as he growled in defiance at the beast in front of him. The beast was a large, five-headed reptilian that was at least four times the size of the youth, with glowing yellow eyes and multicolored dark scales covering its body. Each of its heads had a menacing regal look to them, a queen looking down on her world.

Hercules versus the Hydra.

Then it dawned on me. "Oh shit!" I cursed loud enough to startle some of the patrons eating nearby.

Irini turned to look at me with a small smile on her face. "I assume now you've concluded who my boss is."

I nodded towards the painting. "I'd be stupid not to after seeing that."

"Would you have come if you knew beforehand?" She asked as we made our way through the tables. I snorted but didn't answer.

Anyone with a lick of sense would run the other way, which said a lot about me considering that I wasn't running out of here screaming to high hell. What was it they say about cats and curiosity?

Irini led me to the back of the restaurant. The closer we got to the huge canvas, the more lifelike it felt, and the aura coming off it was oppressing. I didn't know the first thing about hydras, except to not be stupid enough to cut their heads off, but that was the extent of my knowledge. If it came down to a fight, running would be my best option.

Sadly, my dad wasn't an all-powerful god to grant magical powers in my time of need... At least I didn't think so. Seemed unlikely.

Beneath the canvas was a large round table that had a view of the whole restaurant. Sitting at the table was a stunningly gorgeous woman wearing a blood red dress; her short dark blond hair fell just below her chin and her light brown eyes, small button nose, high cheekbones and olive skin personified beauty. She was the type of woman that turned heads.

She saw us approaching and smiled a thousand-watt smile, making a nearby gentleman choke on his wine as he gaped at her. "Irini, thank you so much for bringing Mr. Mercer. That will be all for tonight."

Irini nodded and left, and the woman motioned to the chair next to her with a perfectly manicured hand. "Mr. Mercer please, have a seat, dinner will arrive shortly."

Walk into my parlor, said the spider to the fly. *Come on Nathan, man or mouse, which are you?*

I took the chair next to her and smiled amicably at her. "Thank you for your hospitality, Ms..?"

"Anastasia Pantazis, but just call me Anastasia." She patted my arm and I fought the urge to step away. "The nerve of those witches trying to stir up trouble in my city," She said miffed, "And to bring mortal authorities just because they got outwitted? Poor form, I'll tell you that."

She flicked her hand into the air, and one of the waiters promptly brought over a bottle of wine with two glasses and a basket of garlic bread. She opened the bottle and poured us each a glass. "You must be hungry so please, dinner is on me."

I accepted the glass and took a slice of bread, chewing it slowly to gather my thoughts. She knew what really went down yesterday with Valentina and that she had called the cops on me. She must want something from me, but whatever it was it wouldn't be easy to do or she'd do it herself.

"Please call me Nathan, and while I'm grateful for the gesture, why did you call me?" *No one ever got killed for being polite*, I reassured myself.

Anastasia took a sip of her wine. "Oh, we can talk about that later." She looked behind me and smiled before meeting my eyes. "Dinner is here, let's eat first then talk business."

A pair of waiters brought a tray filled with food, followed by a slightly older man wearing a chef's uniform. "Ms. Pantanzis, tonight we're serving you salmon with a lemon and saffron yogurt sauce accompanied by honey glazed carrots. As for dessert, we have prepared freshly baked cheesecake ravioli. Please enjoy."

Anastasia smiled at the chef. "Thank you, Vicente. I'm sure it's delicious as always." He bowed and scurried away.

The food looked delicious: the salmon was rosy pink, the yogurt sauce in a star pattern on top of it, and the carrots and potatoes had a golden sheen to them. Anastasia started to eat her food and taking my cue from her, I took my first bite. I had to bite my tongue to prevent an audible moan slipping out as the explosion of flavor sent my mouth into a dancing frenzy.

We ate our dinner in silence, although every so often she would look up to one of the tables before going back to her meal. Once we'd finished with our plates, Vicente brought out dessert. I looked down to a plate of powdered sugar covered ravioli with several dipping sauces, took a tentative bite and groaned in pleasure as the soft creamy filling melted in my mouth.

Anastasia smiled at me. "Vicente is such a marvelous cook, for a mortal he has a gift so rarely seen in their kind." She took a sip of her wine giving me a sideways look. "I had heard that one of your employees was taken captive, such a shame."

Warning bells rang all over my head. "Yes, I've been looking for him. The mortals think he's dead," I said as she put the glass down.

She tilted her head and rested her chin in her hands as she smiled. "Selkies are such a chore to deal with, they travel in pods that resemble a shoal of piranhas more than anything else," She clicked her tongue in disgust, "They believe the sea belongs to them and always toot their own horn about the good old days. Bunch of rats that don't even taste good." She leaned forward and whispered, a wry smile playing across her lips, "Too blubbery."

"Bragging about their past glory is something the fae do as a race." I took a sip of my wine, trying to keep my heart from beating too fast. Where was she going with this? "Along with yapping about how they would one day retake the world."

She nodded, leaning back in her chair, her dress swaying to show a hint of cleavage. "Oh, no doubt, but I do find some of their company enchanting. I had a lovely talk this morning with an old friend of yours," She twirled a strand of hair around her finger and smirked at me, "He highly recommended you to me, to help with my little infestation."

Old friend? Is that what we are, Goodfellow? I thought as I took another sip of my wine and smiled at her politely. "I would hardly call one selkie an infestation, anyway. I'm sorry to say he misinformed you, I'm just a humble innkeeper trying to make ends meet."

She shook her head slightly. "Where there is one selkie there's bound to be many more." She smiled, her eyes shifting from their usual light brown to bright canary yellow with a bold slit down the middle like a tiger. "Someone who can slay a fachén with only his wits and a sword is anything but humble."

Fachén were nasty creatures native to Faerie; standing at twenty feet tall they embodied pure rage and single-minded pettiness. Compared to most giants, fachén were about as smart as a piece of rock. They only had one eye in the middle of their face, one arm protruding from the center of their chest and leg in the middle of their waist.

"They're big and quick on their feet, or foot I guess, but they have only one gear - smash fast and smash hard," I shrugged and put the wine down, "You just have to keep a cool head and never fight them in confined spaces."

"So you don't deny slaying one? It's always a testament of one's skill when a smaller and weaker opponent triumphs over a bigger and more powerful one," She motioned to the canvas behind her, "After all, isn't that what makes humans what they are? That inability to quit, no matter how much the deck is stacked against you."

I looked up at the canvas of young Hercules and focused on the grit and determination in his eyes. "I guess you're right, we can take a kicking and keep on ticking."

She turned to me and giggled. "That you do. Now, please follow me." She stood up and started walking towards the back of the restaurant, leaving me no other option but to follow her to another set of stairs that lead upwards.

As we ascended, the noise and smell of the restaurant faded away as if it wasn't ever there. "I want the selkie out of my city. I don't care how you do it but get it done; their presence here is not welcome. A lot of my people are afraid to go into the sea because of them and it's unacceptable."

"I think you have the wrong idea of what it is I do." I shook my head at her and cursed Goodfellow bald in my head. "I'm not a mercenary or killer for hire, I merely provide a safe place for my guests to get away from their everyday lives."

She stopped in the middle of the stairs and turned to look at me with her eerie yellow eyes. "That's where you're wrong my dear. In the end, we're all killers."

We made it towards a thick wooden door secured with a keypad, and I saw her punch in some numbers before stepping inside. As soon as we entered, an ear-piercing scream rang through the room before I had a chance to acknowledge it.

Anastasia looked towards where the scream came and smiled grimly. "Oh good, she's awake, follow me."

"What the hell was that?" I stood by the door, magic thrumming beneath my fingers. One wrong move from her and we were going to fight it out.

"That is your incentive to do as I ask," She turned around with a cryptic smile, "Remember the reason why you are here, my dear. Now, we better hurry before she dies."

Another scream full of dread and pain rang through the apartment. *What have I gotten myself into?*

Damn you, Puck!

I followed her through the apartment onto a balcony overlooking the Pearl District. In the middle, strapped to a table by her hands and feet, was a selkie. Unlike the one at the morgue which had been mostly intact, except for the huge hole in its chest, this one was horribly disfigured; sections of skin had fallen off revealing the bone beneath and half her face was gone as if someone had poured acid on it. If she wasn't fae, she would've died already from such horrible injuries.

But what could inflict such damage to one of the fae? The only thing I knew was iron, but there wasn't any iron near her as the table was made of wood and she was tied with rope.

I looked at Anastasia, who had had a pleased look on her face. "What did you do to her?" I couldn't hide the horror in my voice. No one should be tortured like this, not even the fae.

"One of my men found her skulking around Crystal Springs Creek, and if they hadn't picked her up at that moment then she would've taken a child that was fishing by the shore. The child's irresponsible parents were not paying attention," Her mouth thinned into a fine line as her yellow eyes burned with power, "They brought her to me for judgement. I wanted to know where the rest of her pod is, but she wouldn't talk so I gave her a little incentive. Then I found out about the one at the morgue and well, you know the rest."

"Couldn't you just kill her and be done with it?" I pointed to the pitiful creature. "What's the point of torturing her?"

Anastasia walked over to the selkie and caressed the unmarred side of her face, the selkie flinching at her touch. "They're nothing but vermin that need to be exterminated. However, this one proved more resilient than I first thought. We beat her, cut her fingers, and stabbed her, but we didn't use iron for fear of her dying. The problem was she just laughed while she healed. So, I poured a couple of drops of my blood over her body and she didn't like that," Her voice took a velvety tone as her gaze hardened, "Did you, darling?"

She caressed the selkie's face again. The poor thing was desperately trying to get away, but the ropes held her in place.

"Your blood?" I pointed to the half rotten face and felt sick to my stomach. "That's what did this?"

"The blood of my kind is powerfully acidic, it will melt skin and bone in a matter of seconds upon contact." She had a forlorn look in her eyes as if she was remembering something unpleasant. "Although, there are some creatures who are resistant and can hold on for hours. Heracles lasted the longest; he hung on to his dear life for a whole day before succumbing." She waved her hand dismissively. "But that was mostly thanks to his divine blood. This little pretty here has been screaming for two hours and is at the end of her tether."

She looked down smiling at the selkie, and tapped her disfigured lips. "Now, my dear, are you ready to talk?"

The selkie shivered at Anastasia's touch, her black eyes swelled as she cackled gleefully through her pain, "My mistress will avenge me! She who is the sea incarnate will bring our kingdom back from beneath the waves," She gave Anastasia a macabre smile, pulling against the ropes, "She will smite you down beast, too bad I won't be there to see how she rips the very skin off your bones inch by inch."

"Either she will smite me down or skin me alive, can't do both darling. Just out of curiosity, who is this mistress you're so devoted to?" Anastasia kept caressing her face like a loving mother. Bile rose at the back of my throat and I fought to keep it down. There was no need to do this to another living being, not even one of the fae.

"She once called the depths her home, with a flick of her hand she could send the sea into a frenzy and those who dwell beneath the waves swam to her court and basked in her power and beauty," The selkie cackled in mad frenzy and pieces of rotten flesh fell around her, "With a mere whisper the seas were hers to claim; she is the Voice of the Tempest, the Queen of the Depths, she will remake her kingdom and plunge your world beneath the waves."

Anastasia turned to look at me. "Is that anyone you know of?"

I racked my brain trying to think but came up empty. "Selkies are not very bright 'up top', if you know what I mean." I tapped the side of my head, trying to keep the ravioli from coming up to say hi. "But, like all the fae, they are a prideful bunch and wouldn't show this level of devotion to anyone but one of their own. I'm guessing that Queen of the Depths is one of the old ones."

Her hand dropped from the selkie's lips and turned to me. "What makes you say that?"

I pointed to the city around us. "The spread of iron made the fae lose a measure of their magic and they were forced to retreat to Faerie. Many of them had their own demesnes, their own lands that they ruled over and could magically influence." I looked at her, trying to ignore the deformed selkie. "Have you ever heard the phrase, 'the land and the king are one'?"

Anastasia frowned and shook her head. "No, what does that have to do with anything?"

I took a deep breath and let it out slowly. "The phrase is from an old movie and applies perfectly to them..." I gestured towards the selkie, "The fae are bound to the land they rule - the more powerful the bond, the more they can affect what happens within their borders." I paced back and forth trying to recall what I heard about them at court. "Some of the more powerful ones could bend time and space, creating rooms that are larger on the inside than they are on the outside to the point where entire oceans could be found inside them. You could step in as a child through one door and come out an adult through the other, that kind of stuff," I stopped pacing and shrugged, "But the fae lost the ability to create a demesne in the mortal realm when iron spread."

The selkie cackled and turned to look at me with a deranged, half-skeletal smile. "Lost? We never lost anything, you insignificant ape!" I rolled my eyes, *here we go again with the ape thing.* "The knowledge was hoarded by the courts to keep us under their thumb, but our lady found a way," Her smile grew wider, "Oh yes she did, two have already fallen to her sway, she only needs two more to complete the ritual, come the new moon and you mortals will drown."

I rushed forward and grabbed the selkie by the shoulders. "Is that why you took Lucas? For this queen of yours?" I shook her hard, her weakened body offering no resistance and her head slamming against the table. "Where is he!?"

The selkie started laughing. "Are you talking about the boy who smells of ozone, and storms rage in his blood? Oh my mistress is having so much fun with him."

I shook her harder by the shoulders now, my patience was wearing thinner by the minute. "Where is he!? Speak you wretched thing!"

She continued to laugh, and I slammed her against the table again but she didn't care. Anastasia walked to the other side. "Sounds like you have a lot of faith in your lady, so give her a message for me when you see her: stay out of my city."

Faster than I could react, Anastasia turned her hand into a claw, ripping the selkies throat out and nearly decapitating her. A stream of dark blood sprayed all over her as the selkie gurgled for air for a second before what little life she had in her eyes faded. Blood pooled around the table and fell to the floor in slow drops.

I looked at her and felt my control slip by a fraction as my magic coursed through my body, and I felt my bracelets grow warmer as anger and frustration bubbled inside me. I had wanted answers, even if she was on her last legs. "What have you done? We could've gotten the location out of her and if not, we could've let her go and followed her back to this queen. That was stupid."

Damn it! That was my best shot at finding Lucas.

Anastasia scowled at me as she finished cleaning her hand. "I won't hold that insult against you since you are clearly emotionally distressed, but insult me again *mortal* and I'll be picking your bones from between your teeth." Her yellow eyes hardened and I fought the urge to draw my morningstar. "Did you forget that she was already afflicted by my blood? She had maybe another hour to live and she wasn't going to tell us anything," She looked back to the dead selkie, "What do you think she meant by the new moon?"

I glared at her and was about to make a snide comment but my self-preservation kicked in for once and killed it. "Powerful magics are tied to the phases of the moon. The new moon symbolizes new beginnings and starting anew." I said, scratching the back of my head, thinking back when I heard Cassius teach Lucas the basics. "I'm guessing if you wanted to create a new dimension, it's as good a time as any."

She walked over to a small bar just off to the side and poured herself a drink while looking at the sky. "In other words, whatever this queen is planning will happen tomorrow night" She turned back to me, her eyes had gone back to their usual color. "Seems you've got your work cut out. Let's make it official, stop whatever this queen is plotting, get the selkie out of my city and your debt to me will be paid."

"What debt?" I growled at her.

She gave me a predatory smile. "Why, my dear Nathan, the debt of knowledge. Without me, you wouldn't have known that young Lucas's time is so limited."

I glared at her and bit back an insult as I walked away. One of these days my mouth was going to get me into serious trouble especially with this terrifying, reptilian woman.

10

By the time I got back to the inn it was already close to midnight, and my little visit with Anastasia had left me a little... jittery to say the least. I had seen the fae torture prisoners before; they usually relished inflicting pain on others, especially spies, but the way she had looked at the selkie was cold, detached even, like it wasn't even worth caring about the life she was about to end.

I shook my head as I entered the inn.

The living room was empty, not that I'd expected anything different. Roel was probably in his room, Julia could be who knows where, and Xaris rarely left the attic. While the dragon could take human form, he preferred to remain in his dragon state, and luckily the attic was spacious enough to accommodate him. I walked upstairs to my room and found Sabine lying on my bed, without a care in the world.

I crossed my arms and leaned against the door frame, quirking an eyebrow. "I'm glad to see you missed me."

She gave me a doggie grin before rolling on her back and presenting me with her belly.

I scowled at her. "You know, I've had one hell of a day. I could've been eaten or shot but all you care about is getting pets?"

She huffed at me.

I placed my hands on my hips, the nerve of her. "Yeah well, I don't care if you knew that nothing bad was going to happen, a little concern might be nice."

She gave me a series of low whines.

I looked at her incredulously. "You were emotionally traumatized and need comfort? I was the one that had a crazy dinner with a hydra, I'm the one who needs comfort."

She rolled her eyes at me.

"Is that really all you got out of that? No, I didn't bring you a doggy bag, I was a little busy trying to track Lucas down."

She sneezed at me, jumped off the bed and trotted out of the room, purposely looking away from me.

"Love you too." I rolled my eyes and shook my head.

I pulled my shirt over my head and dumped it on the floor, kicking off my shoes before I threw myself on the bed and closed my eyes. The small staccato of nails on wood caught my attention and I felt as Sabine jumped up and reclaimed her spot on the comforter. Her cold nose pressed against my cheek.

I smiled and scratched the spot behind her ear that made her leg kick. "I missed you too."

She huffed at me and rolled herself onto her back, as I shook my head and laughed. "Fine, I'll bring you a doggy bag next time, happy?" All I got was a tail wag in response before we both fell asleep.

THE SKY RAGED AS BOLTS OF LIGHTNING RAINED DOWN INTO THE SEA, THE waves rolling and swelling as the wind started to pick up around me, sending a shiver down my spine. Standing at the edge of the cliff with his back to me was a boy with short blonde hair, his t-shirt and jeans hanging in tatters on his thin frame.

The boy raised his hands and caught a bolt of lightning as it crashed into him. The lightning took the shape of a snake and wrapped itself around the boy's waist like a belt. He slowly turned around and it was then that I recognized him: Lucas!

I felt myself stop, my body running on pure instinct. The bloated flesh of his face had become a violent green and had split in places, oozing dark liquid. Empty space filled his eye sockets, the same dark liquid leaking from them and down onto his shirt. I gagged as the wind carried the scent of rot and decay.

He opened his mouth revealing a set of jagged black teeth and wailed over the roar of the wind.

"Naaathaaannn! Whyyyy?"

Out of the sea rose a massive pale green tentacle dripping seawater and gray slime. Barnacles encrusted the tip, giving it an almost spear-like appearance. I raised my hands to protect my face, where the heavy rain and wind felt like it was trying to rip my skin off. "Lucas! Hang on, I'm coming!"

The tentacle slammed into the ground, sending chunks of stone flying everywhere before it wrapped around Lucas's body. I ran forward, jumping to avoid the huge crater in the ground, and grabbed him by the arm. His skin was cold and slippery, it felt like trying to hold onto an eel.

"I got you, Lucas! I'm not letting you go." I dug in my heels and tried to pull him towards me, but my grip kept slipping. Lucas turned to look at me with his empty eye sockets, and began to laugh, a desperate maniacal laugh that chilled me to the bone.

"It's your fault, Nathan." Lucas grinned, his hand clasped around my forearm before he embraced me. The smell was unbearable, and I fought not to vomit all over him but it was a losing battle. He leaned into my ear and whispered, "Now suffer as I have suffered."

The tentacle tugged us over the edge, and we plunged into the waters below. The sea was freezing, and I struggled to get free as Lucas's hold on me was like a steel vice.

I screamed in panic, the water that rushed into my throat burning as it went down, and the maw closed around us.

I SAT UP ON THE BED, CLAWING AT MY THROAT GASPING FOR AIR.

A dream, it was just a dream. I rubbed my forehead, wiping the sweat from it. A flash of light from outside the window caught my attention before the room returned to darkness again. Sabine was nowhere to be seen; another flash of lightning lit up the sky before a slow rhythmic tremor shook the inn.

What the hell? As I got up from the bed, an ear-piercing screech rang through the grounds and my head exploded in pain. I felt my knees hit the floor as the pain reached a crescendo and the inn's outer protective wards tore as if they were made of paper. Something warm trickled down my lips, filling my mouth with the taste of copper, as several red drops fell to the floor staining the dark wood.

Using the bed frame for support, I managed to push past the pain and get to my feet, feeling the tremors getting stronger and closer. A resounding roar tore through the night - whatever it was, it was big and not at all happy.

"Fuck me, what now?" I cursed and sprinted downstairs, wiping away the blood.

I met with Julia at the bottom of the stairs. She was wearing a pair of baby pink jammies and had Sabine in her arms, who was busy barking at the noise.

"Nathan, what the hell is going on?" Julia frowned, trying to steady herself amidst the shaking.

"No idea, but whatever it is, it broke through the wards," I said and rushed towards the living room, passing by a bewildered Roel who was leaning against a wall by the fireplace, wide-eyed and trying to not to fall. He was wearing a new purple shirt and pants, and I briefly realised that Julia must've gone to buy him clothes while I was out.

I opened the door and looked up. Dark clouds were circling above us, streaks of light piercing the sky followed by an imposing boom. Gusts of wind wailed through the woods, ripping leaves and branches from the trees. An acid smell of rotten fish and burnt ozone flooded the air.

Julia stepped next to me and was about to say something when another booming roar rang through the night. I looked towards the source of the sound and froze. Through the trees, although about a quarter mile from the inn, a colossal emerald beast was approaching the entrance. The creature stood at twenty feet tall, its smooth reptilian face hid behind a vast mane made of seaweed, its imposing bronze-colored eyes glared at us with malice.

Electricity sparked from its mane before a glaring bolt of energy vaulted from it, splintering one of the large trees and setting several others on fire. Julia looked at the burning forest with her fists shaking and turned towards the great beast, her eyes glowing with murder.

"I'm going to boil that fucking turtle into soup." She started charging towards it, but I grabbed her by the shoulders and held her back, Sabine hot on our heels.

"Hold your pegassi there Julia, that's an Arrachd and an old one at that."

I looked at the monstrosity and cursed. Julia glared at me, her eyes were two burning coals of fury.

"You know what that thing is?"

"I know of them." I covered my ears as the Arrachd roared again, slowly creeping towards the inn. "They're storm spirits that make their home in the waters of the Summer Isles. According to mortal history, they used to sink ships and torment Gaelic fishermen."

Sabine wagged her tail at the incoming monster and growled at it. *Of course she would enjoy this.*

The mane around the Arrachd's head crackled with electricity before another bolt of lightning scorched a wide section of the grass, and all the while it swung its pincers left and right digging out a section of the forest.

Julia's face paled and a trickle of green blood dripped from the side of her mouth.

"Nathan, how do you kill this son of a bitch?"

Every dryad had her life force intrinsically tied to a tree or forest depending on how old she was; as long as the tree lived so did they. To destroy this forest, as the beast was now, was to destroy Julia. We needed to stop him and fast.

"I haven't seen one as old as this - the older they are the bigger they get. They grow about a foot every century, but like any of the fae they are weak to iron or magic." I channeled my magic into my bracelets.

"Ag Fás!" White light shone from them as the buckler and morningstar grew to full size, the pounding in my head grew worse as my magical reserves diminished, but we could worry about that later.

Movement from the corner of my eye caught my attention, and I found Roel standing next to me rolling his sapphire ring around his finger, his eyes never leaving the turtle-lobster.

"If you need my help, I can..."

"You're a guest, this is my business, we'll handle it." I shook my head and cut him off.

The beast was halfway to the inn and we couldn't let it get any further. "Roel please, go back inside, the wards around the building are still standing and are strong enough to hold the beast at bay if it gets passed us." I said to him before turning to face the Arrachd. I also hoped that the dragon will get off his butt if it comes to that. Roel nodded and ran back to the inn. Good.

"Julia, I need you to get me as close to its face as possible." I turned to her, she still looked pale but there was resolution in her gaze. "Think you can do that?"

She scoffed at me before kneeling on the ground, placing her hands on the grass. Her skin shimmered with a faint green glow and the scent of olives mixed with junipers drifted off her as a massive dark green vine as thick as a man's head rose from the ground. The vine wrapped itself around my waist, and I tightened my grip around my weapons as the vine pulled me off the ground.

"Nathan, get ready, this is going to be a bumpy ride!" Julia yelled before the vine's hold grew tighter.

Bumpy ride? It took me a moment to figure out what she meant but it was too late, the vine swung around once, twice, three times before launching me to the monster like a cannonball.

The wind rushed through my skin so fast that for a moment I thought it was going to peel my face off. I fought against the wind pressure, bringing my morningstar in front of me as the gigantic Arrachd loomed closer, the inn reflected in its bronze eyes like the moon on a placid lake. The fae roared with unrestrained violence, its pincers opening and closing as the emerald beast shone with light.

The throat of the monster grew closer. I tried angling myself higher but I was going too fast and crashed into it with a resounding splash. A shrill yowl of pain erupted from the beast as it took several steps back. Dark brown blood drenched me from head to toe, and I tried standing up but found myself buried up to my elbows in the fae's throat. The rancid smell of rotten fish and dried seaweed was a hundred times worse up close.

I tried pulling free from the Arrachd's neck but my morningstar was stuck deep inside the thing.

I groaned, putting my feet against its neck and pulled with all my strength to free myself. The flesh of the creature pressed against my arms in an attempt to heal itself, although unfortunately my morningstar was made of iron and poisonous to his kind.

The harder I pulled, the deeper my weapon sunk into the Arrachd's flesh. In my efforts, a faint sizzling noise caught my attention, and I looked around to see the skin of the beast taking on a dangerous blue glow.

"Shit, shit, shit!" I started pulling and pushing like a mad man.

The morningstar wiggled a little and with another great pull I managed to kick myself free from its neck just as the beast lit the night with an earth-shattering lightning bolt. I plummeted to the ground, my arms spread to the side in a pitiful attempt to slow my fall. From a nearby tree a thick branch stretched and snatched me from the air by the waist.

I could feel my heart pounding like a bucking bronco, and found myself hugging the tree a little harder than necessary. The Arrachd roared again, swiping at something near his feet with its claws. I squinted, trying to get a better look through the leaves of the tree, and saw dozens of thorn-covered vines wrapping themselves around its legs. Dark brown blood gushed out of a dozen different wounds, but the beast was frustratingly still standing, using its claws to cut the vines and stumble forward.

Julia was still kneeling on the ground, her hands pressed against the grass, sweat matting her forehead and the side of her mouth bleeding green again. *Damn it all to hell, we're barely making a dent in the thing!*

I tightened my grip around my morningstar, my body covered in all kinds of nastiness, realising we were still so far from getting rid of this beast.

"Julia, I need to get to the head!" I screamed over the sound of the wind as it surged around us tearing several branches off their trees. Julia had managed to slow the beast down but he was still getting closer to the inn, just another two hundred meters and he would destroy my home. I wasn't going to let it happen.

Julia turned towards me, her eyes glowed like two blazing suns. She nodded her head slowly as the branch around my waist tightened before stretching itself around the body of the Arrachd and placing me on the back of its head.

As a new wave of vines snaked themselves around the huge beast, the Arrachd roared in fury and tried to shake them off.

I stumbled to get my footing and noticed Julia struggling to keep the beast away from the inn, where Roel was inside like I told him, holding Sabine who was barking like mad and trying to free herself.

The Arrachd shook itself, trying to get free, but the more vines he cut with its claws the more Julia summoned. I didn't know how long she could keep this up, but if the beast got freed he would make the last hundred meters to the inn. Its mane started to glow dangerously white, and I ran forwards to the front of the head, jumping over a weed knot and grabbing a strand of it to rappel down. I landed face to face with the beast's right eye and winked at him. I quickly kicked myself back to gain momentum, and the fae yowled in annoyance before I came back, swinging my morningstar into its eye. The eye exploded in a cascade of brown blood, drenching me completely.

The monstrous fae before me shook after the blow to its eye, tearing down the trees and ground surrounding it. Using the branch as support, I swung on to the beast's neck and ran towards the front, smashing my morningstar down again. A stream of dark blood flowed from the wound - finally I was doing some real damage. Suddenly the branch holding me was yanked back into the air, just before the meaty claws of the fae landed hard at the spot I had been standing in. I could see Julia panting with the effort of summoning more vines to keep the beast from rampaging. It looked down and saw me, its one good eye filled with fury, and the beast's entire body glowed with light before the thing opened its mouth and shot a storm of power right at me.

"Sraonadh!" I roared and extended the buckler to shield myself, a soft silver glow emanated from a rune in the middle of the shield, but it wasn't enough to protect my entire body. Some of the current got past my shield, scorching my shoulder and burning the branch that was holding me in the air. Gods it hurt, and black spots began to cloud the edge of my vision. A second blast blistered the surface of the shield before reflecting it back on the Arrarchd, blowing a huge hole in its shoulder.

I was falling too fast and would break every bone in my body if I didn't do something. I pushed past the pain and curled myself into a ball before crashing through branches and skidding next to Julia.

The massive beast roared in pain, staggering back trying to stop the bleeding from his neck and shoulder with its claws. *Good luck with that buddy.* I looked at my shield, still warm from the blast, and felt myself grin like a mad man.

"Nathan!" Julia and Roel screamed at me but they seemed far away for some reason... *is the sky supposed to be spinning like that?*

"Son of a bitch!" The smell of charred meat burnt my nostrils. Shit, I slowly got up and saw that my shirt was pretty much ruined; the blast had charred my shoulder all the way to my elbow and it hung at an awkward angle, I tried moving it but a wave of pain told me that wasn't a good idea.

"Oh, thank the gods it worked." I let out a breath of relief and lay my head on the ground. *Mmm, so soft.*

I normally tried to avoid exhausting an item with too many runes, or you could run the risk of the item exploding from overload. As a precaution, I tried sticking to two runes per object. The buckler, however, had three: the runes for growing, shrinking and deflection. I never had the opportunity to test it out and didn't know if it would even work. Who knew my test subject would be a twenty-foot tall fae monster?

Sabine and Roel rushed to me, my little manager growling at the Arrachd.

Suddenly from the ground emerged a colossal thorn bramble, ten feet high and ten across, wrapping itself around the turtle creature like a constrictor squeezing the life out of its prey. The Arrachd shrieked in pain, trying to break its bonds.

"Nathan, where the hell is Xaris?" Julia grunted in pain. "We could use a dragon right about now, I can't hold it much longer."

Roel helped me sit up, careful not to touch my injured shoulder. I looked back at the inn and frowned. "We've been making enough noise to wake the dead, if he were here he would've come out."

The Arrachd shredded the thorn bramble with its claws and began making its way forward once again, the air crackling with power and the smell of burnt ozone filling the lawn as the fae shot a bolt of lightning blowing apart a section of the roof. I waited with bated breath for the dragon to come out and torch this fool, but when nothing happened it felt like a stone had landed on my chest and crushed my hopes of the ten ton fire-breathing guest helping us to defend the inn.

A flash of purple light glared through the chaos of the fight, and I turned to see a tall and muscled man walk towards me, his blonde shoulder length hair reminiscent of an older time. With eyes glowing a deep heather, his expression was unnerving as his robe sparked with vibrant streaks of light. In one hand he was holding a long wooden staff that curved at the top like a shepherd's crook, and the other had a black satin glove with a large crackling amethyst in the center.

Cassius!

11

"**M**ERCER!" Cassius' voice rang with the fury of a hurricane as he strode forward, before he seemingly noticed Julia on the floor, pale and out of breath. Then he turned to look at me, a sorry sight covered in blood and desperately trying to remain upright despite the pain. Finally, his eyes settled on the rampant Fae on its way to destroy the inn and his jaw went slack in surprise. Cassius turned to me with wide eyes.

"What the fuck did you do?" His voice still rang with power, but the anger was gone and instead replaced by shock.

I raised my shield hand and waved at him weakly.

"Hey there, bud. What brings you here at this hour?"

The Arrachd roared, breaking off the last of the vines holding him. Julia screamed in pain before slumping to the ground, unconscious. The beast lumbered forward, its one eye trained on me, the puny innkeeper that was barely able to stand.

"Why don't you go inside and have a nice cup of tea," I gestured back to the inn with my thumb, "I'll be with you as soon as this is taken care of."

Cassius palmed his face, cursed under his breath and strode

towards the beast, standing between it and us. He turned his head slightly to the side.

"We're going to have a long conversation after this." He faced the Arrachd, his fulgurite staff shining with purple light.

The Arrachd looked at Cassius and roared, its towering body glowing with electricity before it opened its mouth and shot a blast of lightning straight at my friend.

"You dare play with lightning in front of a Master?!" Cassius thundered, lifting his gloved hand, the lightning surging through his body and travelling to his staff. "Foolish beast. STREPO!" He bellowed and raised his staff, an arc of purple lightning shooting out of the tip, blasting a hole on the side of its face.

I rolled my eyes at him as he continued shooting bolt after bolt at the fae.

"Always going for the dramatic." I turned to Roel who was trying to get the burnt pieces of shirt out of my shoulder. "Hey, kid you're a witch, right? Got any healing on you?"

Roel shook his head. "Valentina locked away my familiar, and without it..."

He didn't need to finish, I understood. Witches could perform some of the most powerful magics out there, but that was under the prefix that they had access to their familiars. Without their familiars, they were useless.

I saw the struggle in his eyes as he looked at his ring before coming to a decision.

"All I can do is numb your nerves to keep you from feeling pain, but that's only a stopgap measure and lasts for five minutes, max. After that the pain will double and you might lose consciousness."

"Do it."

Ahead of us the Arrachd bellowed in agony, the storm clouds above darkening as flashes of light arched through them. Cassius stood defiantly in front of the beast's path. I didn't know how Roel could perform a spell without his familiar but right now that was the last thing on my mind.

"Are you sure? You might not feel any pain but that doesn't mean that there isn't any damage. You might end up making your injuries worse."

I grabbed him by the shirt with my good arm and pulled him closer. "Listen kid, right now we have a pissed off tesla coil coming at us with enough power to level the city, so do your spell!" I gasped in pain as I let him go.

"Don't say I didn't warn you." He placed the hand with the sapphire ring on my shoulder, and for the first time I noticed a torch circled by three daggers carved into the stone.

"Choris Pono." The stone glowed with a faint light before a refreshing feeling spread through my whole arm, leeching the pain, as the dark blue gem turned a little paler.

I breathed a sigh of relief and tried to move my arm to stretch but Roel stopped me, ripping the rest of my shirt off and tying it into a makeshift sling. "What did I tell you? Just because you can't feel it doesn't mean your shoulder isn't blasted to pieces," He finished tying a knot in the fabric and nodded at me, "Now go do whatever is that you're going to do."

"Get Julia inside, we'll handle this." I let go of my morningstar, it wouldn't do me any good now, and marched up next to Cassius who was standing his ground against the fae.

"I got your message." He looked at me out of the corner of his eye and frowned, his voice sounding vulnerable for the first time. "The police came to talk to me; they said my boy is dead." His hand tightened around his staff, the wood creaking from the pressure, and his eyes darted down to the ground. "Is it true?"

"He isn't dead but he's in trouble. Whoever has him must know I'm on to them," I nodded my head towards the Arrarchd, "Because they've sent big ugly here."

"You're saying that this *thing* was sent by the bastards who have my son?" He said through gritted teeth, his glove and staff now glowing like a supernova.

I took a step away from him and nodded as the beast's mane filled with charge, sending another blast of lightning at us. I was about to use my shield to deflect it again but Cassius beat me to it, walking into the path of lightning and catching it with his gloved hand. Lightning sparked in his eyes and he glared at the Arrarchd with unimaginable fury and pain. "FULMEN BELUA!"

The staff and glove glowed cherry red before exploding into thousands of tiny pieces, which hung in the air like fireflies before flying upwards into the sky.

What was he doing? I looked up to see the thunder clouds starting to swirl faster and faster, converging into a single point in the sky before crashing down into the ground in front of us.

The clouds began morphing and shaping themselves into a dark gray torso with four powerful thick legs, two ears fanned around a large head, and from the center a long trunk coiled around itself between a pair of purple crackling tusks. The overwhelming figure of a twenty-foot-tall elephant stood proudly as flashes of lightning sparked throughout its whole body as it shook, its eyes two white orbs burning with rage and power. The storm elephant raised its trunk, bellowing its fury, shaking the earth with its unrelenting might.

"Fuck!" I threw myself to the ground, thanking the gods for Roel's painkiller spell, dirt spraying across my face as I glared at Cassius.

"What the hell have you just done!?" I yelled.

The elephant charged towards the Arrachd, electrifying the air as it moved. I sucked in a deep breath and felt a burning sensation in my lungs, like drinking fire water. The air was filled with too much magic and it was getting hard to breathe.

Cassius grinned like a mad man. "It's a spell I've been working on. I usually just call her Lola."

The Arrarchd acknowledged Lola, roared its challenge and raised its meaty lobster claws. Lola looked unimpressed and unfazed, continuing their charge.

The two behemoths crashed into each other with a deafening crack of thunder. The Arrachd lunged for the elephant's ears, but its claws went straight through the cloud construct as if it wasn't there. The elephant's body evaporated into a formless cloud, wrapping itself around the Fae like a dark cloak. The monster tried to shake it off, but his efforts were useless as the shroud covering it grew brighter, discharging its accumulated power at the beast. The Arrachd let out an inhumane shriek as the ground beneath them cracked open, forcing it to fall to its knees.

I protected my head between my arms as a gust of wind surged from the center of the crater, blowing up broken branches and stones all over the place. The ground trembled for a few seconds then settled down once more. I raised my head, hearing Sabine barking like mad and Roel cursing in some foreign language.

I blinked several times to clear my eyes of dust before looking up, and my eyes widened at the devastation in front of me. A huge crater, fifteen feet deep and ten across, lay in front of me. Around it, dozens of trees had been knocked down and charred to a crisp. In the center of the crater, the Arrarchd stood beaten and bloody, his carapace blackened, and several missing sections revealing patches of soft greenish skin beneath.

The pungent stench of burnt seafood clogged at the back of my throat; one of its claws had been blown away leaving only a bloody stump. The Arrachd swayed from side to side briefly before catching himself, spitting a mouthful of blood out to flood the ground below. Its remaining bronze eye blinked rapidly, beginning to regain a glint of focus. It looked around wildly before settling on the pair of us. The battered beast let out a roar and began to stand. .

Cassius fell to his knees, his face pale and sweaty. His eyes had gone back to their natural midnight blue, his breathing was ragged, and he looked like he would tumble over at any moment. That last spell had taken a lot out of him and there was no way he was going to be able to cast another one.

I looked back at the Arrachd and couldn't help but think about how pissed Julia was going to be when she saw the crater. It's funny, the crazy ideas you can come up with when you're about to die. I got up, throwing away my buckler and focused on my own dwindling reserves of magic; I could feel my power was there, but it was so small that it wasn't far off non-existent.

Whenever I drew my runes, the magic always came from inside me and it had always been enough to serve my purposes; mostly pre-

prepared combat magic. I'd never needed to look elsewhere for power, but seeing Cassius borrowing the storm clouds above to assist him with Lola gave me an idea. Honestly it might not even work, but when death comes for you, you get creative.

The Arrachd charged, bellowing in a maddened fury. I had to stop it or my inn would be destroyed. I opened myself to the magic of the world around me, lowering every defense and tearing down every mental barrier, chain and wall that I had built since escaping from the fae.

The world suddenly became *alive*. The colors were vibrant hues, the smells permeating my nose; it was like taking your first deep breath after almost drowning, exhilarating and filled with life. I could see the magic in the air and how it connected it to every living being in the area.

I took a deep breath, taking in the magic and spoke to the world around me.

"Please, grant me your strength."

The land around me awoke for a brief moment, pulsing with vibrant life, and my heart thrummed in tandem with it, filling me with warmth and comfort. I let the feeling guide my finger as it sparked and crackled with intense emerald light and slowly a three peak mountain symbol formed in the air.

The rune thrummed with the power of the forest around me, and I could feel the fortitude of the trees that had stood on the grounds for centuries but also the hope of the new flora, waiting for the chance to bloom. Their sorrow and anger filled me at having seen their kin get uprooted, burned and smashed by an intruder on their land. Their hopes and desires bled into the rune, turning it into a beacon of their wrath as it slowly sunk into the ground releasing all its power.

The ground around the entire property shook as a small obsidian spike emerged out of the crater, displacing dirt and tree roots as it slowly extended upwards. I recoiled in shock as the spike continued to grow taller and thicker, gaining speed as it did so. The surface was completely smooth, to the point it looked like a black mirror. Two silver lights were being reflected, and it took a moment for me to realise they were my eyes.

The inn grounds shook again, as the spike continued to grow until it formed a thirty-foot tall stone spire that penetrated the Arrachd as it rose. The beast howled in agony, desperately trying to escape and smash the spike with its remaining claw, but he couldn't get the leverage he needed. It turned to look at us and for the first time fear welled up in its eye as he was slowly split right down the middle. The inhumane screams of agony that erupted from it dissipated quickly as the life faded from its eyes, and each half of the body fell on either side of the spire.

I blinked, trying to make sense of what had just happened.

"Holy *shit* that hurts." The warm feeling of the magic left me in a rush and I nearly doubled over in pain, my whole body was sore and aching except for my left arm. Roel's little spell was working wonders on it.

Cassius blinked several times before shaking his head and making his way towards me. I was about to say something when he pulled back his fist and swung at me.

Pain flared through the whole side of my face.

"Mother of fuck!" I swore, crumpling to the ground. I glared at him, clutching my throbbing jaw. "What the hell?"

Cassius stood over me, breathing in shallow pants.

"That's for not calling me as soon as you knew something was wrong with Lucas."

He then extended his hand and helped me up. A soft growl came from behind me, where Sabine was standing glaring at Cassius, showing a hint of fang. Oh, boy. I raised my hand and rubbed where he hit me.

"It's okay Sabine, I deserved it. Now, let's get inside before we all keel over."

Sabine growled at me then turned around in a huff, kicking some dirt with her back paws and walking back inside.

Cassius looked at me with a curious expression. "What was that all about?"

"She's going to get back at you for that, be warned. Let's get inside before she decides to put us both in the dog house."

I looked back towards the inn and sighed; all the windows had been shattered after the explosion earlier, but I was too tired to care. With that cheery thought, we went back inside.

When a witch tells you that you might feel pain once a spell ends, they're not joking. Roel's numbing spell lasted midway into him treating my arm. The Arrachd's lightning had given me third degree burns and left me smelling like burnt bacon, and on top of that my tumble through the trees had dislocated my shoulder.

The first thing he did was pop my shoulder back in place, which wasn't so bad since the spell was still going. When he started cleaning my wounds, however, the spell came to a close and the pain flared back with a vengeance, a hot pulsing feeling shooting from my shoulder to the tips of my fingers, as if someone had poured molten lead on it.

I gritted my teeth, trying to ride it out, but the pain kept on getting worse. Dark spots swirled around my vision and before I knew it, darkness had taken me into her painless embrace.

I WOKE UP IN MY ROOM, WHERE THE CURTAINS WERE OPEN AND LETTING the sun spill inside. My whole body was sore and hurting in places that I didn't even know could feel pain. There was a warm prickling sensation spreading from my chest to my left shoulder and the pain in my head made me regret waking up. For a moment I had trouble remembering why my mouth tasted like cotton, until I remembered a monstrous turtle had tried to cook me extra crispy.

Note to self: avoid electric turtle-lobsters in the future.

I tried to move my arm and noticed it was wrapped in a strange green bandage that seemed to be woven from leaves. The wrappings went from my wrist all the way to my shoulder and across my chest. I traced my fingers around it and was surprised to find them warm to the touch. When had that happened?

Sabine was lying down next to me, her gaze worried. As soon as she saw me awake, she scooched closer and filled my face with sloppy kisses. I smiled and scratched her behind the ears with my good hand.

"Hi girl, I love you too."

Sabine growled at me, pointing to the herbal cast with her nose.

I rolled my eyes at her. "It's not like I wanted to get hurt. You try taking a bolt of lightning to the paw and tell me how it feels."

She sneezed at the cast before scratching her neck with her back paw.

"I know you're a badass super-dog, but lightning is lightning. Don't get cocky."

She huffed at me and booped me in the nose with her paw.

I gave her an annoyed look, so it was going to be like that?

"Yes, you could've killed the giant turtle in a minute but could you have done it as cool as impaling it with a mountain?"

I still didn't know how the hell that had happened, but when you're trying to one up your dog you kept those details to yourself.

She barked, pressing her nose where Cassius punched me.

I sighed in defeat, there was no arguing with her. "Yes, then I got my ass kicked by a wimpy mage, fine you win."

"Who are you calling a wimpy mage? I'm a member of the New York Assembly's High Circle." An offended voice called from the door.

I looked up to see Cassius looking a lot more casual; he wore a dark blue t-shirt that read 'Eat my Staff', black pants and shoes, carrying a mug of coffee in his hand.

"You were on your knees for the last part of that fight, Mr. High Circle." Sabine gave Cassius a low growl, showing him just a hint of teeth before lying down next to me.

"You try casting a high-level spell without falling on your ass." He stepped into the room and sat at the foot of the bed. "Oh wait, you did fall on your ass, which reminds me - you owe me a new staff and glove."

"I didn't make you blow your war load to kingdom come, that's all on you brother." I said, scratching Sabine behind her ears. "You, on the other hand, owe me who knows how many windows after that trick with the elephant."

He slapped my foot with his free hand. "You didn't call me as soon as the detectives knocked on your door with the news of Lucas's supposed death, nor did you call me when you found out he had been kidnapped by selkies." He glared at me, and I felt Sabine's body tense beneath my hand. "All I get is this weird message from you right before some cops show up to tell me my son is dead. Damn it, Nathan, when were you going to tell me? When you were dead, or worse - enslaved to the fae again?"

"Technically in those scenarios there would be no way to contact you... well, maybe Devon could call my ghost. Or if the fae were being *really* stupid with my capturing," I pointed out, caressing Sabine's back and felt her relax.

He didn't look amused at my attempt of levity. "I'm serious Nathan, what the hell were you thinking?"

"I was thinking that you trusted me with keeping the kid safe and I failed," I took a deep breath and let it out slowly. "Before we found out that Lucas was kidnapped, all I could think was that it had to be a nightmare, that it was my fault for letting him walk out of the inn that day." I looked away ashamed, focusing my eyes on the back of Sabine's furry head. "How could I call my friend and tell him that I failed at the one thing he has ever asked of me? Then we found out he might be alive and all that went through my mind was, I need to find him and bring him home safe. One thing led to another, and well, last night happened."

"You idiot, did it ever occur to you to ask for help instead of tackling everything by yourself?" Cassius took a sip of his coffee and shook his head. "Now the fae knows you're alive. How's that working out for you?"

I groaned, palming my face.

"Don't remind me, though they would've found out eventually I don't doubt. From what I saw at the club, they have enough manpower to storm a castle." I looked at him curiously. "How did you find out about that anyways?"

"Julia brought me up to speed once she woke up a couple of hours ago, a little pale and weak, but I got the general idea of the situation." He took another sip of his coffee before eyeing Sabine. "You talk to your dog?"

I scoffed at the stupid question. "Of course I talk to Sabine, she's an excellent companion and has clever insights on what goes around here." My clever companion started eating her paw with gusto as she wagged her tail.

"I see." Cassius looked dubiously at her then at me.

"Never mind my dog," I shooed at him with my hand, "So how'd the police finally get in touch with you?" A thought suddenly came to mind looking at the sun outside. "How long have I been out? Is today the new moon!?"

I tried standing up but Cassius put his hand on my shoulder. "You've only slept for a couple of hours, it's still morning so take it easy." I laid back down and let out a breath of relief. "The NYPD tracked me down as I was leaving the Assembly just as I was finished listening to your voicemail," He gave me a conflicted look, "You're lucky it was me and not Ava... she doesn't know anything, thankfully, as it was her turn to hold down the fort at the Assembly."

He was right about that. When it came to their only son, Ava threw caution out the window and bombed the building for good measure. A group of foreign mages thought Cassius was the most dangerous of the two since she was an illusionist and not an evocator, and targeted her for an assasination. She went through them like a heated spoon through ice cream.

You could see Cassius coming from a mile away just by looking at the sky, but Ava cloaked herself in shadows and stabbed you in the back before going back to baking cookies.

"Things are that tense? I didn't think anyone lived in the assembly." I slowly sat up to get a little more comfortable. The Assembly convened once a month to discuss the happenings of the mage community, or on special occasions.

Cassius let out a tired breath and he did look tired; heavy bags under his eyes and three-day-old stubble made him look like a grouchy old pirate. "It's rare but it has happened, usually in times of unrest or war, and in this particular case, both." His mouth twisted as if he tasted something sour. "The sleuth has a new alpha with an axe to grind against mages, and he's been fanning the flames between our communities to incite a war. It doesn't help that a couple of weeks ago a bear got into an argument with one of our Sentinels at a bar - both of them are in the hospital, and if either of them dies..."

If either a sentinel - the Assembly's enforcer - or the were-bear died, tensions between both groups would escalate into an all-out war. The New York Assembly and local bear sleuths had a long history, dating back when mages used shifters as slaves and test subjects. Weres had perfect memory and they weren't the type to forgive and forget, even if most of the perpetrators were dead.

"But that's not what's important here." He finished his coffee and put it on the floor by the bed before turning to look at me, his eyes glowing purple with magic. "I hear that some fucking fae has my son, do you know where they have him?"

Sabine raised her head and growled at him; I caressed her head and she quieted down.

"Turn off your headlights Cassius, I'm not some initiate who's scared of the big bad mage."

"Nathan, I entertained your dryad friend long enough and waited for you to wake up." He closed his eyes, taking in a deep breath, but when he opened them again their glowing menace had faded away, leaving only grief and anger. "That doesn't mean I have forgiven you for putting my child in danger."

"Well before the Arrachd made a mess of my inn, I had gotten some information from the local hydra. Turns out that the fae in question has some delusions of grandeur and wants to establish a court here in Portland, and tie the land to her with some sacrifices." His anger subsided a little as I raised my herbal cast and grunted in discomfort. "The ritual is supposed to take place tonight during the new moon."

I brought him up to speed about my conversation with Anastasia, although I didn't tell him about my dream of his son drowning me.

No need to have my friend think I'm crazy. "Also it might be worth checking out Selenic's place after talking with that selkie, as I have a feeling we'll find some clues there."

"A hydra, really? I thought they were land creatures," He said dubiously, crossing his arms, "Why would she care about the sea population? And she owns an art gallery and restaurant? What's up with that?"

"Out of my whole speech, that is what caught your attention?" I rolled my eyes at him and lay my arm down. "The hell would I know, she spoke like some discount mafia godfather, all she was missing was the cat."

He scowled, lightning flashed in his eyes for a brief second. "Not much is known about those creatures outside of myths, so you could be right about the unkillable part. Is she trustworthy? And more importantly, are we really going to find something at this Selenic's place?"

I snorted and scratched Sabine's neck. "Hell no, she's just using me to do her dirty work. Selenic's store is the only place I can think of to get some clues, other than going back to Goodfellow." I caressed the spot where the woman from my dreams slapped me, and shook my head. "That's something I'd rather avoid as much as possible, since there will be a price to pay and I'm not sure we can afford it." I shooed him with my good hand. "Now get out of here so I can get dressed and we can leave."

He arched an eyebrow at me. "We? You're not going to try and convince me that staying away from the fae is safer and all that."

I gave him a droll stare and looked at my herbal cast. "Can't drive with a dislocated shoulder can I? It's not like I can stop you from coming so might as well make yourself useful"

"Fine, I'll wait for you downstairs." He looked at my cast, shook his head and picked up his mug before stepping outside.

I waited for him to leave and let out a tired breath. "This is going to be a long day."

Sabine huffed next to me.

"Yeah, well it's not like I ask for any of this to happen." I stood up and noticed that my bracelets were on the nightstand. With one arm down, I was stuck either defending or attacking, which wasn't good if we ran into the selkies or this mystery queen.

Sabine whined before stretching herself out on the bed.

I looked at her annoyed, everyone was a critic. "No one likes a smartass, sweetie. How about making yourself useful and help me get dressed."

She gave me a condescending look before jumping down from the bed and going out the door.

"Deserter!" I called after her.

I eyed my closet sighed. "Now, how the hell am I going to get dressed?"

1 2

Cassius looked at the batmobile and groaned. "You seriously drive around town in this?"

The black truck was a decade old, with bumps and scratches from everyday use, and the passenger door had been replaced with a charcoal gray one after one of my guests clawed it to hell. I thought it gave my truck character.

I looked at him offended, *what was wrong with my truck?*

"A family of werewolves stayed in the inn a couple of weeks ago and the father found out the wife was cheating on him with his sister.," I shrugged and started walking towards the truck, "A fight broke out and my truck got caught up in the middle of it all, by the end of it there were four pairs of broken knees, a busted muzzle and a dented door," I said while opening the door for Sabine to jump in. "I'll tell you about it later since it was *your* bundle of joy that started that particular mess." Cassius shook his head, got in the driver's seat and drove.

We made it to Selenic's bookstore and luckily found a space to park close to the entrance, which was a miracle given it was almost noon. I clipped Sabine's pink leash on and we made our way out.

I noticed Cassius pull out a twelve-inch dark wooden... *no, it can't be!*

"Is that a wand? Really? What, are you Harry Potter now?"

Color blossomed in his cheeks. "I haven't gotten around to replacing my staff," He said defensively, "This is my backup. It was an anniversary gift from Ava, it's made from a tree branch struck by lightning five times, it's fairly potent."

I snorted and started walking with Sabine. "By your driving, I bet you're a Hufflepuff and for the record no one told you to lose your marbles and destroy your staff."

Sabine looked at the wand and sneezed.

"See even Sabine thinks it's funny."

Cassius's face turned the color of pepperoni. "What does a dog know? I tell you, this is a fairly powerful wand, probably even more so than my staff. Ava carved the runes herself."

"Sure thing, Huffy," I laughed and it felt good after the last couple of days.

We made it towards the front door, where the note was still taped up, although a little weathered now. I tried the door with no luck.

"Okay genius, how are we going to get in?" Cassius asked as he kept a look out for anyone coming near us.

"Aren't you the mage? Can't you spell it open?" I pointed at his wand.

He wiggled it at me. "Evocator, remember. If you want me to blow it open sure, but I think you want to be a little more discreet than that."

"Fine, I'll do it," I muttered beneath my breath, "Useless badger."

I dipped into my dwindling reserves of magic and traced a small keyhole-shaped rune into the doorknob. "Oscaíl."

The rune glowed white before a series of clicks were heard and the door opened seemingly by itself.

We quickly moved inside and closed the door behind us. I turned to look at the store and stopped in my tracks. Normally the bookstore was neatly organized, with gentle lights glowing as soft music played and incense burned, creating a tranquil reading environment.

Torn books with their pages ripped littered the floors, mixed with shards of glass from the broken lights above. Overturned tables and knocked down bookshelves told the tale of a vicious battle. I knelt by one of the bookshelves, running my fingers along the side where a series of deep long groves ran across it. "Something with claws was here," I said, and we slowly made our way further inside, stepping over broken chairs and display models.

"You said that you looked through the window the other day, right? And you didn't see this?" Cassius picked up a ripped copy of *The Lord of the Rings* from the floor; half of it looked like it had been chewed by something. He shook his head, "What a travesty."

I let go of Sabine's leash and she darted between the shelves. "I was more preoccupied about finding Lucas. Selenic is a centuries old merman, he can take care of himself… at least that what I thought at the time."

Cassius nodded, putting the half-eaten book down. I looked around but couldn't see anything that might lead to a clue in this mess. A faint prickling sensation at the back of my neck told me I was missing something obvious.

The room carried a musky-metallic scent that was strangely familiar, but I couldn't figure out why. I circled around the desk where Selenic's wife, Malia, spent most of her time, either reading or talking to the customers.

Her black La-Z-Boy chair had been tossed to the floor like everything else. I bent over and put it back up: it seemed like the right thing to do.

"What happened to you, Selenic, come on bud talk to me." I murmured, although I knew it was futile.

Selenic was usually putting books back into place, or in his office at the back where the really dangerous books lay; grimoires with horrendous spells, ritual books for summoning demons and long forgotten gods. His bookstore served as a vault for every dangerous tome that the Oregon Assembly found. As one of the most powerful mages in the assembly, the old merman kept the books safe away from the main site, although this made him a potential target. If they took him away, then...

My feet started moving before I could finish the thought, and I jumped over the fallen bookcases and tables, making my way to the back. The reinforced steel door had been ripped from its hinges and tossed to the side on top of a fallen table, Cassius saw me move and rushed over as well.

"Did you find something?" He then looked at the office and paused.

"This is bad. Really bad." A shiver ran down my spine looking inside.

Unlike the rest of the store, the back office was neat and orderly, without a single scrap of paper out of place. The large desk made of cypress stood imposingly in the center of the office while a large chair sat behind it and one of the chairs from the outside sat in front. That was strange. Usually the only chair in here was Selenic's.

The walls were covered by three extensive bookshelves. The front of the shelves were locked by thick and warded bulletproof glass, and behind it sat hundreds of the most dangerous books on the planet. The musty metallic scent grew thicker the deeper we went into the office.

I walked behind the desk and fought to keep my breakfast down. The source of the thick smell hit me as I saw the decaying flesh laying in front of me. The ring and pinky fingers were cut at the knuckles, although the large webbing between the fingers and silver scales told me the severed hand had belonged to a merfolk.

Cassius walked forward and noticed the hand, and his eyes grew cold and hard. "Is that..?"

I nodded, swallowing the bile back down again."Yeah, it's Selenic's. I'm guessing they came in when they were about to lock up, it's usually just Selenic and Malia here at that hour," I pointed to the mess outside, "Thankfully their kids are away in college on the other side of the country. This looks like the work of the selkies. They must've stormed their way in and started the fight, probably thought a couple of merfolk wouldn't put much of a fight. Even though he doesn't look like much, Selenic is a powerful enchanter."

Cassius looked towards the shop again with a critical look. "That explains the destruction outside, he must've used the books, shelves and tables to try and fight them off."

I nodded. Selenic was one tough son of a bitch.

"That would be well within his capabilities, and although Malia is not a mage, she is one hell of a fighter." I frowned thinking about the mess in a new light. "They sure did put up a good fight, but something really bad must've happened for them to take Malia and do that to poor Selenic."

Cassius frowned slightly. "What makes you say that?"

I pointed to the extra chair that had been bugging me ever since we entered the room. "That. They most likely captured Malia, forcing Selenic to open the office to get to the forbidden books." I looked around the seemingly untouched shelves. "There's some powerful dark magic and rituals in these tomes but Selenic is a stubborn old bastard and probably didn't want to open them. So, they torture them, cut his fingers off one joint at a time while Malia watched from the chair."

Cassius took in a deep breath and cursed in Latin.

I was feeling pretty angry, too. I wanted to find whoever hurt such wonderful people and chop *them* into a thousand pieces.

"They probably cut Selenic's fingers and when they saw that they were getting nowhere they cut his whole hand out of spite - selkies are not the most patient creatures."

"You don't say? But why would they torture Selenic? If I wanted him to cooperate then I would just threaten the wife and cut *her* finger's off." Cassius said, glaring at the hand.

"Selkies aren't exactly independent thinkers, if they were told to make Selenic talk, they would focus solely on him." I said, looking at the bookshelves to the side.

Cassius followed my gaze, to where both bookshelves were closed with none of the books appearing to be missing. I turned around to look at the shelf behind me, and swore. "Damn it, I was too focused on the desk, come here and look at this."

At first glance the shelf looked locked, but a closer look revealed that the glass was slightly ajar. I inspected the inside but everything looked seemingly normal, although something out of the corner of my eye caught my attention. On the floor next to the shelf was a pile of ashes.

Cassius knelt by the ashes and muttered a few words and spells underneath his breath; a few seconds went by, but the ashes remained inert. "I'm getting a faint magical residue from those ashes, but I can't tell what kind." He frowned as he stood up.

"I remember Selenic saying that the bookshelf at the back was where he kept the really dangerous stuff. The ones at the side were powerful, but not doomsday dangerous as the things in the back." A shiver ran down my spine just thinking what those ashes could mean.

"Let's close this, just in case anyone comes back." Cassius slid the glass panel until the lock clicked in, and a faint purple shimmer passed through the glass as it did.

"Selenic's ward came back up, does that mean he's still alive?" I wondered aloud - I didn't know much about traditional mortal magic. My magic was closer to that of the fae than to human mages, and they could work magic in ways that were impossible for mortals.

Cassius shook his head, studying the bookcase.

"Not necessarily, if it was a ward made from his own blood then yeah, he would need to be alive for the magic to work. But you can set up a ward with just about anything that can hold magic," He pointed towards the books behind the glass, "The only issue would be recharging the ward. If I had to take a guess, given the purple shimmer that just flashed, he used the magic in the tomes to power the wards that would make them stronger and last longer."

I grimaced and looked around. "Let's keep looking, maybe Sabine has found something."

"You do realize that we are looking for a person smart enough to abduct two mages?" He motioned to the shelf and its protective wards. "I would guess Selenic is fairly powerful," He crossed his arms giving me a dubious look, "But you think your dog is going to sniff out a clue like Scooby Doo?"

I was about to make a biting remark when the sound of chains rattling against each other echoed from outside the office as a soul wrenching wail flooded through the whole store. A shiver ran down my spine and I took a step back pressing myself against the shelf. The protective magic singed my shirt and I jumped, startled.

"No, no, no." I hugged myself tightly as the song of grief and misery brought back a thousand memories I had locked away in the darkest corners of my mind.

"Death is here little boy. You can run, you can hide but in the end, death will find you and your voice will join my lovely chorus." A soft gentle whisper ran through the forest, like a father coaxing his misbehaving child to come out of hiding; a fatherly voice that let you know everything will be ok.

My side was bleeding from where Galesh had stabbed me - the wound had reopened god knows how many times, and I had other cuts and bruises that made it hard to keep running but stopping meant death, not just for me but for my companion. I could see a cave in the distance; if we could get there, we would be safe, even if it was just for a couple of hours. The wailing behind us grew louder and the rattling of chains grew closer, we weren't going to make it, we were going to die here. I needed to...

"NATHAN! Nathan, wake up!" Cassius was shaking me by the shoulders, I blinked, and the forest was gone, the voice no longer holding a sway over me, but the wails and chains were still here. The wails surged with anger as a softer growl could be heard, challenging them.

"Nathan, come on, wake up man!"

I turned to look at Cassius and nodded. "I'm okay, sorry, spaced out for a second."

"Don't do that again," He frowned at me worriedly, "I don't know what's going on, but you better get your weapon out, it sounds like all hell is breaking loose out there."

I called my magic to the surface and activated the rune on my morningstar; the familiar weight felt comforting even if it made me a little unbalanced with my arm in a cast.

We were as ready as we were going to be, Cassius with his wand and me wielding my morningstar and casted arm. *What could possibly go wrong?*

~

APPARENTLY, A LOT COULD GO WRONG. ACROSS THE ROOM, TWO BEASTS were fighting, apparently to the death. The larger of the two darted around the room like a shadow - standing at five feet, its lupine mouth opened, revealing a row of razor sharp teeth covered in green foam. Its fiery green eyes regarded the smaller beast with predatorial glee. Translucent chains wrapped around its paws crashed against a nearby chair as the large wolf-like beast stalked us. The smaller beast retreated like a flash of lightning as she evaded the fangs that aimed at her throat.

Four feet tall, with snow white fur matted with blood, the smaller wolf swiped at the black lupine beast, scoring a large gash with her claws across the beast's muzzle. The white wolf's eyes glowed red with calm determination as she rushed forward, snapping her jaws around the wolf's throat only to miss as his fur shimmered and sunk into the floor. A long, drawn out wail was the only warning she got before the black wolf resurfaced from behind her, swiping his paws and hitting her to the side. The white wolf yelped in pain as she used the momentum of his attack to turn around and slash him, knocking a couple of teeth out of the large wolf's muzzle.

The whole room was filled with flying paper and book remnants as the two wolves rolled around in a ball of fangs and claws. If Selenic saw this, he would have an apoplexy.

Cassius cursed beside me and aimed his wand at the two wolves, muttering a spell. The tip of the wand glowed with a dangerous purple light, but before he could release the spell I slapped his hand away. The purple bolt of lightning arched across the room, splintering a nearby bookshelf.

"Are you crazy?" He whirled towards me with anger in his eyes. "What did you do that for?"

I pointed towards the white wolf glaring at him. "I'm not going to let you barbeque my dog, am I?"

His eyes widened as he turned slightly towards the two wolves. "You're telling me that one of those things is your dog?" He palmed his face and shook his head. "Why can't you ever do things the easy way?"

I rolled my eyes at him. Now wasn't the time for theatrics. "Whatever you do, don't hit Sabine and try not to use lightning-based spells. Spectral beings are weak against them but you might hit her. She's the white one!" I edged towards the side, jumping over the remains of a chair and trying to move closer to the fight.

Cassius lowered his wand, his mouth dropping into a frown. "Oh sure, tell the lightning mage not to use lightning spells".

Sabine pounced on the black wolf, sending the beast crashing into a broken table before sinking her fangs into its shoulder. The wolf rocked its head backwards, howling in pain. The green foam covering its mouth spilled everywhere, melting paper and wood with a sizzling sound wherever it landed.

The wolf swiped at Sabine, hitting her in the muzzle with its chain. Sabine yelped in pain and let go of him. As soon as he was free, he squared his shoulders and let out a hair-raising wail that shattered the windows around us. Two other wails echoed his from the outside, turning into a cacophony of misery and pain, and from opposite sides of the walls a pair of smaller wolves emerged. Sabine wearily eyed the newcomers, walking backwards towards an overturned book shelf to avoid getting pinned.

"I was wondering where the rest of the pack was," I grimaced. Sabine could take the large one by herself, but asking her to take on a whole pack was too much.

I ran towards one of the wolves, jumping over a chair and landing on top of an overturned bookshelf as I swung my morningstar in a downwards angle. The wolf turned with its fangs at the ready, but it was too late and my weapon hit it square in the jaw. For a moment there was a slight tug on my arm, like hitting a cushion with a baseball bat, before the wolf crashed into a nearby table which crumpled beneath its weight. The wolf struggled to his feet, his fur shimmering into an opaque grey before it pounced.

I grinned and kissed my morningstar. "Kathour you mad dwarf, I owe you big time."

"Nathan! What the hell are these things and how do we kill them?" Cassius yelled from behind me.

I turned to see him trying and failing to hit the other wolf with a chair. In the middle of the bookstore, Sabine and the alpha jumped through bookshelves, snarling and snapping at each other, before both of them disappeared into the floor.

"Barghests, spectral dogs and omens of death. The fae use them to hunt their victims and capture escaped prisoners," I said, while dodging to the side as my barghest decided it didn't like to be hit and wanted revenge. "They can turn invisible and go through most solid surfaces - like walls - but they can't cross running water."

"Beautiful, but how the hell do we kill them because my table leg isn't cutting it." He'd dropped the chair and was swinging a broken table leg around like a club.

I was about to answer when the barghest snapped at me; I wasn't quick enough and the little bastard ripped a piece of my shirt. *Going to have to be quicker to avoid getting bitten again, those fangs don't look too fun.*

The wolf snarled at me as it moved in for another bite. I swung my morningstar and smacked him on the muzzle which sent him crashing towards the wall, but the little bugger passed straight through it. That was the frustrating part of fighting spectral beings: they had one paw in our world and the other in the spirit world. You couldn't kill such creatures, just banish them.

Cassius was having a hard time keeping his barghest away from him. I tried looking for Sabine, but she was nowhere to be found.

"They can't be killed; you have to destroy their physical body or banish them from this realm. Iron or magic is our best bet."

The barghest had taken a bite of the table leg and wrenched it from Cassius's hands. Green smoke rose from the wood. Cassius swore, pulling out his wand, and magic gathered around the tip as he called on the arcane forces he was most familiar with, purple light crackling throughout his body with increasing force. The barghest pounced, its claws extended, with green foam dripping from its fangs as his eyes zeroed in on the chanting mage.

"I'm a master of the arcane and won't let some flea bag push me around! Displodo!" Cassius roared as he fired his spell.

"Cassius, no!" I shouted, but it was too late.

The tip of the wand glowed red before an arc of power launched from it, hitting the barghest inside its mouth. The force sent Cassius flying backwards through the air, crashing against a nearby bookshelf. The barghest exploded, dark green goop splattered against and coated everything near it, Cassius and I included.

I braced, waiting for the imminent burning and melting of my flesh, but after a moment of nothing I opened my eyes. Whilst everything was green, slimy and smelt like a sewer, nothing was burning. I sighed in relief. Going out like the Wicked Witch of the West was not on my bucket list.

A sharp pain in my left arm snapped me out of my relieved state, and I looked down to see the remaining barghest clamping its jaws down. The fangs penetrated the herbal bandages and pulled me down towards the floor.

At the last moment, the wolf's fur shimmered and turned ethereal as he let go of my arm, sending me crashing head first onto the floor. Pain exploded in my skull as little black spots took over my vision, blood streaming down my forehead and cascading onto the floor. I groaned and fought to stand up, my arms screaming as I pushed myself upright. "Ugh, I'm never going to live this down..."

I managed to stand up, using a chair for support, and noticed that Cassius was out like a light. "Oh, so you're a one-spell-a-day kind of mage now?" I grumbled before making my way over to him to make sure he was alright. "I want a refund."

Suddenly the large barghest came crashing down from the ceiling, with Sabine following close behind him. Her white fur was stained with dark green blood and she had a noticeable limp on her back leg. The alpha, on the other hand, looked like a mess; one of its ears was missing and there were several gashes around his muzzle and neck.

I was halfway between Cassius and Sabine when the rattle of chains rang behind me. Before my brain could process what was going on, my body was already on the move. I lowered myself, pivoted to the left and swung my weapon in an arc. The barghest had been in mid leap, going for my throat, as the morningstar hit him in the head.

It was a move I had practiced countless times with my sword, and hadn't done in years, but luckily muscle memory served me well. If I'd had my sword with me, the blow would've cut the barghest's head clean off. Morningstars weren't made for cutting flesh, they were designed for crushing bones. As the weapon connected, the barghest's head exploded into a puddle of green goop, covering everything around it. Including me. Again.

I spat a large green glob to the floor, and was about to wipe my tongue with my sleeve when I noticed that it too was drenched in the stuff.

The alpha was looking at Sabine with rage and trepidation. Sabine bared her teeth at him, white mist flowing from her mouth. As if he knew he couldn't win, the barghest made a run for the nearest wall.

One of the problems with fighting their kind was that unless you destroyed their bodies with one blow, they could get away at any time they wanted to. Sadly for him, that trick wouldn't work on Sabine. As soon as he turned to run, Sabine pounced at him, snapping her jaws on his shoulder; the sound of bones breaking reverberated through the room as she pulled him back.

The barghest yelped in pain as it crashed against the desk, trying to move despite the fact that now both its shoulder and back leg were maimed. He would need some time to heal all that damage; time Sabine wouldn't give him. She walked towards him with the slow gait of a conquering predator, her eyes glowing red with menace and judgement. The barghest whimpered, trying to crawl away. Sabine locked her jaws around its throat and, with a quick jerk of her head, snapped the creature's neck. The barghest's final slow, pained breath was cut short, and it melted into a puddle of green goop.

Sabine raised her muzzle and sang her victory, her body slowly shrinking back to her usual beagle appearance. She turned to look at me and limped her way over slowly as she wagged her tail. I went to pet her, but she skittered away.

Offended, I said, "Oh, come one, it's not like you didn't get any goop on you during that fight."

She huffed a little before turning around in a circle; her fur was indeed clean of any goop. The only sign that she had been in a vicious fight was the slight limp which was visible when she walked.

I sighed in defeat. "Fine, you win. I'll clean up before giving you pets."

She wagged her tail furiously before walking away and returning with Cassius's wand in between her teeth. "Oh, right, Cassius. I almost forgot about him."

The mage was slowly coming back to consciousness as we walked over to him, where a stack of books had fallen on top of him. "Here, let me help." I gave him my good arm and pulled him up.

He seemed to take note that he was covered in green goop, grimacing and shaking it off his arm. "What the hell is this?"

I took stock of any injuries we had, but aside from Sabine's limp and my pounding head, we had come out of this without too much damage. I looked down at my cast, which was now slowly closing itself up where the barghest had bitten. "Well, that's convenient," I murmured beneath my breath before turning to Cassius.

"Ectoplasm, beings from the spirit world are made of the stuff," I said, waving my mace and splattering a nearby table. "They're one of those monsters who clean up after themselves… kind of." I pointed to the bodies of the barghests which were slowly evaporating before our eyes. "While we don't have to worry about getting rid of any bodies, they do always leave gunks of the stuff if you manage to destroy them and return them to the spirit world. We were lucky that there were only three of them. Barghests usually travel in packs of ten or more."

"Ugh, you owe me a new wardrobe, and it better be a nice one - not one of those farmer shirts you seem so fond off." He tried to wipe the gunk from his shirt, but it had begun to dry and was now pretty much impossible to get out.

I shook my head, ignoring the dig at my clothes. "I told you not to use lightning. Most of this is because you decided to play demolition man." I was sore, exhausted and uncomfortably slimy. "We're not far from the mall, let's go get some new clothes and regroup."

He nodded at me, then noticed Sabine had his wand in her mouth and was chewing at it with gusto. He was about to yell at her but stopped, presumably remembering Sabine's other form and thinking better of it. "You mind telling her to give it back? I'm kind of defenseless without it."

I looked at Sabine who was now chewing at the wand with her back molars with a very satisfied look on her face. "Sabine, will you please give the grumpy mage his stick back?"

Sabine ignored us and continued to chew, growling something to me.

"Are you serious? Fine," I turned to Cassius, "She wants you to apologize for punching me and also she wants a steak." Another growl. "A big juicy one."

He blinked at me in surprise then turned to her. "Are you blackmailing me?"

Sabine took a hard bite of the wand, something audibly chipping off. Cassius winced as she growled again, and I tried to hold in my laughter as I said, "Two steaks."

He looked at me, jaw slack. "You're bullshiting me?"

I raised my hands in defeat, but couldn't stop a smile from slipping out. Another growl came from my hostage-taking dog. "We're up to three steaks and a rack of ribs. Take it or leave it," I translated.

Cassius's face shook with frustration and I could see that he wanted to say something but was swallowing it down with visible effort. "Nathan, I'm sorry about overreacting and punching your smug face. Would you please forgive me, and allow me to compensate the both of you with dinner."

I grinned, turning to look at Sabine. "Satisfied?"

Sabine got up and delicately placed the wand at Cassius's feet. The whole thing was covered in drool and bite marks, and the chip was extremely visible. He snatched it back quickly, wiping the drool off on his shirt before glaring at Sabine. "Terrorist."

Sabine wagged her tail and huffed a little breath, tongue lolling out. "She won't care what you call her as long as you get her the steaks." I clapped him on the shoulder and nodded towards the door. "Come on, I have an idea about who can give us information on what was taken from here, and with that we'll be one step closer to finding Lucas."

Cassius looked at Sabine with a tentative new-found respect before promptly storming out the door. I waited until he was out, and immediately dissolved into laughter. After finding out what happened to Selenic and fighting the barghests, it felt good to laugh.

13

W e stopped by the Lloyd Center a couple of blocks south of the bookstore to buy a new set of clothes that weren't covered in ectoplasmic crap. An elderly couple who were just coming out of the mall looked us up and down with a weak smile.

"Dear me, what's happened to you two?" The woman asked, her eyes widening behind her horn-rimmed glasses.

I gave her a welcoming smile. "We were helping my kids with their science project," I motioned to both of us covered in green, crusting gunk, "It didn't go as planned."

The woman smiled at her husband, patting him on the arm. "Oh Richard, do you remember the time you got an allergic reaction making that volcano for the kids?"

The man groaned and rolled his eyes, pulling his wife towards the exit. "You're never going to let that go, are you? Come on, we need to go or we'll be late for the doctors."

The couple waved at us before going about their way. I smiled at them and followed Cassius into the first store we saw. I grabbed a shirt and a pair of jeans from a rack and went into the dressing room to change. Cassius followed suit.

We paid for our clothes (the cashier nicely binned the old ones), and were walking out of the store when a loud squeal cut through the commotion.

"Uncle Nathan!"

I turned around to see a little girl running towards us at full speed, weaving between the crowds. About nine years old, with long brown hair and pale blue eyes. My face widened into a genuine smile and I knelt down with my arm wide open, bracing for impact.

The girl jumped when she was about a foot from me, leaping into my arms where I caught her, spinning her around. She was giggling madly, wrapping her arms around my neck and squeezing. I gave her one more spin and kissed her on the cheek. "Margie! What are you doing here?"

"Uncle Nathan, guess what? I'm going to be a big sister!" She beamed, showing me a wide smile that was missing two teeth.

A curvy woman in her mid-thirties rushed over to us, a stern expression clouding her face as she grabbed Margie's arm. "Margie, I told you not to leave my side for anything."

Margie looked at the woman with a frown. "But mom, it's Uncle Nathan! He needed to know that I'm going to be a big sister, it's important."

I laughed and kissed the side of her head again. "A stóirín, you need to listen to your mom." I smiled at Alice and gave her a hug. "Devon told me earlier, congratulations!"

Alice's smile lit up her entire face. "Who would've thought after all these years I'd be a mom again?" She turned to Cassius and gave him a comforting smile. "I heard about what happened to your son, and I'm sorry. I'm sure Nathan will do everything possible to get him back safely."

Cassius froze before giving her a stiff nod. "Thank you," He then turned to me, "Nathan..."

I nodded and gave Margie one last big hug. "Okay, A stóirín, be a good girl for your mom and I'll promise to tell you a story when I next visit."

"I promise!" She nodded enthusiastically, sending her hair flying everywhere about her head as she went hopping back to her mother.

Alice turned to me, her eyes flashed with mint light before frowning. "Nathan, Hope needs to know sooner rather than later."

"Thanks Alice, Hope's my next stop." She nodded, her eyes returning to their natural hazel color, and led Margie away.

"How did she know about Lucas?" Cassius asked as we made our way back to the car.

"Devon could've told her, he was there when I broke through the illusion, or she could've picked it up from my mind - Alice is the strongest telepath I've ever met." We had left the car running so that Sabine could rest in the A/C, and when I got in I scooped her sleeping form into my lap and slowly caressed her head.

He nodded, and pulled the car out of the parking lot. "Who's Hope?"

I scratched Sabine behind the ears. "She's the head of the Oregon Assembly, so if anyone knows what Selenic was guarding it would be her. Plus, her husband makes a killer BBQ, and I don't know about you but I'm starving."

Russell's was a small restaurant near the corner of Graham St and 7th Ave, and although it looked like a simple log cabin on the outside, the inside was where the magic really was. Tall arched windows breathed light into the spacious open floor that hosted several tables, where people delighted themselves with the best BBQ sauce in the state.

Cassius was just turning around the corner when the car began to sputter before slowing to a complete dead stop. He turned the ignition several times but the car wouldn't start, or even rev. I looked over at the needle and saw that we still had half a tank of gas. "What the hell?"

I looked around and noticed that every car around us seemed to be having the same problem; the street was filled with stalled cars. The strangest part of it all was that no one was getting out, or even reacting at all to the situation. Instead, they appeared stuck in their cars, staring straight ahead with glazed expressions as if nothing was wrong. "Yeah, that's not creepy at all." I murmured.

Cassius muttered a few incantations beneath his breath and waved his wand in a forward motion. The wand let out a few purple sparks but nothing obvious seemed to happen. "There's an area wide spell around us, and I can't break it."

The thought of that disturbed me: Cassius was a powerful mage. He could easily be ranked within the top ten in the New York Assembly in terms of raw power, so if there was a spell that even he couldn't break, we were dealing with some *serious* magic.

"It's gotta be Hope, there's no one else that powerful for miles." I opened the car door and dashed towards the restaurant, Sabine and Cassius hot on my heels.

Whatever the spell was, it got stronger the closer we got to the restaurant until every step felt like walking through molasses. As we walked, the air compressed around us, pushing us back. I gritted my teeth and fought against it. Our progress was slow, but at least we hadn't been stopped cold like the mortals around us. After what felt like an eternity, we reached the restaurant and the air softened, the spell seemingly no longer having an effect on us. I glanced back to check Sabine was alright, and then turned back, realising that we had come upon a scene of utter carnage.

Bile rose in my throat and I struggled to swallow it back down. Half a dozen cars were piled in a semicircle around the entrance to the restaurant, their doors caved in and covered in blood. A white limo splattered with red gore lay upside down across from the restaurant, and the street was covered in broken glass and metal parts from the cars. Mixed with the debris were the mauled corpses of at least twenty people; some were dressed in formal attire, as if they'd been dressed for a wedding or birthday party. Next to the limo the body of a girl in her mid-teens hugged the mangled form of a little boy, who looked no older than five.

"Deus Meus!" Cassius whispered next to me.

In front of the restaurant, a group of six people huddled together, their faces pale and their eyes hollow and sunken. Blood stained their tattered clothes and a couple of them seemed to have fashioned bandages with torn strips of fabric. In front of them stood a woman, about five foot, with olive skin and long, curly chocolate-brown hair. Her dark eyes were narrow as she held a dark staff, nearly double her height, made from Alder wood. The staff blazed with a mustard-colored glow, which spread and solidified into a ten foot tall wall, creating a defense between her and a trio of familiar looking wolves.

We had just fought these bastards not even an hour ago, and while they couldn't be the same beasts they were certainly part of the same pack. I knew there had been too few back at the bookstore to consti-tute a full pack. The wails of misery coming from the beasts cut through the people's screams and the chaos of the fight currently taking place.

The dark-furred beasts were repeatedly running towards the wall, slamming into it with their fangs and claws. The wall flared intensely with the impact, sending arcs of electricity outwards which shocked the beasts on contact. The smell of singed fur mixed with the heavy smell of blood in the air created a nauseating stench.

Across the street from the woman a colossal bear stood on all fours, easily eight feet at the shoulder, with snow-white fur matted with red and green blood. He faced off another four beasts, who had him cornered against an overturned mail truck and were darting in and out of his range, swiping with their claws and leaving deep gashes on the bear's fur.

"Fuck!" I cursed, reaching for my magic. "I was wondering why only three barghests attacked us back at Selenic's." I was too drained from my recent battles, and hadn't given my body a chance to replenish my spent reserves. Reaching for my magic hurt. "Ag Fás!"

Black spots flowered my vision and I shook my head trying to clear my eyes. "Cassius, you and Sabine help Hope and protect those people."

I pointed towards the bear with my morningstar, "I'll help Russell."

Cassius nodded as his grip tightened around his wand, and he ran to take cover behind a tree. Sabine's fur shimmered as her beagle form once again melted away, leaving behind a four foot tall timber wolf with glowing red eyes and ears. She phased into the street and vanished from sight.

I gave one last look over to Cassius before rushing towards Russell. Glass cracked beneath my boots as my legs carried me over the upside down limo. I took a running leap from the middle of the wrecked car, the smell of blood clogging my nostrils. The knowledge that those defenseless mortals had been killed for no reason fueled me as I swung my morningstar over my head and slammed it down into the spine of a retreating barghest.

The sound of bones cracking felt so satisfying, and the barghest yelped in pain. I didn't give him a chance to retaliate, and backhanded him with my weapon, crushing half of his skull in as I went to strike at another barghest. The wolves were surprised only for a moment but soon took notice of me as a threat.

Russell didn't wait another second and pounced at the remaining barghest, his gigantic claw swiping at the beast's head, dragging him across the asphalt and leaving a bloody trail before closing his tremendous maw around it, decapitating the wolf in a single bite.

Together, we turned towards the other two wolves. One had a dislocated shoulder from where my weapon hit him, and the other was suffering with a long gash along its flank. They snarled at each other for a moment before levelling those eerie green eyes at us.

I rotated my wrist, the morningstar whistling through the air and grinned at them.

The wolves growled at me, their mouths filling with green foam that fell to the street below, sizzling on impact. The smell of burnt asphalt mixed in the air with a stench of blood, stinging my eyes and nose. They rushed towards us from opposite directions, the one with the lame shoulder coming from the left while the other ran to us from the right. I stood my ground with my back to Russel, who roared at the approaching wolf.

Out of the corner of my eye I saw Sabine chasing down one of the barghests whilst Cassius was evidently muttering a spell under his breath; one of the wolves already lay on the ground, a charred corpse. Reassured that they were doing alright, I whipped back to my own battle to see the barghest pouncing at me, wicked sharp claws extended from its paws.

I rolled forward over my shoulder, bits of glass piercing my skin, but I ignored them and came up swinging my morningstar to connect with its back leg. The wolf spun in the air and landed on its side, skidding next to miserable bodies of the girl and boy. It tried to stand up, but with two injured legs all it could do was stumble forward. I took one last glance at the bodies, praying to the gods that they were in a better place, and slammed my weapon with all my strength into the wolf, caving the murderous beast's skull.

I turned around to see Russell in a scuffle with his beast, its jaws locked around his paw. The huge polar bear roared in pain before rising up onto his hind legs to his full, towering height. The wolf snarled, trying to rip his paw off, but the bear was much stronger than his opposition and grabbed the wolf by the spine, biting it in half with the power of his jaw. The barghest didn't even have time to yelp in pain; it hung limply like a rag doll on each side of Russell's maw.

The bear shook the wolf in the air like a toy before throwing it across the street with such force that it slammed into Hope's barrier, releasing a spark of energy on contact. I turned to see Sabine dodging to the side of a pouncing barghest before quickly leaping forward and clasping her jaws around the other wolf's neck, twisting it with one swift movement.

The last wolf standing took a swipe at Cassius, who was busy conjuring a spell. The lightning mage moved with the speed and grace of a trained fighter, dodging out of the way, using a car door as a shield to hide behind. As the barghets's claws raked the metal, it yelped in pain; looking around, he appeared to realise he was alone and outnumbered, and made for a hasty retreat.

"On no you don't," Cassius pointed his wand, glowing purple at the tip, "STREPO!"

An arc of lightning fired from the wand, but firing at an awkward angle meant Cassius only managed to blow the wolf's ear off before it turned incorporeal and vanished into the ground. I took a deep breath, and the adrenaline of the fight flowed out of me as I examined the carnage around us. I suddenly felt old, and tired. Was there a need for so many people to die? And for what? Mortals should never get caught in the struggles of our world. Was this fae-wannabe-queen really crazy enough to attack the Head of the Oregon Assembly in her own home? *Damn her! Damn all the fae!*

I saw Russell turn towards Cassius, battle-rage still evident in his eyes. He slowly stalked towards him, and sensing that something was wrong, the mage turned towards the huge bear and squared his shoulders.

Oh, shit.

I stepped between the two and turned to Russell. His head and jaw were so massive that he could bite me in half without even flinching. I looked into his icy-blue eyes and raised my hand, forgetting that I was still gripping my morningstar. Oops. The bear roared at me, his mouth stinking of blood mixed with BBQ. It was a... *unique* scent, to say the least.

I dropped my weapon to the ground, spreading my now empty hands in front of me to show the bear I was unarmed. "Paix mon frère," I pointed towards Cassius behind me, "He's a friend, and on my honor he will behave himself."

The bear glared at me, and I felt a brief need to prostrate myself and submit, but I quashed that feeling quick. I had stared down dragons, giants, and every nightmare the fae had ever thrown at me. An alpha bear wasn't much compared to that, although of course back then I had full use of my arms and wasn't drained of my magic.

Russell looked back at Hope, who was touching the tip of her staff to the survivor's foreheads; their eyes grew glassy before they slumped to the ground, fast asleep. Russell growled at me.

"I promise he will keep silent about this," I said and fought to remain on my feet even though my knees felt like jelly.

A spasm passed through the bear's body as it began to twist upon itself. The sounds of bones cracking and popping filled the street again, and flesh and fur warped and shifted, finally revealing a naked pale man before me. At least six and half foot tall, his muscular build was covered in wounds that were already slowly beginning to heal. His strong square jaw and a closely trimmed beard softened his hard gaze.

His blue eyes stared down at me. "You better make sure the magus keeps his mouth shut to his *copains* in New York, or I'll make you into my special sauce." He said with a rich French lilt before making his way towards his wife.

I let out a breath of relief and picked up my weapon. I was too spent to shrink it back into my bracelet, so I had to carry it the old-fashioned way. Cassius walked towards me, looking between me and Russell, who was hugging his wife close to him.

"The head of the Oregon Assembly is married to a bear shifter." He stated matter-of-factly.

"Yes, though only a select few know," I nodded, resting my weapon on my shoulder, "From what I heard, every Assembly works independently of each other unless a national emergency occurs right?" Cassius nodded. I sighed and nodded towards Hope hugging her husband. "The Assemblies' secular nature allows them to live happily and in secret."

Given the strain and bloody history between mages and shifters, it was almost unheard of for them to marry or raise a family as Hope and Russell had done. Then again, they were special.

I turned to Cassius and looked at him seriously. "You have to swear not to spread this information to anyone." This was a risk I knew before coming here, but I did really need to talk to Hope. "If the more radical Heads or other shifters find out, they will do everything to break this family apart."

Cassius looked at me, annoyed. "I know that, dumb-dumb," He sighed and rubbed his shoulder, rolling it with a wince, "This is what I've been advocating in New York for years, peace between mages and shifters."

I smiled and nodded. "Good. Now, let's go and find out what the hell happened."

The doors to the restaurant suddenly opened and a small white shadow blurred towards Russell, who smiled and easily caught the shadow in his arms. He began to sing a little lullaby.

In his arms was now a little girl about six years old, wearing a pink dress, with curly salt-and-pepper hair like her dad and dark eyes like her mother. A beautiful mischievous child, Dana could never sit still for long.

Hope saw us approach and smiled at me before giving Cassius a wary look. "Well, the last thing I expected waking up this morning was getting attacked in my own home. And now I'm meeting a High Circle mage from New York."

Cassius gave her a small bow. "Madam Hope, on my power I swear to you that I bear no ill will towards you or your family, and it would be my honor to keep your secret."

Russell glared at Cassius while continuing to sing to Dana, then turned to his wife. Hope regarded Cassius for a long second before she nodded, and the wariness in her eyes was replaced with the warmth I was used to.

"I'm glad to hear that, Cassius, and please accept my condolences towards your family," She raised her hand and caressed Dana's hair, "I don't know what I would do if anything happened to one of my girls."

At that moment, Dana raised her head and looked at her dad. "Papa, are you going to die?"

"Oh *mon ange*," Russell chuckled and tickled Dana's belly, making the little girl giggle, "Your papa is a big strong bear, there's no way a bunch of flea bags are going to kill me."

Dana looked at her mom for confirmation as soon as she stopped giggling. Hope nodded, kissing the girl in her cheek. "Yes my dear, your papa is the strongest bear in the world."

Dana nodded, laid her head on her dad's shoulder, and began to suck her thumb.

Hope turned to me with a smile. "Not that not I'm grateful for the assistance, but I have to ask: why are you here Nathan, and with Cassius Gray by your side?"

I chewed on my words for a moment, considering how to summarize everything that had happened in the last couple of days. "A couple of days ago, the police knocked on my door to notify me that Lucas had been found dead," I showed her my injured arm, "We discovered that he isn't actually dead, but has been kidnapped by one of the fae to be sacrificed in some messed up ritual. We also learned today that Selenic and his wife have also been taken, and his office was broken into. We came here to see if you'd know why the fae might be interested in him and the vault."

Hope's eyes widened before they hardened into a cold stare with a dangerous light. This was not the caring mother from a second ago. I was now truly facing the Head of the Oregon Assembly in all her fury.

"No wonder Selenic failed his usual check in, I was about to visit him when this happened." She motioned to the carnage around us, where the bodies of the barghests were starting to evaporate. The only signs of the battle that would be left were the mangled corpses of the unfortunate mortals caught in the crossfire, the damaged cars and all the blood. "They dare come into my city, take my people and kill mortals under our protection," Her voice thundered with power, "This is a declaration of war. Do you know which court is responsible?"

I shook my head. "I talked to Goodfellow, he says it's not Winter, and from the information we gathered this seems to be a rogue fae that wants to raise a court here in Portland and plunge the city beneath the sea."

Hope frowned pensively, her voice losing the initial timbre of power. "I didn't think it would be Goodfellow, it wouldn't make sense for Winter to request permission to operate in the city only to try to stab us in the back." She must've noticed the look of surprise on my face because she arched an eyebrow at me, quipping, "You didn't think the fae could settle such a large force in the city without me knowing, surely. We struck a deal."

What!? "Hope, you can't be serious!" I pointed to the dead bodies around us. "Look around you, this is what happens when you deal with the fae. Trust me, I know what I'm talking about." Was she crazy? Any deal with the fae was a ticking time bomb. "What is so important that you need to make a deal with them? You're the Head of the Oregon Assembly for the gods' sake!"

Her eyes gained a dangerous light, and she stared me down. "That is my personal business, Nathan."

A low growl came from Russell, and I knew something serious must've happened, but now wasn't the time to go down that particular rabbit hole. I'll just write it down on my growing list of things to worry about later.

"I'm sorry if I overstepped, it wasn't my intention to offend you." I gave her a small nod. "Is there anything in the vault that could give the fae the power to raise a court, especially one that would require a sacrifice?"

Hope tapped the end of her staff on the ground twice, and a black and yellow ledger appeared in mid air, its worn yellowed pages flipping themselves back and forth before stopping. She peered at the contents and frowned.

"You have to understand, Selenic was the Vault Keeper for our most dangerous and unstable items," She looked at us from the top of the ledger, "It was his duty to hunt new items and then seal them for study and hopefully neutralization. It's why the vault is located outside the assembly - no one would've expected it, and only the head of the assembly and the keeper are privy to the vault's location."

Cassius crossed his arms and frowned pensively. "Yet somehow this queen targeted your keeper. It can't be a coincidence, but where could they have gotten his identity?"

Hope's eyes hardened and her staff glowed with faint yellow light. "I don't know, but I intend to find out." She turned back to the ledger, her finger dancing across the page. "The problem is that there's too many rituals that could give someone the power to drown a city. But one that would give her the power to create a court and destroy the city... there's only two, and both require human sacrifices."

She muttered something under her breath and the book shone again with black and yellow light before a thin sheet of paper appeared in Hope's hand. She gave it to me and I perused it for a moment before cursing, "So if I'm reading it right, this bitch will sacrifice both Lucas and Selenic to either summon a demon from the eighth circle of hell, or free an ancient god of war and carnage from his prison. Beautiful."

Cassius tapped his bicep in thought. "The eighth circle is where frauds and con artists go, if I remember my Dante."

I shrugged. "I guess. I'm not exactly an expert on demons, but I can't see a fae stooping so low as to make a deal with their kind. It must be this god-"

Hope slammed her staff down and cut me off. "Don't say his name Nathaniel. Even locked up, saying his name will draw his attention and give him power over you."

I nodded towards her, snapping my mouth shut before opening it again. "Thank you Hope, for everything. With this, at least we can form a plan to stop them."

"Forming a plan is not that difficult, the problem is finding them," Cassius said as his voice tensed with anger, "We have no leads and the clock is ticking."

"*We* might not have a lead, but I know someone who can get us one." I nodded towards Sabine, who was sniffing the unconscious people, presumably to make sure they were okay.

Cassius arched a dubious eyebrow at me. "Really?"

I nodded. "Her kind were bred to guard the gates of Annwn, to escort the souls of the dead and to hunt evildoers." Sabine came over, wagging her tail as if to acknowledge her proud heritage. I smiled at her and knelt to scratch her behind the ears. "If there's anyone who can track the barghests, it's her."

Russell grunted, and I turned to him. "If you're going on a hunt, then you need some food. You both look ready to drop at any moment." He handed Dana over to Hope. "Give me five minutes to prepare you something for the road."

"Thanks Russell," I grinned, genuinely grateful. My body felt sore and starving, the result of too much magic expended with no time to recover.

He nodded and walked towards the restaurant. I looked around the carnage around us, sadness and rage bubbling inside me. "What's going to happen to the survivors?"

Grief clouded Hope's eyes, and she kissed the top of Dana's head, surveying the broken, sleeping people. "I'll keep them asleep until a team from the Assembly gets here, and then we'll alter their memories. Make it seem like an animal got loose from a zoo transport or something."

I nodded. There wasn't much that could be done; there were too many dead to sweep this whole thing under the rug. The needless death of innocents pissed me off. This bitch had come into my city, hurt my friends, and murdered mortals - all for what? A crazy power trip?

Five minutes later Russell came back, still naked, with a couple of foam containers, handing them to Cassius. "There's half a dozen pulled pork sandwiches inside, along with two cups of baked beans, cherry pie and three T-bone steaks for Sabine."

My stomach growled at the sweet smell coming from the containers. "Thanks again Russell, we'll keep you posted."

Hope nodded, her gaze softening as she moved to stand with her husband. They really were a beautiful family. "Be careful Nathan, something about all of this is giving me a bad feeling."

"We will," I turned to Sabine. "Think you can track the barghests trail?"

Her eyes sparked with a reddish glow and her fur began to shimmer and dissolve as she stepped halfway into the spirit world, keeping one paw in our mortal world.

It took her a moment to gather the scent before she bolted across the restaurant and through the doors. Cassius and I ran to the truck to follow her.

14

F ollowing a floating spectral dog through the afternoon traffic
  was a new experience for me. I'd battled dragons, giants, mages
and the worst of the fae, but none of that scared me like Cassius's
driving. For all the grief I had given him over the years for driving
slowly, I realised that I now preferred it to him trying to kill us.

"Would you slow down? You're going to get us pulled over!" I
screamed as a cat ran in front of us.

Cassius swerved to the right, almost losing control of the car, and I
held on to my sandwich as the crazy mage tried to kill us. *Damn it!*

"I would if your little beast wasn't popping in and out of existence
at the drop of a dime." He grumbled while taking a hard left onto
Lombard St. "Tell her to wait for us."

I swallowed another bite of my sandwich and glared at him, crazy
driving or not my stomach demanded food. "Sure, let me just peak my
head out the window." I looked at the passing cars blaring their horns
at us. "Oh wait, I can't."

I rolled my eyes at him and clenched as Cassius swerved to the
right, narrowly missing another car.

Sabine had suddenly turned left, passing through the back of a
semi truck. Cassius cursed and jerked the wheel, other drivers and

passengers be damned. I tried peeling myself off the passenger window when I noticed someone following us.

An old, white sedan had nearly crashed into a minivan before settling a couple of cars behind us. I tried getting a better look but Cassius's demon driving made it impossible.

"Don't look back, but I think we're being followed." I said after finally sitting upright, not that it mattered, and took a bite of my sandwich. "I don't know by whom, but they have been keeping up with your crazy driving for the last five minutes." Cassius's shoulders tensed and his grip on the steering wheel tightened.

"You think it's our fae friends?"

"No, the car looks too old." I took a quick peek before shaking my head. "The fae can drive some of the newer models since they don't have nearly as much metal as they used to, but they can't drive the older cars, too much iron." I started noticing the street signs and had an idea where we were going.

"Slow down. Damn it," I slammed my hand on the dashboard, "I know where she's going." I gripped the dashboard as Cassius mounted the pavement following my crazy dog.

"Care to share with the class, Sherlock?" He asked as he finally slowed down the car. The white car that was following fell back a little, but was still obviously on our tail.

"If you were looking to kidnap a couple of mages, what better place than the one where hundreds of them gather to drink, smoke, have sex and learn a bit of magic," I said whimsically.

Cassius frowned for a moment before the lights turned on that big noggin of his. "The College."

The College of Mages sat on the bank of the Willamette River, between the St. John's Bridge and the Railroad Bridge. As one of the leading magical institutions in the country, thousands of mages gathered to learn about the different schools of magic and earn their various degrees. Some went directly to work for the Assemblies, others struck out on their own and tried to make names for themselves.

Mortals had no idea that in what seemed like an empty plot of land, a building as old as the United States stood. Founded shortly after the first European settlers arrived from the Old World, the college was protected by centuries-old magic. If a mortal did ever manage to step inside the grounds, the magic would alter their memories, making them forget everything they saw.

Sabine waited for us by the side of the curb, her nose sat between her paws. *Oh, my poor baby girl.* She saw us park, and floated through the door, landing on my lap and rubbing her nose against it.

"It's okay, girl, I know. You can stay here and take a nap and eat your steaks." I said while stroking her back.

"What's wrong with her?" Cassius looked between us and the college campus.

"There's too much magic in the air, her nose is getting overwhelmed." I explained while opening the food container. "Sabine's nose is very sensitive to magic. It's why Lucas always had to shower before coming to work."

He groaned and sat back with his arms crossed over his chest. "What are we going to do now? If we can't follow the scent, how are we going to find anything in this place?"

"I don't know, give me a minute to think."

"A minute? Nathan, my son has been taken by some crazy fae on a power trip, he might be hurt or worse..." His voice broke a little. I turned to see him fighting back tears.

"He's my baby boy, I can't lose him." He took a ragged breath and the pain in his eyes cut me to my core. "I don't know what I would do if anything happened to him. I thought he was going to be safe here, away from the craziness with the shifters. I thought he was going to meet a girl and drive me crazy before coming back home, he was supposed to be *safe*."

Cassius's eyes turned glassy as he started pounding the steering wheel. "Why couldn't he stay safe? Why? Why? Why?" Each word was punctuated by a hit to the steering wheel.

I grabbed him by the shoulder and made him look at me. "Cassius, you didn't do anything wrong. This is what the fae do, when you're at your most vulnerable and feel safe they come at you and turn your world upside down just because they're bored." I pushed back the memories, now wasn't the time for my pain. "I lived with them for years, I know how they think and I know how to hurt them. I promise you that we're going to get him back safe and sound."

Cassius looked at me with a torn expression, and I was really hoping that I could at least keep this one promise.

Kid, hang on a little longer, we're coming.

I got out of the car and let my friend compose himself. It was the middle of the afternoon, so the college was filled with students coming to and from classes. I didn't see our pursuer, but I was sure they were around.

The magic in the air was too thick for Sabine to get a good read; the barghests could've gone to any number of places. Using runic sight was a bad idea for the same reason but it was the only way I could pinpoint where they'd been. I just needed a controlled space without the overwhelming magic, or I would run the risk of over-loading my mind from an excess of information. But where?

The gravel beside me crunched as Cassius got out of the car looking as calm as he could be, but the burning rage was still present in his eyes. My friend was falling apart at the seams and I wasn't sure how long he could keep it together. His emotions were on a roller-coaster; one second he was teasing me about being a bad passenger, the next he's attacking my steering wheel.

"I think our best lead would be to check out Lucas's dorm room," I said, slow and calm, keeping an eye on him out of the corner of my eye. "There's no way they could've taken him from the inn or college without anyone seeing anything. They must've waited until he was between places before grabbing him and even then, he took one of them out, so maybe we can find something there to help us."

Cassius nodded stiffly. "Let's go."

The sky darkened as rain clouds slowly moved, blotting out the sun; there was a moist scent in the air that precluded a heavy rainfall. Great - from what Lucas told me, his dorm room was to the west, on the opposite side of where we parked. I looked at Cassius to see if it was his doing but he was focused on the dorms ahead of us.

After the last couple of days, even regular Portland rain was starting to look like a sign of the apocalypse. Maybe I'll get a vacation once all of this over, somewhere tropical perhaps.

As we got to the dorm rooms, we were stopped by one of the teachers; young and probably in her late twenties. She stood a head shorter than me, her strawberry blonde hair falling below a heart shaped chin that made her features seem soft and almost adorable. It was a welcoming face that inspired trust. Her almond-shaped eyes hid behind a pair of pink glasses, and wearing a peach sundress with matching heels and umbrella she embodied the warmth of a summer's day.

"Excuse me, who are you?" Her voice was soft, almost lyrical, her eyes focussed on the spots of green gunk and my herbal cast, and she raised an eyebrow at us.

I looked towards Cassius, and then back to the woman with a mournful face. "Hi, my name is Nathan. This is my friend Cassius. His son is a student here, we're just here to pick up his things. Could you help us by any chance, Ms..?"

"Professor Arelis White, I'm a teacher in the evocation department," She said, polite and welcoming. "Which student might this be and why would he need his things picked up?"

"Lucas Gray, I'm sure you heard what happened?" I said tentatively, it had been a couple of days. Bad news always spread fast.

"I see," She murmured, her eyes softened as she looked at Cassius, "My condolences, his loss is a tragedy to the magical community." She touched her chest. "He was one of my best students. Please follow me; I'll escort you to his dorm room."

She turned around and marched towards the dorm rooms, and I was about to follow when Cassius caught me by the arm. "What's wrong?" I asked, confused.

"How are we going to look for clues with her watching over our backs." He whispered, a hint of frustration tinging his voice.

"We need her to get us into the dorm with the least amount of suspicion." I shrugged off his hold and patted him on the shoulder.

Professor White had gone ahead a good twenty feet or so before we caught up to her. The dorm building stood imposingly at five stories tall, a blue-gray monstrosity. The entrance had two large trees to the side; one was an apple tree, the other a peach one. Both trees were blooming with fruit, even though the season had passed.

Lucas's teacher must've noticed the look on my face because she nodded towards the trees. "The building is surrounded by all kinds of fruit-bearing trees. The success of a joint project between the conjuration and enchantment departments." She went to the peach tree and plucked two of them, handing them to us. "They were to create an environment that would allow trees to bear fruit year-round. Besides the protection wards around the dorms, now they have an extra enchantment to help the trees."

The peach was soft to the touch, its sweet smell tempting you to take a bite out of it right away. I nodded my thanks to her but didn't eat it. "They look delicious."

Professor White looked at me for a second before giving me a brief smile as if I had passed some kind of test. "Follow me, I'll take you straight to Lucas's room."

The lobby of the dorm room resembled the reception desk of a hotel. A stout man with a large handlebar mustache and receding hairline was leafing through a novel. He looked up for a split second, noticing Professor White who approached him asking directions to Lucas's room.

Behind the reception stood an elevator that took us to the first floor. While the dorm building looked big from the outside, it was nothing compared to the inside. As soon as we stepped out of the elevator, the hallway before us stretched on for hundreds of feet as well as to the side.

"Huh, well that's convenient. I'm guessing you don't have to worry about ever running out space," I commented.

"It's a simple application of transmutation magic, Nathan, don't you do the same thing in your inn?" Cassius educated me.

"Hardly a simple application, Mr. Gray," Professor White clarified, "The spell around the dorm rooms is linked to the College's database. As soon as a new student enrolls and wants to live at campus, the building automatically creates a room for them." She then turned to me with an inquisitive look. "Are you a mage as well, Nathan?"

"I'm merely a dabbler in the arcane." I shook my head.

"I see." Her tone was noncommittal but there was something about the way she looked at me like she knew more than what she was saying. "Please step outside and watch your step, make sure you don't fall."

We got out of the elevator and onto the carpet floor, but before we could question what she meant the floor started moving, pulling us through the left hallway and continued on for about ten minutes before stopping by a dark wooden door. All the doors looked the same and had no numbers to identify them but, being a professor of the college, I'm sure Ms. White had a way to know. Once we stopped in front of the dorm, she pulled out a red wooden wand and traced a few symbols in the air before touching the tip to the doorknob.

As she finished she put the wand back in her pink purse and turned to us. "Alright gentlemen, the wards have been disabled. Take as long as you need, once you're ready to leave come and find me by the elevator and I'll escort you out."

With that the floor started moving again, only this time it only took the professor away. "Well, that was as disconcerting as riding an airplane." I murmured before looking at Cassius who nodded at me before stepping into the room.

LIKE THE REST OF THE BUILDING, THE ROOM WAS BIGGER ON THE INSIDE than on the outside. The room was a statement of the wealth and prosperity you could only have if you became a certified mage; the canopied bed, work desk and furniture were all made of the same dark oak. I shook my head at the extravagance of it all. Did a college kid really need all this? On the desk sat a carving knife, sanding paper and a five-foot-long staff which was halfway done. On his nightstand, a half-opened book lay, filled with theories on evocation magic and its relation to the different elements. The kid was always a hard worker.

Outside the bedroom, there was a spacious sitting area with a sofa and several video games hooked up to a large flat screen TV that was mounted over an unlit fireplace. A small kitchen area was tucked in a corner with a fridge and stove.

"I'm seriously having some décor envy, and this is just for the freshmen," I looked around and shook my head, "I don't want to know what the senior's rooms look like. Gold-plated toilets? Waitstaff? How much are you paying for all this?"

Cassius walked over to the bedroom and was caressing the unfinished staff with a small smile on his face. A small tear rolled down his cheek. "You really don't want to know; it will just make you cry." He frowned at the staff and shook his head. "He was making a staff out of ash, typical youngling going for a big boom."

I walked over to him and looked at the staff that had some runes carved into it. Unlike mine, these were rigid with jagged lines and crisp turns, the result of mages testing different elements over the years to bring about the ultimate expression of their power. My runes felt more fluid and freer. I would just think what I wanted, and the magic guided my actions to draw the appropriate rune.

"What's wrong with ash?" I frowned at him pointing at the staff. "I remember seeing a couple of those at your house."

"These runes are for augmenting power," Cassius pointed to the runes, "Put those together on a staff made from an ash tree and you would find yourself with a temperamental staff that a novice like him would have trouble controlling." He slowly traced the runes with his fingers. "Ash is already a good material for spell augmentation, so coupled with augmenting runes I'd be surprised if he didn't break his arm with the simplest of spells. If you imagine a five-year-old firing a shotgun, you'll get the idea."

"So, he would get thrown across the room and fall flat on his ass?" I remember our earlier fight with the barghest. "Like father like son."

A bit of color crept up the side of his face. "It's been years since I've used any equipment other than ones I've personally made. I had forgotten how much of a kick my wife's wand had." He waved the unfinished staff in the air. "Staffs have the length necessary to allow magic to circulate through it, that's why most mages use them. A wand on the other hand compresses magic inside it, so if you're not used to them then you will most definitely be thrown across the room and fall flat on your ass."

"So, you like to move it while she likes to compress it? That's more information about your love life than I needed to know man. T.M.I." I said with a grin, taking a step back whilst ducking the incoming staff.

"Would you keep your mind out of the gutter? Merlin's beard man, for illusionists the more real their illusions are the better, that's why they prefer wands." He tapped the staff to his chest. "I'm an evocator with plenty of juice in the tank, using a wand would be overkill," He said, as his cheeks turned a soft pink. I was having a hard time not laughing at him.

"Sure, and it's less impressive to fry someone with a three-inch stick of wood rather than with a twelve foot one. I didn't know you cared so much about size." I smiled at him. "Don't they say that size doesn't matter, it's all about how you use it."

His hand clenched around the staff; the unfinished work started glowing with purple light. "Are you trying to piss me off?"

"A little bit yeah, but I need you focused on the here and now." I walked towards him putting my hand on his shoulder. "I know you're worried about Lucas, and trust me I know the feeling, but getting lost in memories and feelings is not going to help us find your boy." I made him look at me. "Hold it together for a little longer, just until we find the bitch and you can shove that staff someplace really uncomfortable."

The rage and guilt in his eyes scared me, and for a moment I thought we were going to go for another round of 'fry the innkeeper'. It took him a second to get a hold over himself before he shrugged my hand off and crossed his arms over his chest.

He didn't say thank you but that was okay, thanks wasn't something that needed to be said between friends.

"Selenic's place was ransacked because they wanted something from his private collection." I frowned and looked in the closet but found nothing. "Sabine traced the barghests here, so they must've spent a good amount of time here. I don't see any signs of a struggle and they clearly haven't ransacked the place." I turned around and gave the room another look, finding it clean for the most part except for the unopened book and staff. The room was in pristine condition, unlike Selenic's place that had been tossed to hell and back.

Cassius frowned. "Why didn't the wards keep the beasts at bay?"

That was a good question. "Barghests are like Sabine, half in this world and half in the spirit world. Unless she wills it and changes her shape, she passes for a normal, awesome dog." I grimaced tapping my finger on the table. "I'm guessing the barghests are the same, they could turn into their corporeal dog forms and follow Lucas like that, although they'd be weaker and vulnerable."

"What if you're wrong and we're just wasting our time?" Cassius growled in frustration. "And didn't you say my son was taken by selkies?"

I groaned in exasperation. "Yes, a selkie was made to look like Lucas but as we have found out, the selkies and barghests are all working for the same fae." I took a deep breath and let it out. "She probably sent the barghests to spy on the kid before sending the selkies to retrieve him." I braced myself for the drain of magic that was about to happen. "I have a way to see into the magical spectrum, it's the only way I can think of to see if they were here."

Cassius's frown became more pronounced as he tapped a finger on the staff. "You don't sound so sure."

"Of course I'm not sure, last time I faced a barghest they made their intentions of turning me into kibble very clear." I tightened my fist and let out a breath, I was too wired and the fight with the pack had brought back some very unpleasant memories. Cassius opened his mouth to say something but I cut him off. "All I know is how to kill them. I never had the need to track one before, this is uncharted territory for me," I walked over to him, "If it looks like I'm going to kiss the floor, grab me." I closed my eyes and began channeling what little magic I had recovered into my eyes. "Féach"

An itching feeling started to take hold of me; it felt like putting a pair of contacts in and scrapping your eye with the plastic. I opened my eyes to vibrant colours swirling and twirling into beautiful shapes. It was like stepping into a new world, and the whole room glowed with a soft, blue light. Next to me Cassius crackled in a vortex of red with streaks of purple.

"Ugh, I forgot how disconcerting this can be." I said, holding tight to him.

"What are you talking about?" Cassius turned to look at me. "Why are your eyes glowing?"

"Side effect of this kind of magic, ignore it." I waved my hand dismissively and focused on the room. "It lets me see the true magic of things. Now to see if I can spot our barghests."

Barghests could shift between their spiritual and animal form, which was a kind of transmutation magic which didn't help me at all since the whole place was glowing blue. Animal magic usually took on a green color, so in theory a barghest should be a combination of both. Like Cassius; the red and purple vortex was a combination of red from his evocation magic and purple from his affinity with lightning.

So green and blue should be cyan right? I looked around for a different shade of blue. At first, nothing popped up, except when I turned towards the fireplace. Next to it was a fading splotch of lighter blue which was different from the rest of the room.

"Gotcha, you bastard!" I grinned. Now that I knew what to look for, it became easier to filter out everything else except for that faint trail.

"Get some of Lucas's things quick so that the teacher doesn't ask questions, I got something." I said to Cassius before bolting out the door.

The trail was faint, almost mixing in with the rest of the magic in the dorm room. I followed it closely, sensing that Cassius was right on my heels. The trail led us to the elevator where Professor White was waiting for us, shrouded in the blazing red aura of her magic.

"Were you able to find what you were looking for?" She stepped in front of me and frowned, "Why are your eyes glowing?" She asked, blocking our way to the elevator.

I was so focused on following the trail of magic that it completely slipped my mind that my eyes were glowing like silver neon lights. Before I could come up with a good excuse, Cassius beat me to it.

"Professor White, there has been a misunderstanding. We're not here to sort through my son's belongings." He said in a low tone.

"Oh, so what is your purpose here then?" She asked with an edge to her voice, and I could see her magic swirling around her, ready to vaporize us at any moment.

I turned to Cassius. "Are you sure about this?"

He looked at me and reasoned, "If that trail leads directly to the people responsible for this, we're going to need all the help we can get, and having another powerful evocator might tip the scales in our favor."

Lucas's teacher cleared her throat as she crossed her arms tapping her elbow with her finger.

The idea of telling a complete stranger what was going on didn't sit well with me. But there was no use stopping him now that he'd opened his big mouth. "I hope you're right."

"Professor, my son did not kill himself." He turned to Professor White and said seriously, "He was kidnapped by the fae and we came here to find some clues as to where they could be keeping him. Please let us through, we don't have much time."

"How do I know you're telling the truth?" She asked as the swirls of her magic spun faster. "You could be thieves using a false pretense to come into the college."

"It's a bit late for that now isn't it?" I couldn't help but say from the side, earning a glare from both of them before Cassius turned to her again.

"Professor, I know we lied to get in here, but we did it because it was the only way to find a way to save my boy." Cassius pulled out his phone and started swiping through dozens of pictures of him with Lucas and Ava.

"Okay, gentlemen, I believe you." She looked from the phone to me and then back to Cassius before nodding, stepping out of the way and into the elevator. "Lucas is a student of the college and it is our obligation to make sure our students are safe, and if something were to compromise that we will punish those responsible. I'm coming with you to find who has the gall to target those under our protection."

"Thank you, Professor." Cassius said as he walked inside the elevator.

"Plus, if you're lying to me, I can deal with you immediately instead of having to track you down," She said nonchalantly.

The doors slid shut as Cassius and I shared a worried look whilst a smirk crawled across the professor's face.

15

"Bollocks."

We hit our first snag when we got back to the truck: it only had space for two. One of us had to make do with sitting in the back. I sat on the truck bed while the professor took the passenger seat. Sabine saw her and flopped on her back for a belly rub.

The professor looked at her for a moment before smiling and giving in. I looked at my dog and gave her the stink eye; she had never been this nice with a stranger before, especially a mage. I shook my head and tapped my hand on the roof. Cassius lowered the window and yelled, "Where to!?"

"Take the next left, grandma. The trail seems to go for about another two miles or so."

The trail led us back towards the main road away from the college, which was good - the farther away we were from the dorm room, the clearer the trail was without all the transmutation magic in the way. I still had to filter out a lot of information where Portland was a magically rich land with so many mages, shifters and other supernatural beings. The land was soaked with magic.

We crossed over the Willamette River using Saint John's Bridge and turned south along the river side. It looked like the barghests were going towards the Pearl District, and we circled the district for a good twenty minutes before the trail suddenly veered right towards the river.

We got off Pacific Highway and parked in the parking lot of a nearby hotel. My magical reserves were almost completely drained, and I desperately needed to shut off my rune, but we were so close. Once we got out of the truck I turned to Sabine.

"Girl, can you pick up their trail from here?"

Sabine sniffed the air a couple of times before the soft glow of her magic flared up and for a moment, I could see two Sabines: the cute beagle form she preferred and the majestic white furred wolf that was her natural form. Her beagle form faded into the imposing shadows, leaving the large wolf in her place.

Her red eyes turned to me and softened with a hint of warmth and love. I reached out and stroked her red ears softly. She closed her eyes and leaned into the touch.

"I love you too girl, now go and find us a scent."

Sabine nodded as she blinked out of existence and stepped completely into the spirit world. I closed my eyes and slowly released my rune sight. When I opened them again the world was back to its usual dull self. Cassius was leaning against the truck while the Professor was to the side.

She saw me looking and gestured at where Sabine had disappeared. "Not a regular dog, I see."

I chuckled and went to lean against the truck next to Cassius. "She's anything but regular. If there's a trail to be found, she'll find it."

Cassius pulled out a granola bar from his pocket and handed it to me. "Here, you were already running on fumes, I'm guessing you must be feeling pretty empty right about now."

I looked at the bar and my stomach suddenly growled in protest. I had been slinging runes left and right since this whole thing started and even with the food Russell gave us, I was still starving. Usually I only reached for my magic when a guest came in order to prepare their rooms or on the odd occasion if one of them got rowdy. But those cases were few and far between, and I was usually at full magical capacity all the time. Now in just a couple of days I'd done more magic than I would normally do in six months.

The last time I was using my magic like this, I was back with the fae. There, it was imperative to my survival that I was ready to sling a rune at a moment's notice. But afterwards, I didn't need to use my magic to survive. In fact, I could go weeks without using it. Magic was like exercise: the longer you went without doing it, the more out of shape you got.

I took the bar and bit a chunk out of it. I felt sore and rusty, now that the fae were back in my life I was going to need to make some time for training again. I suspected that Goodfellow wouldn't leave me alone now that he knows I'm alive.

"Thanks, I might not be able to cast a rune, but activating the ones I have on me shouldn't be a problem… maybe." I had several weapons on my bracelets and still had the two cards I'd made a couple days ago.

Cassius sighed and crossed his arms over his chest. "It's better than nothing, but if we do get into a fight, you're running on empty with only one working arm and without my staff, it's going to be tough."

I sighed dramatically. "It's been a trying couple of days you know." I nodded towards the Professor. "Besides we've got some back up now haven't we?"

He took a deep breath in and out. "What was I supposed to do? We don't know how many people this fae queen has with her, the more people we have the better." Cassius gave me a sidelong look. "Besides, what were you going to do? Knock her out?"

A soft chuckle came from the side. We turned to see the professor twisting a strand of her hair in one finger. "If you think you could've taken out a professor of the college without people finding out, I seriously overestimated your intelligence."

I thought about it for a moment and had to admit she had a point. "Touché."

Silence stretched for a few minutes before Sabine shimmered back into existence in her beagle form, a patch of dark fur in her jaws. I picked it up and brought it to my nose; the smell was undoubtedly that of a barghest.

She wagged her tail before turning around and running for the outside. We followed her closely and exited the hotel parking lot before crossing the street towards the Waterfront Park, a nice green space close to Hawthorne Bridge that the locals used to pass the time.

The sun was beginning to set, and the sky was painted in a myriad of oranges and yellows. The park was fairly empty except for a woman walking her Saint Bernard and two old men fishing in a corner, smoking cigars.

Sabine led us to a spot between two trees close to the river's shore away from the bridge. I walked between them but couldn't see anything that looked like a clue or hinted at being useful.

"My ongoing theory is that Lucas managed to kill one of the selkies that was attacking him and after they took him, they made the selkie's body look like Lucas with glamour." I looked around frowning, something didn't feel right. "It's possible that they did the same thing here, the glamour on the body was very powerful. I managed to break through it before, but now..."

Cassius nodded in understanding. "I got it. I might not be an illusionist, but you pick up a few tricks after being married to one. Give me a second and stand back."

He pulled out his wand and I instinctively took a couple of steps back. Professor White saw me and followed without uttering a word.

The early evening air felt hot and sticky as the tip of Cassius's wand began to glow. He made several hand motions towards the trees. The colors around them began to warp and twist into themselves like looking through a kaleidoscope.

"Apstergo!" Cassius yelled with a final flicked of his wand. The tip flared with light, and for a moment I thought he was going to be sent flying like last time, but all I heard was a grunt of pain before the distortion around the trees vanished and the illusion was shattered.

"Well damn." I said through gritted teeth.

The once beautiful and scenic trees were nothing more than charred corpses. One of the trunks had a crack that went from the base all the way to the top. All that remained of the one next to it was a burnt stump about a foot tall surrounded by singed pieces of wood.

174

The whole ground was littered with broken branches, cracked stones and several deep holes, evidence of the vicious battle that took place here. I had to give it to the kid; he went down but he had made the bastards work for it.

The kid gave as good as he got from the looks of it.

"They must've weaved a very powerful illusion to keep the battle and its aftermath from the humans." Professor White commented as she walked around one of the holes in the ground. "He fired at least five or six spells in rapid succession before they took him down."

I walked towards one of the trees and traced my hand around the missing bark, looked up to the wilted canopy and whistled. "Way to go, kid."

Cassius walked towards the other tree and picked up a broken mage's staff, similar to the one Lucas had in his room.

"This was his going away present from us," Cassius's voice was hollow, "We made it from willow. For balance and learning."

"A staff to learn how to use your magic instead of one use to bring the house down," I guessed.

"You have no idea how many times he short circuited our power grid." He said as his fingers slowly caressed the broken staff. "He has power in spades, what he lacks is control. Guess he didn't think he had enough of the former and was confident in the latter."

I was about to say something when the sound of a branch breaking caught us off by surprise.

What made it worse was who made the noise.

I turned around to see Detective Penelope Garcia standing a dozen feet away with her eyes widened and jaw opened. Her hand was half-raised pointing towards Cassius, and behind her two older men wore similar expressions.

"What..? How..?" Her finger pointed from the trees back to us. "Those trees were fine just a minute ago! What did you guys do?"

Shit! She saw us casting magic. We'd been so focused on finding Lucas that we neglected to see if anyone was close by. I racked my brain trying to think of a logical way to explain what happened but came up empty.

"There's a perfectly reasonable explanation for what happened here." I raised my hands and smiled at her.

She looked at me as if I was crazy. "Really? I didn't just see your friend here waving a stick and turn this place into ground zero?"

Oh damn it all to hell. "It was like this when we got here, but you couldn't see it because there was a magic spell over the area."

"Mr. Mercer ,your attempt at humor is not amusing." Detective Garcia turned towards Cassius and raised her shield. "Sir, Portland PD. Please put the stick down and step away from the trees." She pointed to the professor. "You too, ma'am."

"Detective, I know this is going to sound crazy but you have to listen." I pointed towards Cassius. "This is Cassius Gray, Lucas's father. Lucas isn't dead, he's been kidnapped and we're here to find clues about where they took him, so if you could please let us work."

Her face locked into that stern cop expression. "Mr. Mercer, I don't know what game you're playing or if you've taken something to cope with your grief, but Lucas Gray is dead. I saw his body myself."

"Detective, this is a matter of life and death." I asked, pointing at the burnt stump. "Look, we're not harming anyone and will just have a look around."

"Mr. Mercer, I won't repeat myself again." Her hand moved towards her holstered gun. "All of you, please step away from the trees and walk over to me."

Cassius took a step forward. "Detective, what my friend says it's true. My name is Cassius Gray, I'm Lucas's father." He raised his arms and continued to speak. "My son has been taken by a vicious monster and if we don't do anything he will die. All I ask is that you don't get in our way."

Detective Garcia's stern face cracked a little. "Mr. Gray, I am sorry for your loss but like I said before, your son is dead. I'm sorry but that is the truth."

Cassius shook his head. "Detective, that wasn't my boy, that was one of the kidnappers who was made to look like him by magical means."

"Enough of this magic nonsense," She said, her voice taking a hard edge, "I don't know what you did to those trees but you're going to come with me and answer some questions."

A velvety laugh filled the air. "I do love mortal stupidity, they would go to any lengths to deny that which is in front of them. Maddening, don't you think, sister?"

"You're right sister, but then what can you expect from a bunch of rats running in the maze?" A silky voice answered her.

Detective Gracia spun on her heel with her gun ready at her side. I looked towards the street and saw two women walking over both in their mid-twenties. The one on the left had short pixie blonde hair and was wearing a black and red corset dress. Her companion, wearing a pair of cutoff jeans and a yellow tank top, had long wavy dark hair tied into a ponytail which highlighted her sharp features.

What the hell?

The two fishermen still smoking their cigars sensed something wasn't right, picking up their rods and walking away. There was something eerie about the way the women moved, not to mention the way they spoke. I tensed, readying myself for anything.

"Ladies, please step away, this is official police business." Detective Garcia ordered, firmly holding her gun to the side.

The blonde girl smirked at the detective, licking her cherry red lips. "Oh, but isn't she adorable! Sister, can I take her home to play?"

"I don't think so, sister," The dark haired one replied, "The last pet you brought home didn't last more than a week, and by the end of it she was so delirious that she wanted to rip out her own eyeballs."

Detective Garcia was about to issue another warning but before she could the blonde woman waved her hand and shouted. "Aichmés!"

The ground behind the detective started trembling as two stone spikes rose from the ground impaling her from back to front. Shock washed over Detective Garcia's face as she spat a mouthful of blood, her gun falling to the ground. She moved her head to look at me, her eyes fierce and determined before the life faded from them, and she slumped lifeless on the spikes. Everything happened so fast that none of us knew how to react.

The blonde one smirked, walking towards the detective and

pinching the dead woman's cheek before she turned to her sister and pouted. "Guess you were right sister - she didn't last that long."

The dark haired one shook her head and walked over to the other side of the detective and smiled. "Mortals never do, but don't worry, we'll find you a new playmate soon."

Witches. Were these the ones Roel warned me about?

My magic bubbled inside me like boiling water. How dare they kill a mortal in broad daylight and then play with her like she was a doll, were they insane?

"I see Valentina sent her two lackeys to do her dirty work, is she too afraid to come at me herself?" The witches glared at me as I spoke. "Guess I was right, you're part of Valentina's little coven. What does the Puddle of the Goddess want now?"

I had to buy some time for Cassius and Professor White to get ready. Taking down one witch would've been simple enough for the three of us, but two of them working together would be a lot harder.

The blonde one sneered at me. "Our mistress was right, you're nothing more than an insolent monkey." She then gave me a wicked smile. "I'm going to enjoy playing with you, you'll wear the cutest dresses as we strip the flesh from your bones and use it to make soup! And by the time we're done with you, you'll tell us where that mongrel is." She turned to the woman next to her. "Right, sister?"

"Paximadi!" The dark hair girl yelled, waving her hand in the air and suddenly the temperature plummeted; the cold bit into my skin like sharp needles. A row of razor thin icicles condensed over the head of the witch like a macabre crown, and with another wave of her hand she hurled the deadly ice spikes right at us.

***

I threw myself to the ground behind a tree while Cassius dropped the staff and ran for cover. I analyzed what options were available in my head, and none of them were good. We didn't have time to mess around with these psychopaths, but from the looks of it the witches had other ideas.

Okay Nathan, think, what do you know about witches besides them being wretched beings? They gain their magic through their familiars, and without them they are basically useless: they conjure them from the spirit world and, depending on the ritual and strength of the witch, the familiar would grant them power over an element of nature. From what I just saw, those two hussies had powers over ice and earth.

Another wave of icicles crashed into the tree I was hiding behind, splintering what remained of it. "Damn it all to hell!"

I reached for my magic and at first there was nothing, then a wave of pain. Gods, it hurt so much to gather a trickle of magic but I managed to gather enough to activate the runes on my charms. "Ag Fás"

A silver and red glow enveloped my bracelets, the runes on my charms shining like a beacon in the dead of night, before the two items materialized on the ground in front of me. I grabbed the herbal cast that had been slowly healing my busted arm throughout the day and ripped it off. A snowfall of dead skin fell off my arm as the leafy wraps fell to the ground, leaving behind pinkish tender skin. Moving it *hurt*, but I couldn't afford to battle two witches with one hand tied to my chest.

The ground beneath me suddenly started to shake, and years of fighting for my life suddenly took over. I grabbed my weapons and rolled out of the way before a stone spike shot up from the ground right where I was taking cover.

As I moved from the safety of the trees, the other witch didn't waste any time in sending another wave of icicles towards me. Cassius moved to my left, his wand in hand. Magic gathered around him like a lightning rod. "Strepo!"

A blast of arcane lightning shot from the tip of the wand towards the dark-haired witch and for a moment it looked like it was going to hit its target but the witch simply smirked, murmuring something beneath her breath before a wall of earth rose upwards, intercepting the spell. I didn't have time to think, and used both my buckler and morningstar to smash the icicles coming my way. Every swing of my weapon brought another stab of pain down my whole arm, making it hard to breathe.

"Nathan! If you have any ideas, now would be a good time!"

Cassius yelled as he swung his wand again, sending another arc of lightning towards the witches only for it to crash into another earthen wall.

"Look at them dance, sister! I'm tempted to ask the mistress to change them back into monkeys so we can keep them. Aichmés!" The blonde one said as she made another hand motion, creating a row of earth spikes before sending them towards Cassius. "Dance for me, little chimp."

Cassius swung his wand again, magic heavy in the air. "Malleo Tornitura."

The clouds above him turned pitch black, crackling with intense light as a massive war hammer composed of pure lightning thundered into existence, crashing into the incoming spikes and leaving behind a huge crater. The blonde witch looked at Cassius with a smile on her face.

"Sister, don't interfere with this one, he's all mine," She said as she licked her lips, her eyes glowing with magic.

"Sabine! Find their familiars!" I shouted while throwing myself to the side before another icicle wave hit me.

Sabine had been staying at the edges of the battle, trying not to get hit by anything. I saw her pass into the spirit world before I focused back on the witches.

"Isn't he a clever little beast?" The dark haired witch said as she made another hand motion, her eyes glowing with power.

"Kataigida!"

The temperature in the surrounding area plummeted at an insane rate, thick dense clouds formed above us as a frozen wind raged through the park. I looked up to see snow begin to fall, and although slow at first, it quickly built into a fierce blizzard erupting around us. A soul chilling cold descended over the park, a small cloud of frost condensed beneath my breath. The wind screamed through the battlefield, cutting off my ability to hear anything. I tried looking for the dark haired witch but she had disappeared into the blizzard.

I had spent most of my life living in the Winter court of the fae, so this blizzard wasn't enough to stop me; it was more annoying than hurtful. *Although hypothermia might do me in before the witches do if this goes on any longer*, I thought. The cold bit into my arm, sending sharp needles of pain through my body every time I swung my weapon.

I raised my buckler in front of me, hoping the runes that deflected the spells would hold out if she decided to throw something particularly nasty at me. A flash of light cut through the blanket of ice and snow in the distance, and I found myself letting out a breath of relief. Cassius was okay, for now. I sensed something out of the corner of my eye and barely managed to get out of the way before half a dozen icicles stabbed the ground where I was just standing. I groaned at the stab of pain running up and down my shoulder. The cold helped to numb the pain but it made moving difficult.

I slipped on a patch of ice and fell against something hard that was protruding from the ground. I turned to look and saw the two stone spikes that had pierced Detective Garcia; her body hung a few feet above the ground and was now completely frozen. Entrails and assorted gore coated the spikes, but were slowly being covered by frost and snow. Her lifeless eyes stared at me, betraying the fear and the pain she'd felt in her last moments. Seeing her like that sent a wave of rage through me. Mortals should be protected from the savagery of the supernatural world, not victimized by it.

A wall of ice condensed around the witch, obscuring her from view. I took a deep breath and focused my senses inward; if my magical reserves usually resembled a thriving forest then now it was withered and barren, with barely any signs of life. I squeezed as much magic as my body could give me and activated my runic sight.

It hurt, gods it hurt so much, like getting your eyeballs pricked by a hot needle. My body barely had any magic left, and forcing the magic was a bad idea if I didn't let my body rest and recharge; it would forcibly shut down out of self preservation. My chest felt heavy and it was getting harder to breathe, red spots appearing in my vision before I felt the runes in my eyes heat up and activate.

Once more the veil separating the mortal and magical world parted, letting me see the true nature of things. I didn't have much time; every passing second that my runes were active would make it even harder to maintain.

I could see the swirling violent vortex of purple and red that was Cassius to my left, fighting a dark brown spike that I assumed was the blonde witch. To my right, there was a glowing light blue shape that was slowly walking over to me. *Gotcha, bitch!* I released my hold on the magic and waited for her to get closer. I let my instincts take over, pivoted to my right and swung with all my strength.

The broken bones and grunt of pain that I was expecting never came; my morningstar connected with a block of something solid. It felt like hitting a wall, the vibrations from the blow reverberated back through my arm, making my shoulder scream in pain. I tried to move my morningstar back but no amount of pulling could wrench it free. A sharp, cold sensation shot from the tips of my fingers all the way to my wrist.

The white wall parted around me, revealing my morningstar encased in a wall of ice. Both my hand and weapon were encased, making it impossible to move out of the way. Stepping out from behind the wall, the dark hair witch smiled at me.

"You really thought that would work? How painful it must be, being so stupid." She raised her hand, her ice enveloping her nails and sharpening them into five-inch-long claws. She slowly caressed my cheek with an adoring look. "Don't worry my dear, this won't hurt me at all, but you on the other hand..."

The loving look in her eyes sent more shivers down my spine than the storm could ever do. I was stuck in place with no strength to pull myself out and my magic was completely drained. Was this how I was going to die?

A lance of searing flames pierced through the blizzard, hitting the witch square in the chest before the air shimmered around her, extinguishing the lance. The attack was so unexpected that it sent her careening to the side, tongues of flames scorching her shirt and her hair catching on fire. The witch screamed in pain and started rolling from side to side, trying to put the fire out.

I turned my neck, trying to look at my would-be savior, and saw

Professor White with her hand extended, a small smile on her face. "Well this has gone on long enough, don't you think? Step away from the man and be on your way."

The dark haired witch managed to put out the flames but not fast enough to save her hair; most of it was charred with some completely bald and blistered patches. She stood up, unadulterated rage burning in her eyes.

"You will pay for that, bitch; I will rip your tongue out and cut it to wear as earrings. Katepsygméno!" She screamed as she waved her hand again in a chopping motion towards Professor White.

A sword of ice formed in front of her and flew straight at the professor. She didn't make a move to get out of the way. I tried to scream a warning but the pain in my hand got worse as the ice encasing my wrist started moving upwards. I yanked my hand back with all my strength, but it wouldn't budge.

I turned back to see the professor calmly raise her hand and touch the tip of the incoming sword with her fingertips. The sword glowed with bright light for a moment before it shattered into dust.

"Is that it? I'm actually quite disappointed." The professor said with a raised eyebrow and the best look of derision I had ever seen.

"Psychrí Gi! Paximadi! Katepsygméno!" The witch howled in rage, stomping her feet hard on the ground. Condensing above her head were half a dozen, eight-foot long frozen spears heading straight for the professor. Not satisfied with that, she made another motion with her hands. This time the snow hardened into double bladed swords, as well as a ring of razor thin icicles, which raced towards their intended target.

Lucas's teacher smiled at the witch and raised her hand, a pulse of indigo light flowing from the center of her palm and shattering the ice spells to dust. I never heard her utter a spell and this time she didn't even move. Mortal mages couldn't work magic like she just did without a focus or spell. The only ones who could do that were the fae, and no one could command ice like that except for Winter's.

No, it couldn't be… Arelis White… *No, gods, please, let me be wrong.*

The professor looked at the witch with a taunting smile. "If you're done, dear, then I guess it's about time for me to make my move. I'm starting to get bored."

The witch was not in good shape. Her skin was pale, with heavy and dark circles marking her eyes, and she was practically panting. From behind her waist she pulled a thirteen-inch dagger with a wavy blade etched with strange symbols: an athame.

"You think you've won just because you dealt with a few of my spells? Conceited bitch, let's see how you deal with this." She placed the tip of the athame against her palm making a deep cut letting the blood flow dying the snow at her feet bright red. A blood red sheen coated her eyes. "Cheimónas."

The word cut through the storm, the wind and snow immediately dissipating as if they hadn't ever been there. From the other side of the park I could see Cassius bleeding from several cuts, and he seemed to be favoring his left leg to hold his weight. The blonde witch hadn't gone unscathed either; she had a hand pressed against her side where a hole in the dress showed the charred skin.

They seemed at a standstill but the witch quickly noticed what her sister was doing. "Ariana, are you crazy? Stop this at once. If you finish that spell it could kill you, you can't control it in your current state!"

"Shut up Veronica, I know what I'm doing." Ariana gave the professor a deranged smile before making another cut in her hand. Thick crimson tears began to fall from the corners of her eyes, staining her pale cheeks red. The tip of her tongue snaked out tasting the blood, a look of euphoria draped over her face.

"Arachni."

A soul wrenching howl rang through the park, and my muscles tensed as the air between the professor and witch folded into itself before a crack appeared in the space. *No, it couldn't be!* How stupid could she be? A creature from the darkest of nightmares peered from it - the monster was so grotesque and horrifying, just looking at it would be enough to make you insane.

The enormous beast rose from the portal on eight razor sharp and thin legs. Standing at twelve feet tall, it had pale white fur and thick yellow bone protrusions rising all along its back and covering its entire body. Its large lupine head had eight pale blue bulbous eyes which darted around, looking for prey. Green venom dripped from its fangs as it howled in fury.

A Damhán Búraló - a wolfspider.

Dread and horror filled me as I suddenly felt very small and weak. She'd summoned one of the deadliest creatures to roam the lands of the fae. They were indiscriminate killers that hunted more for pleasure than for food. They were savage beasts of carnage that ravaged entire towns, turning them into web-covered hunting grounds where they lured travelers to eat at their leisure.

Ariana laughed maniacally. "Oh, if only you could see your faces, such sweet terror. Now my darling, kill them all."

The creature clicked its mandibles together, thick globules of green liquid falling to the snow below, and from where it landed, a thick pale yellow gas rose. The beast stood still, making no move to attack. Ariana walked to it and snapped her fingers in its face.

"What are you waiting for? Kill them all!" She roared at the beast.

Professor White clapped slowly. "Well, this has been educational. Who would've thought that a deadbeat witch could have the juice to summon this beastie?" She crossed her arms over her belly. "Too bad you don't know how to control it."

Ariana glared at the professor. "Shut up! This is my beast, I control it."

"Prove it." The professor taunted with a knowing smirk.

"Ariana stop, you're too weak to effectively command it. Don't get near it." Veronica started to walk towards her sister, but stopped as she eyed Cassius.

I felt my eyes widen as the stupid witch ignored her friend and marched over to the creature pointing towards the smiling professor. "Listen, you moronic beast, go over there and kill-"

Before she could finish speaking, the damhán búraló raised one of its needle thin legs and pierced the witch through the chest. The witch looked at the beast with hysterical eyes as she desperately clutched at the beast's leg, trying to push it away from her chest. She tried to say something but the creature brought her close to its muzzle and ripped her head off with a single swift bite, swallowing it whole. The monster then began to gnaw at the rest of the body, pieces of flesh falling from its mouth and onto the ground, covered in that green liquid that melted away with the snow. The ground began to shake as the blonde witch screamed her heart out and fell to her knees, covering her mouth with her hands.

The sound drew the attention of the wolfspider as it slowly moved its head towards her, but before he took another step his eight luminous eyes focused on me as I desperately tried to get free from the ice. It changed its path, and began to walk towards me.

16

The beast moved slowly. Every step dragged Ariana's body along like a broken doll. I tried to free myself but the ice encasing my arm kept spreading, my fingers burning from the cold as panic surged through me. The beast's pale, round eyes were trained on me as blood dripped from its mandibles. The smell of wet fur and blood permeated the air, making me want to gag.

Veronica stood up. Mascara ran down her face, staining her cheeks black. "Ariana, you stupid bitch!" She glared at the monster with palpable fury. " Die! Aichmés!"

She flicked her hand towards the beast, but the earth remained still. She frowned at her hand and slashed the air with it again. "Aichmés!" she shouted again with no success.

"What the hell is going on? Aichmés! Aichmés! Aichmés!" She screamed herself hoarse, but the earth just wouldn't respond.

From the corner of my eye I saw a familiar shimmer appear in the air and Sabine jumped out of it, a large green and brown badger hanging dead in her jaws. Sabine had a few cuts and scrapes, but other than that, she looked okay.

Veronica saw the dead badger and shrieked like a wounded animal. She raked her face and neck with her nails, drawing blood. I felt myself smiling; *that's my girl*. With the witch's familiar killed, she was practically harmless.

Two down. One big ugly to go.

The damhán búraló's muzzle was caked with blood and venom. As it made its way towards me, its mandibles clicked against each other relentlessly.

A deep sigh sounded from somewhere to my right.

"After all the effort I made to keep him safe, do you think for one second I'd let you feast on him? Céim ar shiúl." The professor moved next to me, shaking her head. She touched the block of ice encasing my arm, and it turned into snow and fell away.

The sudden release unbalanced me. I tried to steady myself but my legs wouldn't cooperate and I fell on my ass, the snow melting into my jeans and souring my mood further. For its part, the creature only clicked its fangs in anger. It didn't like being told what not to do.

"I would rather not kill such a prime specimen, but if you continue on this path, death is the only thing that awaits you. Céim at shiúl. Anois!" *Step away. Now!* My brain translated the words almost on instinct, there was something so familiar about them. The command in her voice was undisputable; anyone who defied her would find themselves turned into a popsicle.

There was no one else who was crazy enough, or even had the power, to stand face-to-face with a damhán búraló and order it to go away. As I looked at the professor with her strawberry blonde hair, dressed perfectly in pink yet commanding a nightmare, a decade's worth of rage and hurt erupted suddenly within me.

"Silera?"

A slight tensing of the shoulders was the only reaction I got before she turned her head and smiled at me. "I was wondering when you would figure it out, Rún."

Feature by feature, her looks shifted. The shoulder-length strawberry blonde hair began to darken to auburn and fell below her waist in rich curls, her hazel eyes darkening to a golden color and the sun-kissed skin faded to a softer, paler hue. While the professor had been pretty before in a librarian sort of way, the woman now standing before me was breathtakingly beautiful. The pink glasses faded away, along with the sundress, revealing an indigo gown made of spider silk.

"*You're* the woman from my dreams." I growled.

Princess Silera arched an eyebrow at me and smiled. "It seems you've learnt a bit of flattery after all these years. Better late than never, I suppose."

I stood up; her head reached just below my chin. "You know exactly what I mean. You've been messing with my head for days."

"Hardly, I merely pointed you in the right direction. It's no fault of mine that you thought I was a figment of your imagination."

"What took you so long to help?"

"You needed proper motivation and I wanted to see if your skills had rusted after all these years."

The monster roared, tired of being ignored, and lunged at Silera. Instinct took over before I realized what was happening. I pushed her behind me, parried one leg with my buckler and brought down my still-frozen mace on the monster's muzzle. A mandible broke off and skittered across the ground. The beast howled in pain, retreating a few steps before opening its bruised face to let loose a deafening roar. Hatred and pain flashed in its eyes.

"It seems that my safety is still a concern for you, Rún," Sirela noted from behind me.

I turned to her and raised my shirt, showing her the scars from her betrayal. "I stopped being your love the moment you sent me to my death."

Silera looked at the scars with a stoic expression. She was about to speak when the beast roared again. She raised her hand casually and a torrent of turquoise flames pierced the monster's head, engulfing it in a blaze of scorching heat. She lowered her hand, burning through three of its legs. The wolfspider howled as it fell to the ground, its body recoiling from the heat. I shook my head, pitying the beast. This was what made Silera so deadly; no other Winter fae could call fire to them. That was her own unique talent, inherited from her father.

"You were warned." She regarded the beast with an intense look as blue flames simmered on her palms. "You should've listened."

189

Another torrent of blue flames gushed out, incinerating the beast. There was a deep howl as it rolled on its remaining legs trying to get away, but it was no use. Winter's Princess had sentenced him to death.

The screams faded as the once terrifying beast burnt to ash. I had forgotten how much magic the Fae nobility could wield. She had turned a twelve-foot-tall monstrosity into a pile of ash within seconds.

After a moment I asked her, "How long did it take Goodfellow to snitch about my being alive?"

Silera turned around and walked slowly towards me. "Do you really think I needed Robin to tell me you were alive, Nathaniel?" She stopped in front of me, raising her hand and caressing my cheek. Her touch sent every cell in my body on fire. *Gods, how I have missed her touch.*

"Have you forgotten? You bear my mark upon your skin." Her voice was soft and tender; a small pulse of magic flowed from her fingertips to my cheek and a fresh cooling sensation washed over me. I didn't need to see it to know that her mark was shining for the first time in a decade, an indigo-primrose with an amber center. It was her favorite flower - she had always joked I was her next favourite before placing the symbol on my skin. I closed my eyes and leaned into her touch. Her voice was just as soft as her stroke as she murmured, "I've always known your whereabouts, Rún."

She pulled my head down to meet hers. I wanted to resist, I wanted to pull away and never see her again, but her scent flooded my senses, winterberries and primrose that was so uniquely hers. How many hundreds, if not thousands, of nights had I woken up in the dark, wishing she was there, only to have my heart break time and time again? Even now, I couldn't go near them.

Her mouth, soft and cold, touched mine and that was all it took. Her kiss broke through all the pain and weariness, years of resentment and anger shattered with the soft caress of her lips. Her tongue brushed against mine, filling my mouth with the sweet taste of warm honey. My breath caught in my chest as I drowned in her lips, meeting her passion with mine. She purred, pulling me closer.

The kiss lasted both a lifetime and a fleeting second; I didn't want it to end but our lips eventually parted. Her golden eyes shone with so many emotions, their intensity burning. "Rún," she whispered.

A booming sound broke through the moment, a single shot in the silence. Silera went limp in my arms. "Rela?" I called out.

Her eyes fluttered while her mouth opened and closed, but no words came out. Blood pooled down the side of her dress. *No, no, no!* My breath caught in my throat, and all I could hear was the flow of blood rushing through my head. I turned to see the witch aiming a gun at us. Cassius lay limp at her feet, the hair that covered his eyes matted with blood.

"Not so tough now, are you?" Veronica smirked.

My heart thundered in my ears. Silera was a Sidhe, a full-blooded fae; iron, steel, lead, those were all deadly to her kind. I had to remove the bullet now, or she was going to die. I gripped where the bullet had made a hole in the dress and tore. Her dark blood, a vivid shock against her pale skin, fell and tainted the snow beneath us. It pulsed from the wound alarmingly fast, and I couldn't do anything but cover it with my hands and try to slow the bleeding.

"Get away from her. She deserves to die for what she did to Ariana." Veronica pulled the trigger again, and Silera jolted in my hands as the bullet grazed her arm.

I looked around for a piece of ice, sharp enough to make a cut, when I remembered the shrunken dagger dangling from my bracelet. I cursed and tried to squeeze out a drop of magic but I was tapped out. I was beyond tapped out - there wasn't a single shred of magic left in my body.

"Don't you dare die on me! We still have a score to settle." Tears began to fall down my cheeks but I didn't care. I tried calling the magic in the air around me like I did with the Arrachd but nothing happened. What was I supposed to do? I couldn't let her die, not now. I still had so many questions for her.

A sharp stabbing pain pushed me forward and I almost fell forward onto Silera. I managed to steady myself so as to not hurt her, gripping her closer to me. I looked down to see a small red line streaming from my shoulder. I growled in frustration, laid Silera softly in the snow and picked up my morningstar before running towards the witch.

She shrieked, her short hair standing on its ends as her eyes darted around from Silera to me. Her face was covered with scrapes and cuts, the bottom of her dress hung in tatters around her thighs, and blood trailed down her right leg from a nasty gash just above the kneecap. Clearly, Cassius has got some shots in. "Stupid monkey, why don't you just die with her as well?!" She trained her gun on me, braced and fired twice.

Two sharp impacts pushed me backwards, and a violent pain spread through my shoulder and abdomen. I pushed past the pain, my legs burning with the effort of keeping me upright but I forced them to run, swinging my morningstar over my head. Nothing was going to stop from caving this bitch's face in for Rela.

Even though she ordered my death.

Allegedly knew I was alive and didn't send someone to finish the job.

Then she kissed me. *Gods, that kiss.*

I didn't know how numb and gray the world had become for me until her lips grazed mine. I had so many questions and conflicted feelings. I wasn't going to let a two-bit wretch take her away from me and I'd be damned if I was going to let that kiss be the end.

"Tough little baboon, aren't you?" She lowered her gun and fired twice more. I tried to dodge but a wave of exhaustion came over me and the floor rushed up to meet my face. Snow and dirt filled my mouth with a salty, bitter taste. My morningstar rolled away from me. My mind desperately called for me to get up but my legs wouldn't answer.

I pushed myself up onto my hands and knees and crawled over to my weapon, my vision beginning to blur. I shook my head. *No.* I couldn't let myself pass out. If I did then Rela, Cassius, Lucas and Selenic were all going to die.

Snow crunched beside me as I wrapped my hand around the

handle of the mace. I raised my head, only to see the butt of a gun strike me - darkness took over.

I woke up to the sound of waves and the feeling of being drenched in icy water. I gasped in shock, trying to get my shivering under control.

I looked around, trying to find anything that might look somewhat familiar or give me a clue as to my whereabouts, whilst also distracting myself from the constant sea spray that had made it its mission to turn me into a popsicle. True to the prophecy, tonight - assuming that I had only been out cold for a few hours - was a new moon. Unfortunately, this meant it was as dark as a dungeon. Luck must have taken pity on me though as the stars were out, shining like tiny diamonds and stretching as far as the eye could see. This at least let me see that I was surrounded by the ocean. If there was a shore to be seen, I couldn't make it out through the darkness.

I located the familiar Little Bear in the sky and then the sailors' delight itself Polaris, or more commonly, the North Star. Knowing that I was at least still in the northern hemisphere of Earth helped to calm my rapid heart slightly. Another wave crashed into the island, drenching me from head to toe, and I gritted my teeth as the cold water took what little heat I had managed to regain. At least my body was numb; I could vaguely recall being shot but that wasn't a feeling I was anxious to remember.

My eyes had started to adapt to the dark conditions and I could just make out a circle around me. I was tied to a post in the middle of it, but there were other posts, all placed at each cardinal point. The pessimist in me warned that this was a classic summoners or evocation circle, while the dwindling optimist hoped that I was just in the middle of a very cold and wet prank.

Evocation circles usually required large, open spaces to channel as much power as possible all whilst keeping an even flow of magic. From what I could make out, the posts were no more than a few meters apart which made for an unstable circle and a snug summoning. Another wave crashed against the cliff, soaking me in the icy spray. I gritted my teeth and breathed slowly through the shock. I knew that keeping my breathing calm was key in this situation.

I guess I could count myself lucky that I wasn't in any danger of being washed off, thanks to an oddly-tiered building that I could see out of the corner of my eye, and the thick chain tying me to the post. I tested the chains, but stopped as the movement triggered a wave of pain that no amount of seaspray could numb. I clenched my teeth as my vision darkened for a moment. I breathed deeply and waited for the pain to subside before giving the chains another look. My wrists were clasped by a pair of thick manacles, linked by a foot long chain. A two-inch nail had been driven into the post. My wrists were otherwise bare; they had taken my bracelets. *Assholes.*

I felt a familiar tightness, suggesting that someone had bandaged my shoulder and abdomen. I hoped that they had also taken the bullets out, but the intensely hot pain coming from the wounds suggested otherwise. Worst of all was my left arm; it felt like someone had poured molten iron over it. Then again, it had been electrocuted, dislocated, shot and nearly frozen - all in the span of twenty four hours. On the bright side, I could feel that some of my magic had returned. Being unconscious had some benefits it would seem.

I craned my head around to try and identify some more features of the silhouetted building. It looked familiar, the thought annoyingly on the tip of my tongue. I wracked my brain trying to think where, when it suddenly hit me. They had taken me to Tillamook Rock, or 'Terrible Tilly', as the locals knew it; an old decommissioned lighthouse off the Oregon Coast that sat on a small speck of land.

The island could be seen from Ecola State Park where I had accompanied Devon and his family for a little get together last summer, where I had spent the entire time entertaining Margie with pirate stories.

"Well, it's remote enough to kill someone without anyone knowing." I muttered to myself.

The ocean air suddenly felt heavy and tense, the silence of the night broken only by the sound of crashing waves against the island. The cold sea breeze slid across my skin like the sharp edge of a butcher's knife. I let my gaze rest on the huge expanse of water, remembering my dreams of the past couple of nights, and something tightened in my chest. They were just dreams. I wasn't a precog so there was no reason for a giant tentacle to rise from the water and drag me into the depths below... *Yeah, and pigs fly south for the winter.*

I heard a door creak open before an orb of pale yellow light flashed above each of the wooden posts and hovered a few inches above them. The sudden light after the darkness brought a flash of pain as my eyes adjusted. I could vaguely make out the soft clicking of heels on stone as my senses tried to recover. A wave crashed on the cliffside and I tensed, expecting the hellish rain of icy spray but nothing fell. All I heard was the tut of a tongue, and the waves around the cliff calmed to a near silence.

"Nathaniel Mercer, Winter's Wolf and Champion of the Frozen Spire. We thought you were dead, yet here you are, shivering on the floor."

I squinted, my eyes still adjusting to the light. A tall and curvy woman stepped into view. Long ebony curls framed her gentle face and the yellow light only added to the glow of her skin. A strapless dress accentuated her figure, enticing yet elegant. She tucked a stray curl behind her pointed ear and smiled. The hairs on the back of my neck rose with the corners of her mouth.

"It's been sometime, dear captain," She crossed her hands over her stomach. "Imagine my surprise when they brought you in."

I shrugged my shoulders, ignoring the stab of pain it cost me. "You know how the saying goes, rumors of my death... largely exaggerated and all that."

The woman nodded. "Extremely so. I had heard from my children that someone had been snooping around our business." She tilted her head to the side. "Never would've guessed it would be you."

"Yeah well, life is full of surprises." At least I knew she was from Winter now. The battle at the Frozen Spire had been a savage bloodbath that forced the Queen to issue a gag order on the whole court.

"Indeed it is." She took a step closer to me. The salty sea and olive scent grew more intense as she did—it was a disconcerting combination. "While I have many questions as to how you're alive, my most pressing concern is why you're interfering in my business."

I looked into her sea green eyes and saw honest curiosity. "You took some of my people and I intend to get them back."

Her brows furrowed. "Was it the boy or the merman?"

"Does it matter? You abducted two mages; one of them a student from the College, the other a member of the Oregon Assembly. You sent your hounds to assassinate the Head of the Assembly which resulted in the deaths of dozens of mortals, including children." The rage spilled over and I snarled at her. "Lady, I would've hunted you down for just one, but all of them together? I want to rip you apart."

The woman calmly nodded. "I see your sense of altruism still holds true to this day." She clasped her hands together. "The important thing is that you're here now, but where are my manners? Terribly rude of me." She raised a hand to her chest and smiled. "I'm Muirín, Queen of the Depths and Mistress of the Waves. You, my dear captain, are about to become part of something greater. Your assistance is most appreciated, I did have someone else in mind for this position but using you is proving more tempting by the minute."

She rested her index finger against her chin and gave me an inquisitive look. "Though now that I think about it, this could be a perfect opportunity to raise some capital for my court." Her smile widened, turning predatory. "You left so many enemies back in Faerie who would pay anything to get their hands on you. I think an auction for the infamous Winter's Wolf would be a marvelous event."

A shiver ran up my spine that had nothing to do with the cold night air. I scowled at her. "I wouldn't get ahead of yourself, once I'm free from these chains, your ass is mine."

Muirín clicked her tongue. "So crass and uncultured. Then again, what can you expect from a race that rose from the mud?" She crouched down and caressed my cheek. I moved my head, turning away and making no effort to hide my grimace. "I never understood why Silera would raise a slave above his station. We were all glad when she cast you out."

My chest tightened again; even after all these years the mere mention of that day was too much to bear. I had locked up those memories in the darkest corner of my mind but seeing Rela again, and kissing her, brought it back to the forefront. My head was a mess. I didn't know what to think or feel about her anymore.

"What were the exact words she said? Let me think..." She pretended to mull it over before snapping her fingers. "Oh yes. 'I'm finally relieved of that loathsome swine'. At least she proved herself a proper fae in the end."

"For someone so high and mighty, you pay a lot of attention to what happened to a simple slave. I don't know if I should feel flattered, or call the cops."

Muirín smiled, her face inches from mine. "You should feel honored that your insignificant life is finally worth something. If I were you, I would enjoy my final days in silence. Soon, all you'll be able to do is scream."

I laughed, I just couldn't help it. She frowned. "I wonder what part of that you find so amusing?"

"The part where you think that I'm going to go down quietly," I grinned. "Listen, here's what's going to happen. I'm going to get free from here, fight my way through your precious children and free my friends." I let Nathan the innkeeper slide from my face and brought Winter's Wolf to the surface. It had been a long time since I'd been Winter's Wolf, but I fit back into the role almost too easily. "By the time I'm done with you, the fae will remember why we don't welcome your kind here."

Her eyes flashed with cyan flames. Her hand caressed my face again, traces of magic leaking from her fingertips. I could feel Silera's mark flare to life. My stomach knotted and my skin wanted to crawl away from her touch. "I do love punishing mortal arrogance." She dragged her nails across my face, leaving hot white pain flaring across my cheek and blood beading down my face. "I'm going to enjoy watching you squirm." She flicked her hand away, splattering blood across the floor as she got up and left.

I waited a moment before wiping my cheek against my shirt. "Damn them all to hell," I swore under my breath.

Come on Nathan, you've survived worse, think, what can you use? I looked around for something to free myself. *If you could survive the Frozen Spire and the The Crooked Man's forest then a chunk of metal is not going to be the death of you.*

A huge wave raged from the stormy sea, surging against Terrible Tilly, drenching the island. I spat out a mouthful of seawater, the salt sending a new wave of pain through me. Shock hit me from both the cold and pain. I clenched my teeth and looked back at the building. "Damn that witch."

The loud scraping of a metal door rang through the air, followed by the steady sound of heavy footsteps.

A looming figure stepped into the light, carrying a person carelessly over its massive shoulders; eight feet tall, its slick black head looked like a seal's with dark, fathomless eyes above a large snout that resembled a bottlenose dolphin. Seashells of every color coated its skin like iridescent scales but stopped just under its chin. The fighter in me knew this was armor, and the shells would make stabbing this thing too difficult to attempt, but I could barely draw my eyes away from how beautifully dangerous this creature was.

"Where did they pull you out of?" I said.

The beast turned its head to look at me, his lips pulled back, showing me a forest of triangular white teeth the length of my pinky.

The staccato of heels announced Muirín's return; she was escorted by an army of selkies carrying spears, hatchets and tridents. She looked at the large beast and smiled at it before turning to me.

"Beautiful, isn't he? The Shellycoats were nearly hunted to extinction by human fishermen. They were a mighty race, although sadly he is the last of his kind."

The Shellycoat dropped the battered person it was holding.

It couldn't be.

Tied up, bloody and bruised was Travis, groaning in pain as the silver chains burned his flesh. Several selkies grabbed the chains, dragging him to the post behind me, tying him up against it.

Another group of selkies emerged from the ranks with a limp body, and tied them to the post to my right. It was a slender humanoid, his sharp angular features marred by a collection of bruises that had left half his face swollen. His long black hair had been completely ripped from his scalp, and cobalt blood was streaming down the side of his face. His whole body was covered in silver scales, but some of them had been pulled apart and were oozing with blood. I noticed that they had only tied one of his hands above his head, the other one lay limply at his side ending in a stump where his hand would be. The man tried to move his head only to be punched by the selkies before they stuffed a dirty piece of cloth into his mouth.

"My gods, Selenic, what have they done to you?"

A third group moved to my left, carrying between them a half-naked man in his late twenties with golden-brown hair that fell to his waist. His piercing sapphire eyes glared at the selkies manhandling him. If not for the gag, he probably would've cursed their mothers and all their ancestors. His whole upper body was a map of green and purple bruises. As his eyes landed on Muirín, hate made them blaze brighter still.

Valentina Hall stepped through the horde of selkies, wearing a gown similar to the one she had worn to my inn, only this one was violet with black trimmings. Her platinum curls were pulled back in an elaborate bun that resembled a tulip. Behind her, a couple of selkies were dragging a screaming woman by her hair. She tried to break free only to be backhanded by one of the selkies. They hauled her to her feet and tied her to the wooden post across from me.

She had long dark hair that hugged a soft motherly face, and was bleeding from a jagged cut that reached from her jaw to her ear. Around her neck was a strange white leather necklace that glowed with a faint blue light. Unlike Selenic and the young man, her mouth wasn't gagged. She cursed at Valentina, "When I get out of here, I'll boil your eyeballs, rip your bones from your writhing body and stab your traitorous heart with them."

Valentina looked at her, amused. "Matilda, my dear, you need to read the room, there's no scenario in which you can escape. So be a doll, and shut up."

The selkies moved in and gagged the head priestess of the Portland coven. I looked at the fae and shook my head. "A piece of advice? Walk away and hide in some dark corner of the ocean," I smiled, trying to hide how worried I was for everyone, "As soon as Mab finds out that you've shot her daughter, the hell she will rain upon you would make even Lucifer cry."

Muirín raised her eyes and grinned. "I'm surprised that after living in court for so many years, you would attribute familial love to her emotional capabilities." She clasped her hands above her navel. "You know Winter's law - the strong prey on the weak. She wouldn't care even if she knew."

I shook my head and clicked my tongue at her. "This isn't about love, it's about power and pride. How can the great Mab let some two-bit wannabe get away with assaulting her heir without an appropriate response?" I tilted my head.

She nodded towards the hulking beast beside her and the Shelly-coat stepped forward to ram his foot into my stomach. I doubled over, coughing up several mouthfuls of blood; it felt like getting hit by a car.

Muirín walked over to me, placing her fingers beneath my chin and raising my head. "I abhor that petulant mouth of yours. Say her name one more time and I'll start feeding your friends to my children. Is that clear?"

"Why kidnap Travis and Matilda? The rituals for the demon and the cursed god only required two sacrifices."

"Do I look like one of those theatrical villains that the mortals enjoy so much? Should I tell you my whole plan so you know how to stop me right at the last second?" She shook her head. "No, my dear captain, you will know when the time comes and not a moment sooner." She looked to the sky and seemed to be calculating something.

"Midnight is almost upon us," She turned to me and winked, "Since you're the main event of my upcoming auction, I need to make some adjustments. While I do, why don't you stay here and catch up with the boy and merman. After all you went through to find him, I wouldn't dream of depriving you two of some quality time together."

Reality crashed into me. I looked at the young man as he glared at Muirín with pure loathing, and a lump formed in my throat. It took me two tries to get the word out. "Lucas?"

The young man turned away from Muirín and looked at me. The loathing in his eyes was replaced by shame.

17

"You bitch," I breathed, stunned, "What did you do to him?"

She walked over to Lucas and twisted a strand of his hair between her fingers. "I did what any fairy godmother would do. I turned a frog into a prince." She let go of his hair and traced over his bruised chest with a single nail. "How could such magnificent power have resided in such an ugly package? What do you think, Lucas? Do you like the new you?"

Lucas flailed in his chains, striving for Muirín's neck, but the fae only laughed and took a step back. "He's still adjusting to his new body, not that it matters much for him now."

She blew a kiss at him before clapping her hands together, summoning the hulking form of the Shellycoat. It had been occupied by staring at the cut Muirín had left on my cheek as all the while fishy drool had spilled from its mouth and had now collated into a pool by my feet. Even after it answered Muirín's summon, the stench made my eyes water.

"Now that we have all the materials for the ritual, which I must thank my new allies for gathering, we can proceed. Since you and I have reached a profitable solution, we need our original sacrifice." The sea of selkies parted as two of them carried forward a young woman.

Her dark cropped hair clung to a tear streaked face. I held in a gasp - they had taken Matilda's daughter. I clenched my teeth and scowled at Valentina. *What I wouldn't give to get my hands around her neck and snap it like a twig.*

Matilda raged against her chains, trying to get to her daughter, but it was useless. Valentina looked at her with such glee I wanted to cave her skull in with my morningstar. The selkies ignored Matilda and released the chains around my chest. The heavy chains fell away as they dragged me a few feet from the post. I raised my shackled hands but they ignored me, retrieving the fallen chains to bind and gag Leann in my place.

"Now that we have our sacrifices ready, all that's left is to take care of is a minor inconvenience." She made a hand motion and the unconscious body of Cassius was brought forward and dumped next to me. "After all the trouble he went through to find his son, it's only natural to reward his efforts. A short reunion is better than no reunion at all, don't you think, captain?" I ignored her completely and crawled towards Cassius, putting my head on his chest. Relief flooded me as I heard the faint but steady beat of his heart.

The door to the lighthouse opened and from it stepped Teresa, escorting Silera down the steps. The witch looked emaciated, wearing a black turtleneck and leather gloves that appeared baggy on her frail hands. She had several bald patches and strands continued to fall behind her. Her face was completely disfigured; scars covered every feature, and her hollow cheeks were blistered and oozing something unnaturally orange. Her eyes darted around, not focusing on anything or anyone.

Silera looked paler than usual. She was wearing the same gown as before and the large stain of blood on her side was difficult to look at, but even harder to ignore. As much as she had abandoned me, I'd spent so long protecting her that the urge still lingered - despite the gnawing ache in my side where Galesh had stabbed me. Her hands were bound by handcuffs and the skin beneath the metal had split, leaving a small trail of blood behind her. Despite the obvious pain, she walked with her head held high, her golden eyes clear and defiant.

She stopped a few feet short of Muirín. The sea fae nodded towards Teresa and the witch joined Valentina, standing on the fae's right hands side. The two fae eyed each other before Muirín gave a small nod. "Well, Princess, have you come to a decision?"

Silera looked at her, arched a condescending brow and smiled grimly. "You were actually serious about that? I thought you were jesting. If that is all, please escort me back to my quarters, I was having a pleasant nap."

The Shellycoat growled as it stepped forward, sounding more like a mix between a bear and tiger than any sea creature I knew of. Muirín raised her hand and the beast stopped. "What is your answer? Will you side with me, or your mother?"

For a second everything became muted. She couldn't possibly be thinking she could challenge Mab. *The* Mab? The Queen of all evil faeries. Muirín wasn't missing a couple of screws, she was missing the whole damn tool box.

Silera laughed, full of contempt and derision. "Now I know you're truly delusional. You can't take on Mab. You couldn't even take one of her pinky fingers before she eviscerated you."

Muirín's cheeks colored before she slapped Silera so hard that she stumbled on to the ground next to me. "Your mother may be an all-powerful monster, but she isn't the only one."

She waved her hand through the air, as colors merged and swirled together until they formed a new image. Instead of the open sky, we saw the bottom of the sea, the sandy banks barely visible in the depths. The silhouette of several sunken ships could be seen, centuries old galleons dwarfed by the newer cruise ships, and even an aircraft carrier. They were all nestled tightly within the ocean floor, as if someone had thrown them down like javelins. I looked around at everyone's equal confusion but slowly their faces settled, taking on the appearance of fear-twisted masks.

I looked back to the image and saw the floor was moving, as if disturbed by our presence, but it showed no sign of settling. I attempted to lock my gaze onto a patch of ground but the floor was moving too much to follow. No, not the floor… tentacles. The ships were nestled in tentacles, which had started to stir, and were now being slowly crushed like tin cans.

"Is this meant to be impressive? Shall I pretend to cower for you?" Silera's voice tore my attention away from the vision which had started to collapse in on itself and was already fading, once again showing the starry sky in places. "Oh dear, help me someone, Muirín...." Silera paused for a moment in mock thought. "I'm sorry dear, what titles did you give yourself? Mistress of the Expanse was it?" All humor dropped from her face. "Muirín of no titles given or earned, has summoned a picture of a fish."

The fae's face darkened, her shoulders tensed and I could see moisture gathering around her hand. She drew in a long breath and I willed myself to have the strength to stop whatever she may be about to do. But Muirín had been waiting too long for this ritual; she exhaled and the gathering moisture vanished. She looked at the selkies around her and smiled. "Come, my children, there's lots to do and little time to do it. Let's give them a few minutes of privacy. It will be the last time they'll spend in each other's company after all."

Muirín slowly walked back towards the lighthouse, taking her minions with her. Valentina and Teresa followed. The younger witch paused beside me and knelt down next to my ear. "I'll enjoy watching you suffer. Don't worry about that tree bitch, I'll burn every tree in her precious forest and laugh as she dies."

She followed Valentina, leaving us alone with the Shellycoat who kept an eye on us from a few feet away.

With Muirín gone, the sound of the increasingly aggressive waves filled the silence. Leann and Matilda had given up trying to talk to each other and were silently crying against their posts. To my right, Selenic was still unconscious along with Cassius next to us, and to my left Lucas looked like he'd retreated into a far off place that had become all too familiar recently. That just left Silera beside me, and there was history between us that I wasn't sure I wanted to address that felt heavy in the air. To someone who's lived as long as I had, ten years wasn't enough time to heal the wounds she had inflicted on me.

"Nathaniel, I... There's something we should discuss." Her confident front had dissipated. Silera had never been good at talking about emotions.

"Oh? I'd hoped we were just going to ignore the fact you tried to have me killed." I followed in Matilda's suit and leant back against my post, trying to rest while I could.

"Really?" Silera looked relieved. I could practically see my sarcasm fly over her head.

"That was a joke, by the way. You've spent too much time in court." I closed my eyes, even though the wind and sea spray were ensuring no one would be comfortable enough to sleep. Still, pain lets us know we're alive.

"You've spent too much time around the humans. You never say what you mean, always making snide little jokes." I could hear the petulance in her tone. Despite everything that had happened between us, she was still comfortable enough to drop the icy facade with me.

"Spending time with humans wasn't exactly my plan. But what can you do when the Princess of the Winter Court, the Hunt's Maiden and Winter's Flame, orders you dead?" It was a struggle for me to keep my voice even; the decade old scar burned in contrast to my cold skin. Anger and betrayal ate into my chest, somehow more painful than the gunshot wounds.

"I didn't have you killed, Rún," she whispered in my ear.

My eyes flew open and met hers; the familiar pools of molten honey were always the warmest thing in Winter.

"'The Princess sends her love', hard to miss the message in that. Especially when followed with multiple stabbings and then being stranded in the Crooked Man's Forest." I turned away, not wanting her to get to see the hurt in my eyes. I'd overestimated my importance to her once before, but she wouldn't get to revel in my pain now.

Her shackled hands reached out to cup my face and pulled me in. "Rún, my love, my wolf, my captain, my saviour, my Nathaniel, mine. I swear on everything that I am, that I did not order to have you killed." She looked me in the eye as she said every word.

The pain I'd been suppressing for years surged to the surface, and rage overwhelmed me. My heart tightened to such a point that it felt like it almost didn't exist anymore, cowering from the hope Silera threatened to bring.

"No. You don't get to call me any of those names anymore." I tried to shake my head from her grip, but fae are strong, even when shackled with steel. "Galesh wouldn't have acted on anyone's orders but yours. I don't know how you're lying, but don't do this to me, Silera. I've witnessed fae spouses do worse things to each other than you've done to me. I can live with what happened. Once I'd healed, I can't even say I was surprised. But don't you do this to me, Silera. Don't lie to me."

Silver tears filled her eyes, a sign of the purity of her soul. "Rún, I cannot lie and I wouldn't lie to you. Do you know how wretched this past decade has been for me? No one has come forward to claim they did it, there were no leads and Galesh rode to his father's dukedom as soon as he thought you were dead. I couldn't touch him. All I received was your bloody hair in a box to let me know what had happened to you." She pulled me close. Even wet, the smell of primroses permeated from her hair and I felt myself wanting to give in, to believe everything she was saying. "And then I saw you at the college. You were alive, I couldn't believe it. I could barely stop myself from telling you who I was right then, but I knew you wouldn't believe me."

She pulled my face to hers again. *Gods, how I had missed her.* She was perfect in every way, even the slight asymmetry to her face was perfect.

"I haven't taken anyone else since you've been gone. I've mourned you all these years and now I have you back, you think I'm the monster who banished you." The tears finally broke free and poured down her face. Rivers of silver melted in with the seaspray and meandered down her cheeks. "We might go to the grave tonight, my love, can we at least go knowing that we love each other?"

I leant my forehead against hers but couldn't find any words to say. For once in my life, I was speechless.

"Please, Nathaniel…"

I didn't wait for her to finish before kissing her. Her lips tasted salty and sweet, triggering something within me. My heart flurried in anticipation of kissing her more. She gasped at first but then melted into the kiss, her tongue touched mine as her body released its tension towards me. I felt a wave of fiery heat sweep through me as I pulled her into a close embrace. My hands framed her face, admiring her features that I had so dearly missed, my heart threatening to burst out of my chest but I didn't care. I surrendered myself completely to this moment and to her, and felt whole for the first time in a decade. We ended the kiss and I leant my forehead against hers, breathing in her scent.

"I need time," I muttered.

"I can wait." She closed her eyes letting out a deep breath before composing herself. She leaned back, raising her handcuffed hands. "However, as you previously pointed out, I'm a little tied up at the moment. We should solve that first."

I laid my head against the wooden post and whispered to her. "Our heaviest hitter is tied behind us, our mages are gagged or out cold, and Selenic is in no state to fight. Which leaves just you and me to save everyone and defeat the evil queen."

"We've faced worse odds," Silera said, a smile tugging at her mouth.

"True, but at least I know who we were fighting then. Muirín's clearly from Winter, but I don't remember her - any idea what her deal is?" I had racked my brain but couldn't remember ever seeing or hearing of her.

Silera's gaze switched from Lucas and settled on the vast expanse of ocean on the horizon. "Back in the old days, many of the fae were worshipped like gods. She was one of those." She took a deep breath and shifted her weight where her wound must've been bothering her. "The Veneti worshipped her by making sacrifices, in the hopes she would grant them a safe voyage and a hearty catch. But her cult perished when Caesar invaded their lands with his legions. She drifted for a couple of decades, trying to restart her cult in other regions. But she never succeeded and finally ended up in my mother's court."

That was typical of the fae, a lot of them still yearned for the 'good old days', when they were worshipped like deities, before the spread of iron robbed them of a portion of their powers. Most of them had made the transition and accepted their new lot in life. Muirín wasn't among those.

"Were you worshiped as well?" I asked. Her hair danced with the sea breeze. I could picture her as an ancient goddess, leading her people into victory. She had the charisma and wit that drew people to her and made them want to follow her into the gates of hell itself. Once upon a time I would've been one of them, but now I wasn't sure what I would do.

She smiled and shook her head. "Those practices were before my time. I grew up at court, learning the ways of my people, to one day replace my mother should the need arise. Not that I think it would, you know how she is."

"I know." Scary didn't even begin to cover Mab; she was a force of nature.

A groan came from between us and I looked down to see Cassius's blue eyes slowly blinking. "Ugh, would you two stop flirting and actually figure a way out of this mess."

I let out a breath I didn't know I was holding. "Hey, nice of you to join us. How long have you been up?"

"Since the fish part," he whispered to us.

I turned to look at the Shellycoat who was staring right at us, although he made no move to come forward. Across from us, Matilda stared at her daughter, her eyes full of tears. Selenic hadn't stirred since they chained him up. I turned my head to look at Travis. The shapeshifter had woken up. Smoke rose from where the silver chains had made contact with his flesh but he didn't seem to care. His eyes flashed with intense amber light that told me his other self was firmly in the driver's seat and wouldn't be pushed into a corner like last time. Good.

Lucas had begun struggling against his chains like a wild animal. The Shellycoat turned to him and licked his lips but no made no further move.

Okay Nathan, think, besides a half-conscious mage and injured princess, what else do you have to work with?

My magic had barely recovered, I could maybe activate a rune or two, but they had taken my bracelets. I patted my pants to see if they had left me with anything and felt the soft edges of the two playing cards I had prepared so long ago. I felt myself grinning.

"It seems you have an idea, care to share with the rest of us, Rún?" Silera turned towards me, her movements slow and methodical.

I turned to Cassius and whispered, "How much magic can you do without a wand or staff?"

Cassius frowned. "I can do the simplest spells, maybe enough to cut a link in your chain. It will be difficult without a focus, anything stronger will kill me, but it can be done."

A plan started forming in my mind. "Okay, here's what we're going to do. First, I need you to reach into my pocket."

1 8

Half an hour went by with no opportunity to put our plan into action. I kept an eye on the Shellycoat the entire time, and noticed Selenic and the others coming back to reality. People usually woke up slowly, taking time to come back to their senses, their bodies relaxed. When Selenic woke up, his body immediately tensed, as if expecting a blow any moment.

Leann stirred in her chains and looked around until her eyes settled on her mother, tied directly in front of her. The Shellycoat turned towards them and lumbered his huge form towards Leann. Matilda let out a muffled scream but it fell on deaf ears as the muscular fae ignored her pleas.

The beast raised a clawed hand, taking a loose strand of hair that had fallen off her braid and brought it to his nose, sniffing it deeply. Leann squirmed away from the fae's touch but there wasn't anywhere she could go.

"Get away from her!" I glared at him as Silera sighed next to me. The lumbering form of the Shellycoat tensed before he turned to us on the ground.

"I see you haven't changed much over the years, Rún," She said in an exasperated tone, "Can't you see he's much larger than you?"

The Shellycoat scooped me up from the ground by the front of my shirt and raised me to meet its dark fathomless eyes. His slick dolphin-like snout scraped against the tip of my nose, hot breath warming my cheeks, the thick stench of blood made me gag. His lips raised up into a snarl, showcasing a forest of razor sharp teeth that could render flesh from bone in a single bite.

I glared at the Shellycoat but before I could say anything the fae smirked.

"Meat." It was the first time the fae had spoken, and its deep voice grated in my ears. He raised me above his head and slammed me down onto the ground. Hot blinding agony flared all around me, and I gasped trying to catch my breath and relieve some of the tension, but there was no air to be had; my throat felt on fire and my back screamed at me. I looked up to see the sea troll's immense foot come down on me, and I fought to move out of the way; my brain gave the right commands but my aching body refused to listen out of sheer exhaustion. A sharp whistle cut through the night air as the giant foot stopped an inch above my face.

I looked back to see what had stopped it. Muirín stepped out of the dilapidated lighthouse and walked towards us. "Shelly, stop playing with the merchandise - if he's too beaten up we won't get our money's worth."

The sea troll stepped away from me. I took in a deep breath and turned on my side. I spat out a glob of blood and wiped my mouth with my hand.

"Next time you see something bigger and stronger than you, try not to antagonize it, Rún." Silera sighed next to me. "It's like the fachén all over again."

"My orders were to make it go away and I did." I sat up slowly trying not to injure myself further.

"It was going away; it wouldn't have bothered anyone but you *had* to hit his eye with a rock." She reminded me.

"Its not my fault the stupid oaf turned around at the last second, I was aiming for the bushes next to it."

"Isn't this amusing?" Muirín stood next to the Shellycoat. She clapped her hands twice, and from behind the lighthouse appeared a pair of burly looking selkies carrying a large oval shaped brazier made of what looked like dead coral, bleached white with a roughened surface. It glowed with dark mercury light. Behind them, Valentina, Teresa and Veronica followed closely.

The selkies placed the coral brazier in front of Muirín as one of them handed her a thick leather tome. A spiderwork of white lines sprayed across the wine color binding, and she caressed the binding, letting the book float in the air. The skies rumbled with a faint sound of thunder. I peered at the book, extending my magical senses towards it, and felt a sharp needle of pain stabbed me between the eyes. I swore under my breath.

Valentina glanced at me and smirked. The wind around the lighthouse picked up, opening the book and flipping through several pages before stopping. The book began to emanate a crimson glow, casting a blood colored shadow across Muirín's face. A terrified scream came from the book, its crimson glow swaying and darkening into a deep mahogany color.

Muirín turned towards the assembled selkies and witches, an excited look on her face. "My children, tonight we have gathered on the apex of the new moon to witness my ascension to greatness." She smiled, caressing the book. "Within this book lies the power to awaken the slumbering spirit of this land and bind her elements to my will."

Muirín pointed towards Travis at the back. "The Earth's Beast, to grant me the strength of a titan." A ripple ran through the pale yellow orb above him, twisting and darkening into a deep hickory color, the concrete around the post cracked as its vines sprouted from it, twisting themselves around Travis. A line of pure power shot from the changing orb across to the orb above Selenic. "The Shallows's Knight, to grant me dominion over the waves." The globule pulsed and rippled from a yellow color to a bright electric blue, a small gray cloud forming over his head from which rain began to fall.

Muirín continued to chant, her words vibrating with power. Magic flowed from her as her voice rose to a crescendo, drowning the whole lighthouse with the scent of copper and sulfur. Another line shot from Selenic's orb to the one above Matilda. "The Ember's Witch fueled me with the power of an inferno." The orb swirled and folded into itself, turning into a bright orange color; the wooden post Matilda was tied to lit ablaze, making it look like she was being burned at the stake before another line shot to Lucas's orb. "The Storm's Child, empowered me with heaven's wrath." The globule spun in place, crackling with a deep mauve color. A black cloud formed above his head and a rain of lightning descended upon him as two lines of magic shone from the orb, connecting to Travis's hickory one. Finally, Muirín spoke, "The Magic's Blood, bestow upon me your power." Leann's globule flared with a bright, golden light, shaping itself into a pair of feathery wings.

The orbs merged, creating a circle of their own above our heads. Colors danced and melded, shimmering into each other and back, our very own aurora borealis. As Muirín continued to chant, the borealis flared, each colour beaming into the night sky before spiralling, as if drained, into the brazier that began to flame with each colour of the borealis.

I went over the two rituals that Hope gave me, and neither of them mentioned any of this. I turned towards the sea and felt unsure - I had no idea what she was doing.

Muirín raised her arms into the air and smiled. "With all the elements present, awaken and be mine."

Muirín began to read from her book. The air thickened with magic as each new syllable was uttered. I gazed into the flames, mesmerized by its beauty and felt a wave of nausea coursing through me as my magic screamed in protest. Although I couldn't understand the words themselves, their meaning rang clear through my head.

She had called to the True names of Fire, Air, Earth and Water, tethering them to her with death. For the first time, I knew what she was really trying to accomplish. She wasn't creating a demesne, summoning a demon or releasing an ancient god: she was awakening the spirit of the land, and enslaving it to her will.

The bond between a ruler and their land was one of mutual trust.

The land provided the resources and a home for its denizens while the ruler oversaw its prosperity and protection. What Muirín was doing went against the natural order of things.

"I'm going to be sick." I murmured. Silera looked at me with worry in her eyes, and I told her what was going on.

Her eyes widened and she shook her head. "We need to stop her, now!" I nodded and mouthed. *"Ready?"*

"As I'll ever be," she whispered as I nodded before looking at Cassius.

"You only have one shot at this, make it count."

He handed me the two rune scribed playing cards I'd made in case of a fae emergency. Teresa must've noticed something because she shrieked, "What's in his hands?!"

But it was too late. As Muirín's voice reached a crescendo in her chanting, I gathered the scraps of my magic and poured it into the two cards. "Loinnir! Deataigh!"

The first card's rune detailing a circle pierced by four lines burst into a blinding white light that pierced the dark of night like the midday sun. The second card, a cloud with a spiral inside, released a blanket of gray smoke that flooded the whole area. I pulled my shirt over my nose and felt my eyes tear up.

A multitude of voices screamed through the confusion; Muirín's chanting had stopped as she screeched at her minions. A flash of purple lightning cut through the smoke behind us and I felt myself smile - Cassius had done his job. The smoke parted, revealing a charred and broken wooden post that used to hold a very pissed off shapeshifter.

Thick silver chains fell to the floor, and Travis cracked his neck from side to side before setting his gaze on the fae around us. Pools of raging amber flared like searchlights as he looked at the gathered selkies before his eyes finally landed on the Shellycoat in front of us, and a wide predatory grin formed on his lips. "Hunting time." He growled before releasing an earthshaking roar.

The nearest selkie ran towards him with a raised javelin, but Travis caught the weapon, pulled it from his hold and opened his mouth. Bright orange light flared at the back of his throat and a base-ball sized fireball flew out, incinerating the fae's head; soon the body caught fire and quickly turned to ash. The other selkies recoiled in fear as Travis began to shift into his feral form. Unlike when we fought in his garage, this time the transformation was faster and more fluid, like fire spreading through dry grass. His bones shattered and molded into his new form, and rust colored fur covered his entire body; a nightmarish meld of beast and man.

He stood at equal height with the Shellycoat, black stripes criss crossing along his fur, his feline face reminiscent of a prehistoric tiger. Long canine teeth grew from his upper jaw as his thick black mane sprouted from his neck. Broad shoulders extended into muscular arms before ending in six-inch sharp claws. The king of beasts opened its huge maw, roaring his challenge to the skies above.

"What the hell is he?" Silera asked as Cassius grabbed me by the arm and helped me stand.

I looked at Travis who was taking a running start at the Shellycoat. "A creature born of magic and malice, he was mutilated by the fae to be reconstructed into the perfect mix of lycanthropy and Summer magic, a killing machine against Winter," I said, whilst Cassius worked on cutting me free.

Travis pounced towards the Shellycoat, claws extended in front, his mouth glowing orange as he launched a basketball-sized fireball straight into the Shellycoat's face before slamming the large shell monstrosity into the ground. The Shellycoat shrieked in pain as Travis dug his claws into its shell-covered flesh. Blood and chunks of meat flew through the air as the fae fell beneath the assault of fangs, claws and fire.

Cassius looked at the battle and whistled. "Guess they succeeded."

The momentary surprise had given Travis a slight advantage, but the Shellycoat quickly swung its giant meaty fists against Travis's side - the shifter roared in pain and slashed at the fae's face, ripping several shells off before both of them began rolling around the pavement, knocking several selkies off their feet. A hatchet skidded across the ground, landing next to my feet. The other selkies surrounding them got out of the way, leaving the two colossal beasts to tear into each other.

Cassius muttered something in Latin and I felt my wrist loosen. "Did you really just waste magic to untie me?" I asked while rubbing my wrists.

"It's not like I've got the key," Cassius remarked, "Now move, we don't have a lot of time before the shock wears off."

I picked the hatchet up from the ground; it weighed about a pound with a black wooden handle and sharp edge. "Fine, go untie Matilda, we need all the firepower we can get. I'll take care of Leann."

Cassius knelt down, helping Silera to her feet and freeing her, and rushed over to Matilda. I nodded at Silera, turned around and pulled on the thick nail trapping Leann as Silera went to confront Muirín. The damn nail wouldn't budge.

I gave Leann a reassuring smile. "Don't worry, we're going to get you out of here," I said, using the edge of the hatchet for support as the nail began to wiggle free.

A muffled response was all I got. "Oh right, sorry." I removed the gag from her mouth.

"Look out!" She yelled.

I turned to see Teresa waving a hand in front of her scarred face, making a blowing motion. "Roí Aéra!"

A gust of powerful wind stormed towards us. I cursed and jerked the nail around until it finally came loose, and pulled Leann towards the ground. The gale of wind crashed into the post which splintered.

While Teresa prepared to release another spell, Veronica charged at us with an athame in hand. Her face was a mask of fury as she raised the knife above her head.

"Stay behind me, and keep an eye on the wicked witch," I told Leann, using the post as support. My legs were still weak and couldn't hold my weight for long.

Veronica continued charging with her hand held high to make an overhead slash, but I moved my head to the side as the athame struck deep into the wood. The witch grunted with effort to pull it free but I didn't wait around, punching her in the jaw with all the might I had.

The witch's eyes rolled to the back of her head as she dropped to the ground.

I pulled the athame free from the wood; the handle felt cold and porous in my hand, like holding a piece of granite. I gave it to Lean. The blade, though short, was wickedly sharp. "Better than nothing, I suppose."

Leann nodded, clutching the athame with both hands, her knuckles white as her eyes darted around the battlefield.

A lone selkie stepped forward, his hand shaking where it held a trident; he looked back at his frozen comrades and barked something at them before pointing his weapon at Travis, licking his lips. The selkies barked in unison and began to move towards the feral shifter. Whenever one of them got within striking range, they would have their skulls caved in or throats ripped out.

"Look out!" Leann shouted behind me, but I didn't have time to react as Teresa plunged her weapon into my left arm.

"Fuck!" I shouted in pain as Teresa yanked the blade out and stabbed at me again. I jammed my elbow into her chest, pushing her backwards and enraging her further.

"I'll rip your eyeballs out and wear them as a necklace!" Teresa laughed maniacally as she went for a third strike.

I grabbed her wrist and twisted it; I heard bones snap, and the athame fell to the ground. She took a swipe at me with her nails, but I dodged, slashing at her with my hatchet. She pulled back with unnatural speed, freeing herself before my weapon could hit her.

Warm blood flowed down my arm, soaking my shirt. Finally, the smoke began to clear, revealing a scene of chaos.

A wounded roar came from within the circle of selkies surrounding Travis, which was followed by a wail from the Shelly-coat. Cassius freed Matilda who ran to Valentina, who was skulking at the edges of the battlefield. Cassius turned and ran for Selenic.

Silera was engaged in an all-out power struggle against Muirín, both of them stood a dozen feet from each other. Sweat began to pour down Silera's face, turquoise flames licking the sides of her arms as she blasted at the sea fae. My princess's face turned bloodless and her breathing shortened while Murirín bit her lip and condensed a shield of water from the sea spray around the island, extinguishing the flames. Normally the only fae that could rival Rela would be her mother or brother, but she was wounded and weakened by iron, plus who-knows-what juice Muirín was hopped up on.

A flash of movement caught my attention as Teresa came around for another swipe with her athame. I parried it with my hatchet, and would've cut her head off if not for a scream breaking my concentration. I turned around to see Leann being held at knife point by Veronica. "Now, be a good dear and drop the hatchet, or I give the little bird a nice crimson smile."

She pressed the athame to Leann's throat, prickling the skin, where a drop of blood flowed from the edge of the blade and fell to the ground.

I tightened my grip around the wooden handle of the hatchet. "You wouldn't dare. You still need her for Muirín's ritual." Leann tried to pull away from the blade but the witch tightened her grip around her hair.

Veronica sneered at me as she drove the blade a little deeper. "This isn't a negotiation. Drop the weapon, or she dies. Simple as that."

Out of the corner of my eye, Cassius finished stomping on a selkie's head and stabbing another one with a spear before he ran over to his son. He had managed to free Selenic, but the merman was too weak to move. The selkies had completely blocked off my view of Travis, but from the sounds coming from inside the circle, the battle was still raging on. Teresa was squaring off with Matilda; the witches stood inches apart without moving, the air between them shimmered and waved like heat rising from the street.

Silera raised her hand and a spiral of flames cut through the air, while she twisted her other hand in a complicated gesture, unleashing a storm of ice shards towards Muirín. The sea fae frowned, her eye twitching, and conjured a maelstrom with her at the center. Steam and ice shards exploded as the two faes's magic clashed into elemental chaos.

With each blast Silera's face paled, the turquoise flames growing dimmer, flicking in and out of existence. Her ice had lost its sharp edge and was all but snow at this point. I gritted my teeth; she was losing and there was nothing I could do. Muirín smirked, biding her time until Silera was weak enough to overpower. I wanted to wipe the smug look off her face.

Veronica caught me looking and grinned. "You've only delayed the inevitable. Our priestess will take Matilda's head, the Princess will die and your feline friend will be eaten by the Shellycoat."

I looked around, Veronica's words sounding in my ears as Travis took a brutal hit to the chin from the Shellycoat. Cassius was battling his way towards Lucas, cutting down any selkies that came close, as Selenic's eyes glowed with wild magenta light, the chains previously imprisoning him now in the air, hitting the selkies near him.

Magic saturated the air as the battle heated between the two fae; the elements raged against one another in an immense clash. Razor sharp blades of ice and jets of scorching flames flew through the air, only to be confronted by a whirlpool of spinning water. The temperature around the lighthouse peaked and fell like a dancer mid-pirouette; one second searing heat, the next frostbiting cold. Silera called the elements, demanding their obedience as they bowed to the Princess of Winter. Magic coiled around her like an ancient wyrm, her left hand shrouded in blinding turquoise flames, and I could feel the intense heat licking my face from across the battle-field. Her right hand glowed with a bright indigo light, encased with ice.

The ground shook around us and split down the middle where she stood; one side frozen solid like a polished mirror, the other, a lake of bubbling molten rock, its burnt concrete smell filled the air and burned my nostrils. Magic coalesced between her hands as a spear of winter ice enveloped in sapphire flames erupted from between them. My heart sped up, I held my breath as I helplessly watched the chaos unfold, my grip around my borrowed hatchet tightening. *Come on! You can do it!*

Muirín smiled and raised her arms palms up as a tidal wave rose from the sea and crashed into the spear, shattering it and extinguishing the flames, sweeping Silera off her feet. My heart screeched to a halt.

"No!"

Silera lay crumpled and shockingly pale against the dark floor, perilously close to falling off the edge. Muirín smirked, tucking a loose strand of hair behind her ear. She turned towards the Shelly-coat. "Stop playing with your food."

I turned back to Travis just in time to witness the Shellycoat, renewed by Muirín's command, grabb Travis by the leg and pull him off his feet. The shifter avoided smashing his head against the rocks at the cost of landing on his back and winding himself. He lay on the floor, paralysed by his inability to breathe.

A vicious smile came across the Shellycoat's face as he picked up a trident that had been previously dropped by a selkie and plunged it into Travis's gut. Ice crawled through my veins as time slowed; Travis instinctively clutched at the trident, pain contorting his face. The Shellycoat ripped the trident away and grabbed Travis by the throat, bringing the shifter's head down sharply to the rocks. Travis immedi-ately went limp, and the Shellycoat dropped him with disgust on its face. I couldn't tell if Travis was alive or not.

A shout came from behind me, and I looked to see Matilda and Teresa still locked in their silent battle, with Matilda seeming to have easily gained the upper hand. Valentina was sweating profusely and blood streamed from her nose while Matilda didn't look any worse off than she had before. To their right, Muirín was crouched over Silera, caressing the princess's hair in a motion reminiscent of a mother comforting her daughter, but the expression on her face showed she was gloating in her victory.

Fire sparked within me, and I took a step forward, drawing my magic to me.

"Uh, uh, uh, I wouldn't do that if I were you."

I whipped round to see Veronica as she pushed the athame deeper into the skin on Leann's neck. The terrified young woman stood perfectly still, her eyes focused somewhere behind me.

"Be a good boy and give me the hatchet before you hurt yourself,"

Veronica grinned at me, "You don't want the kitten to be hurt—" A scream cut her off, and as one we looked back to Teresa and Matilda.

Matilda stood over the other witch, a basketball-sized fireball hovering above her hand. Teresa's scorched skeleton crumbled to the ground as the wind carried the ashes away into the night. Everything was still for a moment; even the selkies had paused for where they had been trying to subdue Cassius and Lucas. A small smile played at the corners of Matilda's mouth.

"Mom, look out!" Leann screamed as Muirín moved with unnatural speed and appeared behind Matilda, who didn't have the chance to move besides to turn her head.

Moisture condensed around Muirín's nails, sharpening into claws as she thrust her hand forward, piercing Matilda's chest. The fireball in her hand flickered before vanishing as if snuffed out. The force jerked Matilda forwards, shock and pain splayed across her face. Muirín used Matilda's falling motion to withdraw her hand, ripping Matilda's heart out. Matilda landed next to Teresa's skeleton with a wet thud, her blood pooling underneath her and coating Teresa's remains.

19

"Mom!" Leann shrieked as she broke down into a chorus of uncontrollable sobs, and rammed her elbow into Veronica's side. The witch grunted in surprise and yanked the young woman by the hair. Leann turned and spat on Veronica's face; the witch shrieked and cut a line across her face with the athame. "Try that again and see what happens." She turned to me, smiling. "Shall we get this over with?"

Muirín walked to the brazier, passing by Lucas and Cassius who had managed to be subdued by the selkies amongst the confusion. Desperation seized me, and I looked around trying to figure any way out of this. Lucas and Cassius had been subdued at the eastern post, Selenic had collapsed by his post at the western point and was being guarded by three selkies, all of whom carried tridents. The Shellycoat had returned Travis to the southern post and Leann was still next to me in the center. Despite everything, Muirín still had her complete circle, as Matilda's body lay next to the northern post.

Muirín squeezed Matilda's heart over the multicolored flames. Smoke flowed around the fae, forming a dark crown over her head, the smoke constantly moving and churning. Muirín smiled in triumph as she withdrew her hand from the flames, unburnt, and turned to her followers.

"This is just the start, you're about to witness the ascension-" She suddenly stopped speaking as the flames in the brazier surged upwards, creating a pillar of heat and flame. Cries of pain came from the selkies who had been unfortunate enough to be stood nearby, their skin bubbling as the flames grew brighter. Muirín looked in horror as her crown of smoke collapsed, flowing down from her head and covering her face in a mask of black smoke. It didn't stop moving, swirling and torrenting around her face, angry at being summoned. Muirín coughed and screamed as the hot smoke began to suffocate her; falling to her hands and knees she clawed at the smoke, but her fingers passed straight through.

Selkies attempted to help her, but couldn't get close due to the intense heat. I was enjoying watching the bitch claw at her neck and the heat was welcome in the icy environment. Just as I thought Muirín was about to collapse, the smoke stilled. Muirín sat bolt upright, as if someone had pulled an invisible string. Her arms spread, her mouth and eyes wide open in a silent scream as the smoke flowed into her mouth and eyes.

Foul magic washed over me, bringing bile to the top of my throat as my muscles cramped and I fell to the floor. I writhed as my muscles seized; I could vaguely hear someone calling my name but all I could think about was how *wrong* the magic was. Something deep within me, at the very core of my being told me that this magic was wrong. It was an abomination.

The fire slowly dimmed, and my body finally lay still, the seizure passing. I lay looking at the stars, panting, sweat slicked my forehead but the feeling of 'wrong' persisted. My body felt heavy and my head refused to clear. I turned my head to see Muirín collapse to the floor, retching and gasping for air. Her hair had obscured her face, but as her breathing quietened she turned to us, her eyes aglow with fire. Her skin glowed as if she was lit within.

She got to her feet, her hair now dancing like the flames in the brazier. She looked like the embodiment of fire itself. She flexed her fingers and a fireball, like the one Matilda had killed Teresa with, appeared in her hand. She let out a laugh as she flung the fire at the nearest selkie, incinerating it within seconds. She cackled as she threw fire, incinerating selkies, who were ducking for cover, or just throwing it into the sky and sea. She laughed and laughed, as she exercised her new power.

Muirín turned to the rest of her captives with a triumphant look in her manic eyes.

"Bring them to me now." Her voice was deeper, imbued with forbidden magic.

The struggle between Cassius and Lucas and the selkies resumed, but it didn't last long before the selkies overran the mages and dragged them over to Muirín. Two selkies brought the still unconscious Selenic over while the Shellycoat dragged a bloodied Travis along by the scruff of his neck.

"Witches, bring the welp, I want to get this done quickly." Muirín had the others lined up in front of her. She held an athame now - never a good sign. I willed my body to move, to do anything but remain still. It wouldn't obey me. I didn't have the energy to lift a finger. I felt for my magic but there would only be enough to activate a rune, and they had taken my weapons away. Not that I could have lifted the morningstar or buckler in this state.

Leann struggled as Valentina and Veronica grabbed her by the shoulders and started dragging her over to Muirín. Hearing Leann's mourning cries sparked something within me, and I used what was left of my magic to grab the lifeline. I felt the presence from the Inn. It felt wounded. I needed to kill Muirín; she couldn't be allowed to chain this land.

Through the connection that tethered me to this presence, it siphoned magic into me; just enough to replenish my own magic and lift the fog and heaviness from my mind and body. These last twenty-four hours had been painful, but it was nothing compared to what I felt now. Everything within me burned as if someone was trying to cook me inside out. I managed to pull one knee, getting my breath back.

"Look at the mongrel. Once one of Winter's mightiest Captain's, now brought to his knees by me, Muirín, Queen of this Realm." Muirín laughed and danced to an unheard beat.

"You mad with power or just mad?" I said through gritted teeth. The presence was still slowly filtering power to me, but it did nothing to lessen the pain. I just needed a bit of time.

A familiar shimmer of light appeared behind Veronica's head and I almost sagged in relief.

A white wolf suddenly appeared and landed hard on top of Veronica. The wolf's muzzle opened, revealing a row of razor sharp fangs. Before she could react, the witch's head was mauled and crushed between Sabine's jaws. Leann fell to the ground gasping for air, finally free from the witch's suffocating grip. Sabine stood above Veronica's headless body, raised her bloodied muzzle and howled into the night.

The ghostly song of the hunt made everyone pause as a resounding burst rang through the air. Behind Sabine a lightning bolt split the air in half, revealing a bramble-adorned wall that slowly parted, forming an archway. Stepping through the opening, clad in sunlit forest armor was no other than Robin Goodfellow. His immaculate suit boasted a towering rowan tree engraved on his breastplate, its branches curved outwards protecting his arms while its roots twisted around his legs. But Robin was not alone; closely following were a squad of his elite troops, clad in the same gorgeous armor.

Goodfellow took in the situation before his eyes landed on mine and gave me a smug smirk. "It appears you're in a spot of trouble."

"By the Evernight Robin, attack already!" Silera yelled as she struggled to get up.

Goodfellow grinned at the eager army behind him and raised his slender sword in the air. "You heard the Princess, lads. Attack!"

His men raised their weapons and roared as they charged out of the archway.

Muirín stood by the brazier, her shoulders shaking as she glared at the incoming army, the sky above her darkening and thundering with a barely contained fury. She raised her hand towards the selkies and snarled, "Stop them!"

The selkies ran to defend their mistress, raising their rusty weapons and forming a shield of bodies, clashing with Robin's forces; the line of selkies shuddered for a moment and fell beneath the ferocious onslaught of Winter.

A selkie with a rusted sword charged me and I couldn't help but smile. Its attack was clumsy and I could tell it simply relied on its strength to win fights. I stayed low to the ground as the selkie raised the sword, clasped in both hands, in an overhead slash designed to take my head from my shoulders. Time slowed as the selkie brought the sword down and the adrenaline coursed through my veins. I sprung upwards, my left arm blocking his arms from coming down any further and I hammered a punch into his solar plexus, forcing the wind out of his body. My body rejoiced at the movements - my pain had receded into an ache which I was enjoying stretching out. The selkie dropped the sword as I grabbed the back of its head and brought it down hard. Face met knee, bone crunched, and the selkie didn't get back up. I picked up its sword and charged into the fray.

I'd cut through my third selkie when I sighted one attempting to sneak up to Goodfellow, who was fighting off a group of five others. I ripped a spear out of one of the dead's hands and launched it. It struck true, pinning the selkie into the ground as Goodfellow finished up his group. He looked at me and nodded as a jet of golden flames engulfed his sword, and with the swift elegance of a trained swordsman he danced through the army of selkies, leaving golden ash behind him. He slowly carved his way towards Silera when two burly-looking selkies, both armed with spears, blocked his path. Puck smiled, somersaulting and landing gracefully behind them. The selkies turned, unaware of their imminent beheading by a single swipe of Puck's blade.

I glanced over to Muirín, standing next to the Shellycoat that was holding both Travis and Selenic in front of her. "Let them go, Muirín!" I roared over the clashing of weapons.

She turned to me, her eyes burst into blazing suns filled with fury. "Foolish mortal, you think a cast out from Summer and his band of misfits is enough to save you?"

Thunder rolled across the sky as a bolt of lightning crashed into the dilapidated lighthouse, the rusted metal flaring with a bright light, illuminating the night sky for miles around. Muirín raised her hands, her nails elongating into razor sharp talons before she thrusted them into Selenic and Travis's chest.

"No!" I felt my blood run cold.

Travis let out a thunderous roar; his fur fell to the ground in waves as his muscles deflated before he turned back into his human form. His defiant lavender eyes lasered in on Muirín, the sea fae smirking as she pulled her hand out of his chest, his heart firmly in her grasp.

Selenic lasted only a moment longer before falling on top of Travis.

Muirín wrinkled her nose at the merman and stepped over their bodies, squeezing their hearts over the burning blaze. Dark brown and electric blue smoke rose from the flames. I rushed over to her, carving and slicing my way through her army.

She looked at the smoke hungrily, her eyes wild and mouth open as she inhaled the fumes. A pulse of raw magic surged from the brazier and punched me in the chest, lifting me off my feet and sending me crashing against one of the wooden posts. My back felt like it was on fire, and I tried to get up using the post as support but my foot slipped on something and I fell again. I looked at the fae as her skin glowed with an unnatural light, as if she had bathed in an aurora borealis. Her eyes flared with light; no longer the color of raging flames, they hardened like white marble rimmed with rings of orange, deep oak and striking midnight blue.

I felt the magic take hold of the elements around us; the earth shook like a wounded animal and the water raged against the island as the ritual claimed its victims.

Muirín laughed in delight as she spread her arms in the rain. "Worship your new mistress!"

She looked at Lucas with a hungry look in her eyes "Now to bend the storms to my will. Are you ready to join me, child?"

Lucas raised his chin, squaring his shoulders, his eyes burning with a heather light as he spat on the floor.

Purple lightning cut through the dark clouds as thunder rumbled around us, like an angry god woken from his sleep. Lucas raised his hand as the bolt struck his palm; it curled around his body, hardening into a suit of armor as a gale of wind flew from the north and circled beneath his feet like a centralized tornado, suspending him in the air.

"Lucas, stop!" Cassius yelled, trying to pull his son down. "You're not ready for this yet!"

Muirín smirked. "Defiant as ever I see." The kid might be powerful but he was no match for a millenia-old fae. Too many lives had been lost in this dash for power. The madness had to stop.

The island's death and chaos suddenly muted and I could feel a vast encompassing presence around me. It felt powerful, ancient and vulnerable; it was such a strange feeling that I had a hard time wrapping my mind around it. Quickly, clarity overtook my confusion and I realised what was happening. Muirín's ritual had awoken the Spirit of Oregon, and with each sacrifice it was dying, turning into something perverse and corrupted.

I wanted to heal it, cover it in my embrace, and protect it from harm.

In front of me small silhouettes misted into view, their features shifting and flowing. A warrior holding a spear, a mother dancing in the rain, a boy running with a herd of deer, and finally a little girl huddling in a corner of the ground. I stretched a hand to the last of the silhouettes.

"It's okay, I'm not going to hurt you." The little girl raised her head, a cascade of raven locks parting to reveal a cherubic face with hazel-colored eyes that swirled and spiraled in a myriad of undertones. She took my hand in hers and gave me a shy smile. A shock of electricity shot through me, sending my nerves into overdrive.

The world suddenly shifted; time slowed to a crawl around me, and everyone stopped in their tracks as thousands of images over the course of millions of years passed through my mind. The Spirit was showing me everything it had witnessed before the visions settled in Portland. I saw its rich history, how it was formed after the collapse of frozen dams during the last ice age, how her children, the Multnomah and the Clackamas, threaded upon her soil, fished in her waters and hunted her game.

The Spirit shared with me the pride she felt as she watched over the diverse community that called her lands home. Mortal, supernatural, human, siren, mage or shapeshifter; it didn't matter to her, they were all her children. She shared her grief and rage that some intruder had dared to wake her up and twist her into something that she wasn't. Pain assailed me like a battering ram through my connection with Oregon and I could see why.

Sprouting from Muirín, I could see blood-colored barbed chains piercing the land, the sea and the fire around us. From the center of her chest another set of chains wrapped themselves around the little girl pulling her towards the fae in an effort to subjugate it.

Silera suddenly appeared before me, her golden eyes glowed with indigo flames.

"She's hurting." I said, although not sure who I was talking about.

Silera smiled at me and wiped the tears from my eyes. "Then heal her, Rún."

I shook my head. "I don't know how."

She gently pressed her hand against the side of my face. "Yes you do." She lowered her hand and placed it over my chest.

I shook my head again. "I don't know if I can, last time..."

She put her finger to my lips and smiled. "Yes you can, my love, but you have to hurry." Time warped around us, and the spell that had frozen everyone around us broke. I felt my heart thrum with renewed power and I knew exactly what I needed to do. Silera stepped to the side, her presence reassuring.

I could see Muirín frowning at us as she made a pulling motion with her hand; the chains dug deeper into the spirit's flesh, dragging it towards her. Silver and red sparks covered my hands as I grasped the vicious-looking chains. They felt cold and porous, the barbs extending to pierce my hand as a strong suction force began pulling me towards the sea fae.

The little girl, the Spirit of Oregon, cried out in pain and held on to me, her eyes hopeful and trusting. I gave her a reassuring smile and went to work. I began to pull free the chain around her neck, but they resisted, digging deeper into her flesh. The cold and heavy barbs struggled and I poured more magic into my hands. With a few forceful tugs, the barb chain pulled free.

Muirín screamed, falling to one knee and holding on to her chest as if she'd been shot. I could see a tendril of hickory magic slithering from her towards the little girl; I shaped my magic into a bright double-bladed leaf-shaped crimson sword with a silver hilt and willed it to cut the tendril. The fae began to bleed from her eyes as she tried once more to tether herself to the Spirit, but I just cut the magic again. I summoned a gust of wind that circled around Muirín, keeping her in place.

The Shellycoat rushed over to his mistress but before he could take more than a couple of steps, a bright heather flash stepped in his way, and Lucas stood in his place like an elemental avatar. Lucas punched the sea troll in the stomach, purple lightning coursing through the fae's body, and blackened pieces of shells began to fall to the ground as the Storm's Child channeled the wrath of heaven into an apocalyptic beat down.

The Shellycoat bellowed in pain and moved in to swipe at Lucas, I felt myself tense, and was about to use my connection with the land to help him when the kid moved with unnatural speed, getting out of the claw's path and jumping to deliver a haymaker into the troll's chin. Bone cracked and a forest of teeth flew from its mouth. Every blow released a crack of thunder across the sky that made it seem like it would fall at any moment.

I turned my attention back to Muirín, as slowly the chains binding the Earth to her were wrenched free from the ground, severing her link to the element. The Spirit of Oregon flared with intense light, her skin taking a darker tone as a new element was back in its control, her hazel eyes glowed with a shining new luster, like polished diamonds.

I looked at the little girl in front of me and nodded before moving to the next set of chains that bound her. These ones were around her left shoulder and twisted themselves all the way to her wrist; a flash of sympathetic pain flared in my own arm and I got to work. The barbs, unlike the last ones, were searing hot, and I could feel the heat course through my hands even through the protective membrane of my magic. I gritted my teeth and began to pull them out one by one, while keeping my attention on the magic holding the sea fae in place.

Sweat began to drip down my forehead and I felt my body shake with the strain; I was channeling too much magic, I needed to hurry. I pulled the last link free and could hear a loud shriek over the howls of the wind and thunder. The smell of burnt flesh filled my nostrils and made me gag.

One by one the links binding Fire to the sea fae burst into bright golden flames before fading to ash. The brazier howled and cracked along the rim, small pieces beginning to fall to the ground as the spell lost its integrity. The little girl's form misted and shifted before it settled into the shape of a young woman with long raven hair braided to the side and almond shaped eyes that shone with intense light. Her skin glowed with health, with the exception of the jagged chain piercing her heart. Her very presence grew, flooding the sky above and the earth below as it moved towards the sea; it met some elastic resistance and I saw an annoyed pout form on her lips.

I looked at Muirín and felt my eyes widen. The once beautiful sea fae fought against the gale of wind that had her pinned; she struggled like Atlas holding up the world, her arms strained with the effort, her face pale and bleeding from her nose and eyes. She glared at us, and I noticed that her marble eyes had softened, losing their colored rings, leaving only the electric blue behind. Her skin glowed blue and a pulse of magic tore from her, dispersing the wind over her. She waved her hands through the air, colors merging and swirling together until they formed a familiar image in the sky above. Oregon stumbled and I moved in to catch her; she was shaking in my arms as her breathing turned ragged. She looked at me and shared an image of a dried ocean, the corpses of thousands of fish littering the ground. I turned to Muirín, and saw her draining the ocean of its magic, feeding it to the portal...

"You miserable ants! I was going to elevate you to greatness and you spat on my mercy!" Muirín raged, wiping the blood off her face.

"Come forth, great beast, and feast on their bones! Swallow the city and make it yours!"

Oregon turned towards the portal and took two steps from me; she threw hands that glowed with a golden light into the air as she tried to cut the connection between the sea and the fae. The barbs around Oregon's heart began to pulse with dark crimson light and the Spirit faltered, falling to one knee. My body moved before my mind had time to process what was going on. I grabbed the barb, which felt slick and clammy, and poured all my magic into my hands, pulling with all my strength.

Oregon opened her mouth and screamed. The sound that came from her wasn't something a human could make - it raged and roared like an erupting volcano. I didn't have time to finesse this like the last ones, and hoped to the gods Oregon didn't take it to heart. I gave the last barb another hard tug and ripped it free from her. Oregon cried out, and all around us the sea stopped in its rage. I gasped, looking at the once stormy sea freeze. It looked like a placid lake now; *how much power did one need to do this?* The sheer enormity of the power blew everything I knew about magic.

Muirín screamed in pain as her hair fell to the ground in waves; what remained on her head was wiry and wispy. Her skin greyed, the moisture leaving it as it shrivelled and wrinkled, sagging around her throat. The once beautiful goddess who embodied fire was now extinguished, replaced by the old hag that stood before us.

Out of the corner of my eye I saw the lumbering form of the Shellycoat on his knees. Half the shells on his body were gone, leaving behind charred flesh, and Lucas stood over him like an avenging angel. He raised his hand behind him and the sky rumbled with the sound of thunder, lightning gathering in a single point in the sky; as Lucas slammed his hand down the sky broke, unleashing a torrent of lightning. Like a pillar of light crashing down onto the troll, the world drowned under the thunderous explosion.

I shielded my eyes for fear of going blind. The flash lasted only for a second and when I turned back to look, Lucas stood over a pile of ashes, his skin paled and the lightning armor reduced to a few sparks.

He turned to look at me and mouthed something I couldn't hear before his eyes rolled to the back of his head and he fell to the ground. Cassius rushed over to his son's aid, and I was about to move when a loud bellow surged from the portal. Everyone froze in their tracks.

Water spilled into the island from the portal, pouring off the sides of the cliff, as six tentacles pushed themselves outwards. Pale green and dripping gray slime, they wrapped themselves around Terrible Tilly, squeezing the life out of it. The floor shook, and everyone paled at the sight of rocks falling into the ocean. I felt a stab of pain course through my body as the already small island diminished further under the grasp of the kraken.

I could feel my hold on the land weaken, my body trembling with the effort to keep my tether with Oregon open, but I had expended too much magic breaking the ritual, and both the spirit and I needed to recuperate. The kraken had wrapped itself around Terrible Tilly; that's all I needed. That, Oregon's power and a buttload of luck.

I let Oregon's magic flow through me as a rune came to mind. I drew a three pointed mountain in the air, the rune glowing with mocha colored light. The name bubbled to the back of my throat, struggling to be released. I pulled and gathered my magic to me, the pressure building as Oregon gave me what was left of her magic. I opened my mouth and screamed. "TALAMH!"

The rune spun in the air, diving into the ground, and Terrible Tilly came to life with an earth-shattering roar. The sections of stone that had begun to fall to the ocean stopped in mid-air and flew towards the kraken's tentacles, hammering the beast with fury of a stone colossi. The tentacles writhed and recoiled from the island.

Oregon stood up, her glowing skin dimmed but with a shining new light in her hazel eyes that rolled and swelled with the waves. Her lips curled into a smile and she walked behind me. She put her hands over mine and I felt the sea brimming with rage and pain; this was a creature that didn't belong in our waters, it was something alien and unclean. She lifted my hands and placed them on either side of the portal - even from far away I could feel the break in reality, like a window half closed. I let Oregon guide me, and together pushed against the edges of the portal. It resisted, flaring with bright light. I didn't wait for Oregon to tell me what to do and released all the magic she had shared with me into my hands, and we fought back. At first the portal bucked, twisting around the edges before it slowly began to close.

For the first time since this whole ordeal started, terror washed over Muirín's face as she knelt, clutching her chest. "Impossible! That bloodline was severed, we made sure of it."

The tentacles thrashed around madly, trying to keep the portal open as the edges began to cut into its flesh. Dark green blood streamed from the cuts as the beast's appendages flailed in the air and were pulled inside as the portal finally closed.

Muirín gazed at the portal in shock, the ground beneath her feet beginning to shake; three earth spikes erupted from the ground, piercing her chest. Dark blood bathed the spikes as the fae struggled to move. I turned around to see Oregon with her fist clenched in the air, looking at the fae, triumphant.

A movement out of the corner of my eye caught my attention and I saw Leann stand from where she had been cradling her mother's lifeless body and walk towards Muirín. The fae's bloodless face looked up from the spikes to see the young witch standing over her, an athame in her shaking hand.

Tears flowed down Leann's face as she raised the athame and slit the would-be goddess's throat.

Finally, it was over.

The battle around me had ended, and Goodfellow's forces were rounding up the rest of the selkies. But that didn't matter to me. I walked over to the prone bodies of Selenic and Travis as grief assailed me.

"I'm sorry." Tears slowly fell down my face.

The young woman that was Oregon knelt next to them, her body shining like a beacon. Their bodies pulsed with faint traces of magic as golden light shone from the holes in their chest and a tendril of magic flowed out, wrapping itself around their battered hearts. The hearts absorbed the light and began to beat at a steady rhythm. They rose in the air diving into their respective owner's chests, a golden flash bursting from them as the holes sealed themselves, leaving only a hairline scar that was slowly fading away.

Both men opened their eyes and took a deep breath, coming back to consciousness. Relief washed over me and I nearly blacked out. I was so tired. Oregon looked at Matilda being cradled by her daughter and shook her head, her eyes mournful. I closed my eyes, fresh tears flowing down my cheeks for the mother who did everything to protect her child and the daughter that saw her mother give it her all to save her.

I turned towards Oregon. She looked older now, like a woman in her mid-thirties. She took my hands into hers and gave me a dazzling smile. She was glowing like a supernova. Gratitude and warmth washed over me before the magic ebbed and darkness took me away.

EPILOGUE

I don't know what happened after passing out; I only found out after waking up three days later when Travis came by the inn and brought me up to speed. Goodfellow had rounded up the surviving selkies for Silera to judge. Their guilt was undeniable and they were sentenced to death for treason against Winter and the slaughter of innocent mortals. They were beheaded on the spot.

Leann took Matilda's body away, without saying a word to anyone. Sadly Matilda wasn't the only casualty: Selenic's wife Malia was killed and devoured by the Shellycoat. I only wished that the Shellycoat had suffered more before he died.

Cassius had taken Lucas back to New York. It was time that Ava knew what had happened, and maybe they could find some way to reverse what Muirín did to him. Travis said that it wasn't likely, and Silera and Goodfellow confirmed that the transformation was permanent.

Valentina managed to escape with Muirín's ritual book in the chaos of the battle, which wasn't something I was thrilled about. We told Roel, who guessed that she would probably go back to Texas to recuperate. I asked if he had any plans now but he just shook his head and asked if he could stay for the foreseeable future. We were down a kitchen boy/gopher, so I gave him the job which he seemed grateful for.

Hope had managed to keep the magical fallout of the battle from the mortals; the story of an illegal animal trafficking ring that had let loose some of its animals and how they killed a dozen people was the talk of the town, along with the tragic news that Detective Penelope Garcia of the Portland PD had been first on the scene and fell in the line of duty. She was survived by a husband and twelve year old son. The detective deserved better than what she got, but at least her family would get closure instead of wondering what happened to her.

In other news, a massive storm had hit the Tillamook Rock and had damaged the old lighthouse beyond repair. The building had collapsed on itself and there was no safe place to land anymore since the only way to do so safely was by helicopter. It had been abandoned for years, but no one had expected the infamous building to be gone overnight.

As for me, my injuries were the worst of the lot. I had been shot and stabbed several times, two of my ribs had been broken by the Shellycoat and my shoulder was swollen. What's worse, my body was completely devoid of magic; even after a few days of rest, every time I reached for it there was nothing. Julia had called Devon while I was unconscious and he had stitched me up as best he could before she wrapped me from head to toe in another herbal cast. To prevent me from doing anything stupid, as she put it.

Not that I could anyways. While I was out Detective Kane came by to ask some questions but was stonewalled by Julia. She had made up some excuse that I was down with the flu and he went away vowing to come back at a later time.

It took me a week of bedrest and constant nagging before Julia loosened the casts enough for me to walk around the inn. During that time, Cassius had sent a contractor to fix the broken windows, which was nice of him. I asked to speak with Lucas but he wasn't ready yet. I told Cassius that whatever he needed he could count on me. Anastasia sent Irini with a fruit basket to confirm that my debt to her had been paid in full. I thanked her before closing the door and going back to bed.

The mountain was still there in the backyard, and I honestly didn't know what to do with it. This whole ordeal had left me shaken. I had done things with my magic that I never thought possible; connecting with the primal spirit of Oregon had left me raw and sensitive to the minute changes in the weather around me. Or maybe those were just my wounds, aching before the rain.

Even after a week my magic still hadn't come back. I called Hope worried, and she reassured me that my body just needed to heal, that I should take my time and rest.

I leaned my head back on the couch in the living room and cuddled myself by the fireplace. Sabine was lying on my lap, her breathing slow and deep. Rain was slowly falling, and I was about to nod off when the front desk bell rang. I sighed for a moment before putting my best smile and went to greet our new guests.

"Welcome to Tir na nÓg, my name is Nathan. How can I help you?"

~

SHE WATCHED THROUGH THE MIRROR AS NATHAN GOT UP FROM THE couch and limped his way to greet his new guest. Being an innkeeper suited him.

It had been hell dealing with the fallout of Muirín's failed coup. Her mother wanted to know who had supplied the ritual's location to the sea fae, but sadly the only one who could answer that was dead, and the book had been taken away by the mortal witch who was doing who-knows-what with it.

"I see you're keeping an eye on him." A soft velvety voice said behind her, bringing her back to reality.

"Robin, do you have something to report?" She said, her displeasure clear in her voice and pulled her hand free from Tundra's mouth. The cat yowled and glared at Robin.

"In all my centuries there's only been one person who could wield the kind of magic that he did that night, outside of the fae that is." Robin said offhandedly

"Report, Puck or get out of my sight before I decide to finish what Oberon started." She glared at the summer fae. Tundra hissed, feeling her displeasure.

The spy master eyed her cat, his muscles tensing before nodding. "As you wish, Princess. Initial search of Muirín's abode didn't reveal who provided her with the information about the ritual or where to find the tome."

Silera arched an eyebrow at him. "I assume there's more and that you're not trying my patience in an effort to amuse yourself. Out with it."

"While we didn't find who gave her the information, we did come across this."

He handed her a silver brooch in the shape of a crow in flight, with a crown grasped beneath its talons. The brooch wasn't magical or made of any special materials from what she could tell. "And what's so special about a piece of jewellery?"

"Absolutely nothing, from what my people can tell it's just a plain silver brooch." He pointed towards the brooch and scowled. "What's interesting is that we found it hidden in a heavily warded room. Two of my men died after triggering one of the room's defenses."

Silera noted the hard lines along Robin's jaw and the fury that sparked in his garnet-colored eyes. If there was one redeeming quality about the traitorous spider, it was that he valued the people that worked under him and took any slights to them seriously.

"Now that's interesting." She said tuning the brooch over as Tundra tried to catch it between her paws. "I wonder who it belongs to."

"I don't know, but I intend to find out." He vowed solemnly, and she felt sorry for whoever got in his way to get answers.

Silera nodded and handed the brooch back to him. "I want to know the second you find out anything." He nodded and left her closing the door behind him.

She turned her gaze back to the mirror where Nathaniel had gone back to laying down on the couch by the fire with his hound. A small smile formed on her lips as the remnants of their kiss played back in her mind. After meeting again, there was no way she was going to let him get away from her. She couldn't - not a second time. Nathaniel was hers, he just didn't know it yet.

GLOSSARY

Ag Fás- Grow
Laghdaigh- Shrink
Tost- Silence
Saor- Clear
Oscaíl- Open
Nochtadh- Unveil
Sraonadh- Deflect
Talamh- Ground
Féach- See
Loinnir- Light
Deataigh- Smoke
Fuar Dorcha- Dark Ice
Damhán Búraló- Wolfspider
A stóirín - my treasure
Rún- my love
Apstergo- Strip Off
Strepo- Lightning Bolt
Displodo- Explode
Fulmen Belua- Lightning Elephant
Malleo Tornitura- Thunder Hammer

Choris Pono: Remove Pain
Aichmés- Stone Spike
Paximadi- Icicle
Kataigida- Blizzard
Katepsygméno- Ice Sword
Psychrí Gi- Ice Spikes
Cheimónas Arachni- Winter Spider
Roí Aéra- Air Blow

ACKNOWLEDGMENTS

This book would not have been possible without the support and encouragement of my family and friends. Words cannot express my gratitude to my editors, Loredana Carini and Megan Miller, for their professional advice, patience and assistance in polishing this book. An additional thanks to my proofreader, Maddie Bazin, for her help in the final stretch as well as Matt Seff Barnes for a wonderful job on the cover and bringing Nathan to life. Thanks to Erin for showing me her beautiful city and providing some local expertise. A final thanks to Smashbear Publishing and their team for giving me the opportunity to tell my story and being such excellent people.

ABOUT THE AUTHOR

John Ortega launches his debut novel with 'Storm's Child'. He currently resides in Puerto Rico with his dog, Noah, where he continues to work on new projects and the second book in the Rune Caster Chronicles. Follow him on his social media for book updates and future snippets.

f

Printed in Great Britain
by Amazon